TIMESCAPE

TIMESCAPE

To all the staff at The Hero

Thankyou for your
great hospitality and
lovely meals!
    Hope you enjoy this

Christine Meanwell

CHRISTINE MEANWELL

christinemeanwell@btinternet.com

© Christine Meanwell, 2016

Published by Oakfeld 88 Publishing
oakfeld88@btinternet.com

A CIP catalogue record for this book is available from the British Library.

ISBN 978-0-9935819-0-8

Cover photograph © Josie Baughan

Prepared and printed by:
York Publishing Services Ltd
64 Hallfield Road
Layerthorpe
York YO31 7ZQ

Tel: 01904 431213

Website: www.yps-publishing.co.uk

For Beryl and Peter
with my love

ABOUT THE AUTHOR

Christine Meanwell didn't set out to write a novel. As part of a University of Leicester Creative Writing course, she was assigned the task of producing a first chapter with an ending to motivate a reader to want to read more. By the time this chapter had been written, it was she who was hooked into exploring the lives of the characters she had created. She hopes you find the outcome as absorbing as she did.

Christine lives with her husband in landlocked Northampton. It was their many visits to the North Norfolk coast which inspired the setting for *Timescape*.

CONTENTS

Part 1

"Like a red morn, that ever yet betoken'd,
Wreck to the seaman, tempest to the field . . ."

William Shakespeare
Venus and Adonis

1

PARTING

If she could hold her mind carefully in the gap between the present and the future, concentrating only on the expansion of that nothingness, it could become a peaceful place to be.

Everything felt unreal. The space she took up in the room. The table on which she was tracing the pattern of the wood grain with the tips of her fingers. Yet the reality was that the words spoken to her husband and his son still whispered around inside her head. Those carefully chosen, over-rehearsed words, held on to until the end of their meal, had at long last been said out loud. With her eyes focused on the chicken carcass, which sat like a centrepiece on the kitchen table, she'd made the announcement.

'I'm not coming home with you tomorrow.'

'What?' said Mark, pushing his chair back from the table.

No response from Joe – as expected, living up to teenage predictability.

'I've booked the place for two more months.'

Still nothing from Joe.

'I don't understand what on earth you're talking about?' said Mark.

From within a bubble of unexpected calm, Kate explained

how this holiday had been a last chance for them all, a time to establish whether her relationship with either of them was worth any more emotional energy. It had been a lost cause from the start.

'Why the hell have you waited until tonight to tell us all this?'

'I wanted to be sure …'

'Well good for you – wonderful timing, waiting until Joe has finally condescended to sit at the table with us!'

Kate didn't know whether the blood draining from his face indicated anger or defeat. But, typically, Mark's first thought had been for his son. Getting Joe to the table had been a major feat in itself – to eat with them instead of in his curtain-closed room with the DVDs on his laptop for company. It had not been without deep resentment on his part.

'I knew that if we were alone, you'd talk me out of this.' Kate could hear her voice rising. There was no longer the chance of floating away on the bubble; it had evaporated, leaving her exposed.

'At least you're right about that, it's just the rest I don't get,' said Mark.

'You're the one who taught me to only to give team talks with all present … you two are a team – always have been.'

'You're part of that team …' Mark replied, '… we *need* you …'

Kate almost smiled at his delusion; she said nothing.

'… and what about your job – what will Dominic say?'

The outside world rushed in.

'He knows … knew it might happen.'

'That's true to form then, you discussing *us* with your business partner!'

'I told Dom I might need more time … he thinks it's …
work,' she lied, in order to lessen the blow.

'Are you sure it's not?' Mark muttered.

'Yes, I'm very sure.'

Joe got up and left the room.

Mark glared at her. 'Now look what you've done!'

Then she started saying everything badly; random bits and
pieces that had been weaving in and out of her brain in the
last two weeks which should have been edited from the final
presentation. Kate still couldn't bring herself to look directly
at Mark. Facing her audience was something she usually
did with such ease when submitting an advertising pitch to
prospective customers. *Place your pitch right between their
eyes*, would be her mantra, *it's designed to convince – don't
deviate*. It was second nature to her.

This time she had deviated.

In an attempt to stop herself from saying what would
later be regretted, she ran up the stairs to the living room.
Mark followed. Glaring out of the window, across the creek
to the salt marshes, she soon heard herself ranting on,
complaining about his shortcomings, the emptiness of their
marriage and … about Joe. Past resentments welled up like
a whirlpool tossing bitter words, the remnants of their life
together, drowning.

The sight of Joe silenced her. Hoodie up, he trudged past
the beached sailing boats and onto the jetty where he'd spent
so much of his earlier childhood holidays in the company of
his grandad. Defiantly lighting a cigarette, he leant his long-
limbed body against the mooring post, a body ill at ease with
the results of a growth spurt dictated by hormones. Kate's
tears were near. Attempting self-control, she closed her eyes

tightly. Tears would draw Mark to her and the window – he must be spared the sight of Joe smoking, another blatant act of contempt. She escaped onto the small landing, grabbing her coat from the old oak wardrobe to flee down the stairs and out of the front door. If Mark was given the right of reply, all resolve would be lost.

There was a temptation to turn left to follow Joe, to try and explain. But this would have been self-indulgent, and unwelcome. It would be better, she thought, to go right out to the beach; there would be enough light left in the early September evening before nightfall. She glanced back to see if Mark was watching – to be unnerved, for a second, by a fleeting impression that her actions were being observed, not from where she'd left her husband but from the empty flat above their holiday retreat. Shrugging away this sensation, she set out on her chosen path.

The track stretched along the embankment which followed the muddied inlet out to the sea, a walk of no less than two hours there and back, more if she lingered on the solitary North Norfolk beach. Kate knew that in spite of everything her return would be uplifted by the changing light over the sprawling half-whitewashed harbour buildings and the sea-abandoned fishing boats. Just as surely as the tide would seep back into these moorings, she too would have to retrace her steps.

Kate arrived back from her walk with a clear mind, well prepared for more questioning and reasoning from Mark. But it didn't happen; bags were packed and in the car, her stepson was in the passenger seat, plugged into his iPod. Indoors, Mark sat hunched up at the breakfast bar, scribbling on the back of an envelope. Kate resisted the unforeseen urge to reach out and hold onto that dependable man who spent his whole life energising others – at whatever cost to himself or their marriage.

With all anger burnt out, he ran his fingers through his hair and spoke without looking up. 'You'll have to hire a car. I've found a number ... I'll get something delivered.'

'No, don't ... I'll get a bike ...'

'Look ... I can't drive off with the car and abandon you ... you can't even get a phone signal out here. I'll organise it when I get back – it shouldn't take long to fix up a car.' Kate could see that Mark was dealing with the situation in his usual style: solve the practical problems and pack the emotional ones away.

'Don't – leave it Mark, *please*.'

He picked up her mobile, placed it in her hand and folded her fingers around it gently. 'You can get a signal when you shop in Burnham Market – just let me know you're ok.' His kindness hurt far more than harsh words.

Kate listened to the sound of the car until it faded away. She wandered aimlessly from room to room, unprepared for the numbness which had overtaken her, and ended up in her favourite space – the living room of this upside-down house. While the kitchen and two bedrooms filled the ground floor, this large open area covered the whole of the first floor and enjoyed the endless panorama of a wide window which filled much of the length of the seaward wall. That evening it gave the effect of a cinema screen showing the tide drawing away from the stability of the land. The view diminished her and tears fell within the silence.

Time was suspended.

A vague feeling of hunger pulled Kate out of her stupor; she'd eaten very little earlier while the other two had been demolishing the chicken with their usual fervour. When she'd returned from the beach, the meal had been tidied away, the kitchen left spotless. Any mess from now on would be hers alone.

Heading downstairs to the kitchen Kate reached the landing but failed to see a small, shiny rubber ball on the floor – her ankle turned sharply as her foot sent the offending object flying under the wardrobe. The ball had been a gift to Joe one holiday from his gran, cherished for years and repeatedly polished on his jeans whilst listening to his grandad's advice on where to drop his crabbing line into the water. She'd no idea that Joe still possessed it, let alone that he had brought it with him. The surprise was two-fold: the physical shock of stumbling, together with the discovery of Joe treasuring an 'uncool' relic from his childhood.

'Brilliant,' she said aloud, sitting on the top step and rubbing her ankle. Alone for such a short while and already injured – and talking to herself. Would this solitude send her completely bonkers, now, at the age of thirty-six, long before senility reached out to her? Was it a coincidence that the ball had been left here on today of all days? Had it been left by Joe to taunt her, to underscore the end of his childhood forced by her actions?

The memory of a younger Joe and his love of the ball's marbled mix of colours prompted Kate to kneel down and peer under the wardrobe. It was a solid piece of Georgian furniture on stubby legs, far too big for the cramped space at the top of the stairs but useful to house the large amount of all-weather coats they always brought with them. It was quite a hideous thing with an air of having been dumped there unceremoniously by persons unknown who'd given up trying to manoeuvre it elsewhere. She stood up to test her weight on her ankle, and glimpsed a pale reflection looking back from the mirror on the front of the wardrobe. *God I look haggard!*

Grateful that her ankle didn't seem too bad after all, Kate decided that her mother-in-law's walking stick might help matters. It had been left behind on some past visit and once located at the back of the wardrobe, she used it, not for support, but to rootle about underneath.

All this activity paused the replaying of those earlier words which were still stuck in her head refusing to budge, even though she'd let them loose on Mark.

Kate still couldn't track down the ball. She pushed the stick as far as she could reach: – it must be there somewhere. The stick went further in than expected. Had she found a mouse-hole? She hoped not; the pitter-patter of tiny feet in the middle of the night did not appeal. Not to be beaten, she tried to move the wardrobe, managing to pull it a little from the wall and then attempting to squeeze in behind to push with her whole body. She fleetingly wished for Mark and his greater strength.

The wardrobe grudgingly capitulated to reveal a hidden space, a low archway exposing a further staircase up to the attic. Kate shivered. *Get a grip*, she told herself, pushing away the recollection that throughout all those summers of holidaying in The Old Pilot's House, Joe had called the flat in the attic The Void. Kate shivered again as she experienced emotions rarely admitted: vulnerability and fear. She'd presumed that any internal access had been blocked up long ago. All she'd been aware of until now had been the unstable flight of wrought-iron steps around the back, which led up from the garden to a padlocked door. Although Margret, their landlady, promised each year to have them removed, they were still there, rusting away.

Her hand reached out for a light switch; there were two, neither of which worked. Kate listened, registering that silence does in fact have its own sound, and intuitively made a link between her own emptiness and the loneliness of the space above, a room never occupied. In the past she'd been frustrated by Margret's repeated refusal to let it out to friends of theirs who were interested, without any explanation as to why.

That feeling of being observed on leaving the house earlier, coupled with the darkness of the stairwell, did not conjure up an inviting prospect – yet curiosity still tempted her. Kate made a decision; keeping a firm hold on the walking stick she went back down to the kitchen to get the torch. Reckoning she'd been brave enough already that day to cause such change, she resolved to confront this fresh challenge of her new life.

When she returned to shine the torch behind the wardrobe, Joe's ball was in the corner. She reached for it with the stick, intending to tap it towards her. Instead the ball rolled back under the wardrobe and down the stairs into the kitchen, hitting each step with a reverberating thud until quiet restored itself again. Armed with the stick in one hand and the torch in the other, Kate climbed the stairs to the attic flat. As she reached the top she had a bizarre sense of time not moving forwards into the future. Instead, she was being drawn inexorably towards the past held captive within this house.

2

IMAGININGS

The last well-fed customers left the bistro. Margret locked up the instant they'd gone, finished clearing their table and wiped it down.

'I'll get off now,' she said to Phil, who remained behind the bar giving it one last check over before he could go and "chill out upstairs over the shop" – a phrase guaranteed to be heard several times each evening as he bantered with the customers. Phil was much more popular than her previous employer – "Old Phil", his dour father – from whom he'd taken over the village pub. However, Margret feared that Young Phil wouldn't cope with the quiet out-of-season months, despite all his grand schemes for the place. Not after all those exotic countries he'd worked in, gathering the culinary expertise he displayed each day in the tiny kitchen round the back.

'Ok, see you tomorrow – be careful on that mean machine of yours.'

'Go ahead and laugh … you just wait and watch as those wheels propel me towards a smaller body!'

'It's not going to make much difference – you barely live a stone's throw.'

'Look, every time I come and go,' she said – tugging

on her trainers – 'I do some extra turns around the block. Who needs a gym? I did four laps this morning, and when I arrived you were still wandering around in your pyjamas.'

With that, Margret closed the door on what she guessed was a disbelieving Phil. She retrieved her gleaming bicycle from the back shed – still full of the pleasure of new acquisition – and before climbing on, pulled out several hairpins to shake free her grey hair. It felt good to leave behind the kitchen heat together with the blended aromas of the bistro's gastronomic delights and the wood fire in the bar; the cool night-time air with its salty taste on her lips was a blessing. Organising distribution of weight on the saddle as evenly as possible, she hit the road determined to do two extra laps before reaching her home – Fisherman's Cottage – which overlooked the staithe and the small creek-side harbour. Once there, Margret would put away the bike, leaving it locked up, safe for the night, in the lean-to which relied on the cottage for stability in much the same way as she did – constantly.

* * *

After a few miles even Joe's iPod let him down; with all that angst going on earlier, he'd forgotten to recharge. He swore under his breath, took a sideways glance at Mark and considered his options. If he took the earphones out, he'd be forced to talk to his father. He *could* pretend that it was playing … which he did only for a short while, soon to be put off this deceit by his conscience reminding him of the close bond they used to have.

Still, Joe had another way of shutting out his dad. The silence in the car told a lie. An outside observer would judge that the two passengers had been switched off to life. But any such observer would have failed to hear a continual monologue taking place inside at least one head. Instead of letting sound take over his brain, Joe talked silently to his dead mother, as he often did; a habit which had started after "The Accident" when no one else had been talking to him about what happened. At five years of age he'd been old enough to go to school, but not to have anything explained: lots of voices, kind and sympathetic, but they said nothing of substance – not really.

In school, Joe would recall, it was always him chosen first for important jobs in class – such as taking the register to the school secretary who would greet him like a long lost friend returning from some sort of endurance marathon. There was also *the look* – his teacher forever catching his eye, to check his well-being – followed by the *reassuring smile*. He'd felt continually watched … for something … he hadn't known what. At home (full of people he didn't want) everyone would stop talking when he came into the room. He wasn't fooled; he'd been bright enough to realise the topic of conversation had hastily changed. Sometimes not all the adults had caught on and he would catch part of a mixed-up conversation that made no sense to anyone at all. The sudden random jabbering used to make him smile – until, unfailingly, someone said: "Hi Joe, feeling better today?" Why that question? He hadn't been ill. That term he'd been chosen to play the Angel Gabriel in the Christmas Nativity resulting in the searing memory of thinking *all* the tears of *all* the mothers in the audience were for him. He became really popular, for a while, with his friends in the playground always insisting on letting him be first to line up.

And then little by little, it stopped. His instant celebrity faded away and he never understood why. By the time the spring term started he'd become *ordinary Joe* again and something or someone new had taken precedence in the playground. Recently he'd opened up a letter on the computer from his dad to the school asking for staff to stop any preferential treatment. Looking back, he guessed that his behaviour must have been pretty bad that Christmas. During those early forlorn months of that year, he'd overwhelmingly missed being centre of attention – guilt had followed and hurriedly hidden out of sight. He'd told no one, ashamed of showing what he thought of as his mean character. A decade on from all that, it remained tucked away in his brain in a file marked *Confusion.*

So, with his moment of fame having passed, Joe ran conversations with his dead mother. That evening, travelling home in the dark without his usual stream of sound, the one-sided discussion carried on … *We never wanted Kate around, did we? I've got enough people … Dad, Gran, Batty … and you Mum, sort of.*

'You alright?' said Mark taking advantage of Joe unplugged.

For one instant Joe believed Mark's words were part of his imagined conversation, to be disappointed to find it was not the voice with the sensitive, musical tone so desperately sought.

'I said, are you alright?'

'Suppose.'

'Suppose – what's that meant to mean?'

Suppose – I don't know. Suppose I don't know how I'm meant to feel about anything. Suppose I don't have the words.

Suppose you never taught me the words I need to use … None of which came out loud – instead Joe chose to speak words aimed to send his father off on another train of thought altogether.

'Suppose … we'd better get home,' Joe replied. 'You've only got tomorrow to get stuff ready for school … not me … I've got one more day than you.'

'Oh God, Training Day – all my sun-soaked colleagues will be asking *Did you have a good holiday?* and *How's Kate?* And along with all that I've got to concentrate on work as well.'

'But you'll all enjoy a day of mega-moaning about us lot, won't you,' said Joe, wishing as ever that he didn't attend the school where his father was head of the PE department. 'It's me and my mates that'll suffer the consequences next term.'

'Well, with no Kate, you'll have to be the one to go shopping tomorrow and get some food in … I've got loads to do.'

Joe groaned as reality began to trickle in. It wasn't fair. Only two days left of the summer holidays; he'd planned to catch up with everyone on Facebook as well as his online gaming, having survived the last two weeks with no internet on the edge of the world. But it was cool, Batty would come to the rescue and pick up some shopping – he'd give him a call in the morning.

So two heads travelled, busy with random thoughts, lists of things to do and imaginary conversations. Three hours passed along pitch-black country lanes, cosy home-lit villages and late night sepia-illumined dual carriageways. Finally the vehicle carrying this noisy silence reached Warwick and pulled up outside the house its driver and passenger called home.

* * *

If, after the last two weeks of trying so hard to communicate with both Mark and Joe, Kate had attempted to guess at the atmosphere in the car as they journeyed home, their inability to connect could have been easily imagined. There was, however, no time for such conjecture. While the miles of separation clocked up, she had been standing at the top of the newly discovered stairs, straining tired eyes to make sense of the gloom. The torch lit up the shadowy corners of an artist's studio, rather than a flat, with large canvases leaning up against the wall showing their backs, not their story. Evidence of their creation existed everywhere; in scattered tubes of paint, the debris of colour mixing efforts and numerous paintbrushes left randomly on the floor. Holding the torch, Kate's eyes followed the beam of light as it reached out along parallel floorboards travelling to the window, in front of which stood an empty easel. Not much else; except, in the centre of the room, a bed of faded cushions thrown together.

The mustiness of neglect mingled with a faint smell of recently doused candles ... and a fragrance of ... what was it? Something on the edge of experience, not easily recalled. This sensory potpourri drifted above another odour: overflowing ashtrays and empty beer glasses.

The torch seemed to shudder, the light wavering from object to object as if it didn't want to linger on any one spot. Kate recognised her hands were shaking and passing this message to the torch. With a churning stomach and a brain imploring retreat, she followed this urgent instruction, nearly tripping for a second time before managing to escape that private world which emitted such a strong sense of its past. Pure reptilian flight took over.

Kate's logical mind couldn't understand this overreaction to what was, on the face of it, a vacant room. A panic attack was not anything she had encountered before, and being generally cynical about such things, she'd been taken by surprise at the ferocity of the assault. It felt as though her heart was trying to escape whilst the whole building appeared to vibrate in time to its fearful beat.

Come on, control, breathe …

In the next instant, Kate understood what was happening; the ancient front door knocker and her heart were pounding in unison.

* * *

Margret had been knocking on the door for some time, at first tentatively, and then, when there was no response, with more insistence. Had it been former memories entangled with imagination that had conjured up the lights she'd witnessed? The other alternative was the real possibility of an intruder. The car outside had gone, so perhaps there was no one at home after all. Maybe they'd decided to go out for a meal, or even a smuggler's walk – some visitors to that part of the coast had taken to doing this in the middle of the night, trying to happen upon some type of preternatural experience dredged up from the past. Margret, however, had learnt that there was no point in waiting for such ghosts – it had been many years since she'd peered out from the staithe, across the motionless high tide, on a murky soulless night.

Margret's recollections were broken by the sound of footsteps running down the stairway inside the house and a breathless Kate, shouting.

'Is that you Mark? Why on earth ...'

The door was unlocked with the key, the bolt snapped back. When opened, it revealed an ashen Kate sucking a finger as if the bolt had bitten it. As usual the sight of Kate's willowy body made Margret remember the girl she herself had once been before life's disappointments had driven her to seek comfort elsewhere; battles with a predisposition to put on weight had long been lost. Even at this time in the evening, Kate – with fair hair scraped back and no make-up – still managed to look stunning, although startled and disconcerted.

'Oh Margret ... it's you. I assumed Mark and Joe had come back.'

Kate's relief was palpable and this alerted in her visitor the stirrings of a new interest, of a tale about to be told. Margret didn't wait to be invited in; she headed for the breakfast bar stool where, unbeknown to her, Mark had sat so despondently a few hours ago. She pulled herself back to her mission.

'No, it's me – hope you don't mind me turning up so late? Something spooked me. I'd finished my stint at the pub, did two extra laps on my bike ... and then, instead of going home, something caught my eye ... so I came up the footpath in front of Coastguard's Cottage ... and *that's* when I saw the lights.'

'What lights?' said Kate with her facial muscles holding an expression of complete innocence; Margret began to think that perhaps it had all been in her mind.

'Flickering lights,' Margret replied, vaguely wafting her hands. 'From somewhere around here.'

Kate hesitated before responding. 'I'm fine, honest ...

trying to get used to being on my own.' She opened the fridge door and grasped a bottle of milk with shaking hands. 'I think I'll make myself a hot drink to take to bed.'

Margret was not unaware that her original purpose had been deliberately deflected, but her inquisitiveness concerning the whereabouts of Mark and Joe had taken a firm hold. She examined in more detail the evidence presented in the kitchen – one pair of walking boots by the door.

'They've gone then.' Margret said. She was not talking about the boots.

Kate nodded. 'I'm not expecting them back.'

'Oh, I see, I mean I don't see … when you asked if I could let you rent the place for longer, I presumed all three of you would be staying on … I wondered why, at the beginning of the school year … maybe Mark had lost his job, or something … but then Joe would've been expected at school …' she ran out of words and suppositions. The floor was left open for an explanation.

Kate stepped towards the door. 'It's been a long day,' she said, yawning and placing a firm hand on the doorknob.

Margret conceded that Kate had regained control. Beaten on all counts, she prepared to leave by shifting her weight to the edge of the stool, from which position she launched herself off.

'If you're positive everything's ok,' she said, taking a fleeting look up the stairs towards the wardrobe before leaving. No lights were on. 'Sorry, of course you were about to go to bed.' With that, an affectionate hug was shared while Margret took the opportunity to peer over Kate's shoulder for one more glance in the direction of the stairwell. 'If you have any problems here, you know where I am.'

'Of course I do, anyway it's me that should apologise for being so unsociable – thanks for checking up on me. We can get together for a coffee soon, perhaps later this week,' Kate suggested, leaving Margret's imaginings searching in the wilderness.

* * *

Locking up and leaning against the door, Kate tried to assimilate what was going on. Fear had given in to curiosity. Why hadn't Margret directly mentioned the upstairs flat? If she'd seen light from the torch she must have known that it came from there. Why didn't she say? Kate concluded that whatever that space represented, it preserved within its walls something of strong significance to Margret. All that evasion confirmed that what had been uncovered by the moving of the wardrobe was even more strictly out of bounds than first anticipated.

Kate went back up to the wardrobe, deliberately not putting on the stair lights to give Margret any evidence of a return upstairs. Feeling her way, it was finally pushed back into place. Hampered by the dark she cautiously stepped into the living room intending to close all the curtains, but before she could, there was a noise behind her. The wardrobe door swung open; simultaneously a cloud suddenly permitted light from the moon to catch the mirror. Without a moment's hesitation, she rushed at the wardrobe, pushing the door back firmly with both hands and held it fast; again she was forced to direct her heart to slow down and her brain to think logically.

Kate looked up to challenge herself in the mirror. 'Go home tomorrow, face reality, move out, and start afresh.'

As she turned away, something made her look back; it was as if someone else was there waiting to pronounce their verdict.

'I am not solely guilty, I am not,' she whispered.

Cloud once more covered the moon; Kate stood in darkness.

Imagination running on overdrive ...

Craving sleep, she bolted for her refuge and climbed into bed fully clothed, too tired for normal rituals. Thankful that her bedroom was on the ground floor, she attempted to blank out any thoughts relating to the events of that day by mentally retracing her earlier walk along the embankment out to the beach. It worked: sleep came – with dreams of Margret on a bicycle trying to deliver babies to every house in the empty out-of-season village.

* * *

In Warwick, where Kate ought to have been lying curled up next to him, Mark had not been sleeping well at all. The beginning of a new school year was notorious for many a restless night's sleep, but this time it wasn't work concerns – the after-school fixtures and team meetings – that kept him awake; *this* time it was all about the botched job he'd made at his second chance in life.

In that same house, in those few minutes before sleep took him, Joe had talked to his mother, which soothed any of his immediate anxieties, as it always did. He'd fallen asleep comforted, like a five year old whose mother sits by him until his breathing reflects sleep.

3

CONNECTIONS

'You did it then,' said Dom.

Kate was a mile down the road from the house, perched on a small boulder where she hoped to get a good signal – but every few minutes either a car went by or the connection faded. 'Look I'll phone you later, I've got to shop, there's no food in the fridge … I'll go somewhere with a better signal. I thought I'd confirm I won't be in to work … for quite a while,' she blurted out, hopeful that he'd heard some of what had been said. It was nearly as difficult to pick up his reply.

'Don't leave it … long … I … all the details … need something to spice up … a bit … good gossip … sorry I didn't mean …' at which point Kate feigned complete signal failure and cut off the call, knowing she would eventually have to tell all. It was what they always did, she and Dom, tell all – ever since the beginning, at University, followed by first thing every morning once they had set up the business together. This early morning heart-to-heart cleared the ground for their creative thoughts to nestle and grow. On this particular morning, the side of the road proved not to be the place to unburden oneself – she would phone him later; like a drug, it was a necessity, not an option.

Dom was the sibling she'd never had, blurred in with being

the replacement for her parents who had found themselves a better life in Nice. His listening skills compensated for all those lovers who were wonderful in bed but hopeless when it came to conversation. Until Mark. Mark had, at first, listened *and* talked to her. But Dom had become a way of life and not someone you could discard. There was nothing romantic in their desire for each other's company; Dom was like family – better than family – and was intimate with all her history, having his own special place in it. Mark – good, kind, accommodating Mark – had seen no problem with this in the early days and had taken Dom on board, like people do with family. As things had deteriorated between them, Mark had seemed more than happy to abdicate the listening and understanding part of life to Dom. And Kate had let him.

* * *

When he'd answered his mobile earlier that morning as he was about to leave for work, Dominic McKinley had expected it to be Kate; Mark's number flashed up instead.

'Can you meet up with me tonight? I can't explain now, I've got to get to work, it's Kate you see, she's stayed in Norfolk. I'll meet you at that pub near your office if you like, we could have supper – Kate and I often eat there. It's not bad for pub food. Joe's not speaking to me at all – I need your advice.'

Dom felt anxious about the prospect of being alone with Mark; his own complex feelings about Kate and Mark had plagued him for years. Being well aware of the expectation to work either a miracle to make everything alright or to somehow apply a metaphorical sticking plaster, Dom was trying to think up an excuse when he heard: 'Got to go and get to work, see you at The Foresters then, about six – don't tell Kate if she rings – bye.'

It seemed to be his destiny to end up in the role of counsellor for the zillionth time; a role he definitely didn't want to pursue with Mark.

By 10.30, their usual morning coffee time in the office, Dom was sitting staring at his mobile trying to compose a text that would excuse him from meeting Mark, when it rang again. This time it was Kate sounding like she was standing on the hard shoulder of a motorway. He gathered that she would try and make contact later and was frustrated when the signal vanished. All this made him very much feel like pouring himself a large glass of wine even though it was so early. He unbuttoned his waistcoat – which was slightly too tight these days – rolled up the sleeves of his smart ivory shirt, dragged off his favourite pale blue tie and moved to pick up the unopened bottle of wine under his desk. He kept one down there to celebrate new contracts with Kate, although had never before opened one in the office without there being two glasses to fill. The image of her disapproving face flitted into his mind, so instead he made himself a peppermint tea. They had a new brief to create enticing publicity to seduce young people with the wonders of what had previously been given an unsuccessful strapline by another Agency: *Perky Peppermint – The Tea for Teanagers!* Bloody Kate, this was her job – to taste the garbage they were asked to advertise. He on the other hand prided himself on his refined sense of taste, which included enjoying good wines and avoiding eating at the local pub.

Double-bloody Kate – why did she have to blow off course? He needed her in so many ways, not least with just keeping everything afloat. The effect of the recession was beginning to nip at their ankles, with advertising being one of the first services to suffer as companies endeavoured to cut costs. They – McKinley Nichols Advertising – had to be better than anyone else out there, and without Kate he would struggle; Dom accepted he was somewhat mediocre compared to her. It was ironic, his name coming first on the billing – it should have been hers. They'd argued about this when their union had been conceived. Eventually alphabetical order had solved the problem but after working together for so many years he'd grown to accept that due to her vast creative input, Kate deserved to have her name far above his. He would never concede that to her face (it sounded better the way it was anyway, flowing off the tongue more readily) as it would be stating the obvious – that the Agency would be nothing without her.

In the end Dom decided not to cancel Mark. And by the time he climbed into bed that night in his meticulously tidy water-mill conversion, he had listened sympathetically to Mark's plight. There'd been no further phone calls from Kate. Only a text: SORRY SPEAK SOON X. It was the *speak soon* that surprised him. Not *tomorrow* or *in the morning*. Just soon.

* * *

There was no way Kate could talk to anyone about her experience that day. She'd woken up with a clear head, but famished, and remembered that there was virtually no food in the place as they had organised their meals in the last few days so that there would be little left to pack and take home. Investigating the fridge, all that faced her was the carcass of the chicken and somehow she couldn't bring herself to pick at that. Kate chucked it in the bin, grabbed a lone apple which was well past its eat-by date and went upstairs to study the view to see what weather the day was bringing.

What greeted her was an overcast sky which gave nothing to the observer and made a scant impression on the canvas. Nevertheless, it soon became evident that even a dull sky had a purpose. Instead of her eye being drawn to the vast beauty of that natural dome and its effect on the earth below, her line of sight dipped and absorbed the foreground, as it would in a town. So a reverse observation began beneath her window and worked its way out to the horizon; a different perception of the new day emerged.

Kate deduced what had happened over night. The first clue was the row of pearl droplets poised to fall from the taut plastic washing line. The second clue? Birdbath brimming. Third? Wet slate pathway. She became absorbed in the full value of the cheerless sky and its powerful influence on the spectrum of colours enlivening the scene below: shocking-pink geraniums boasting their last bloom before the autumn set in, hanging on to summer, yellow roses with their heads still lifted – having defied the cloudburst – and red crab-apples cluttering the dark earth under blue-brown branches. It was role-reversal, with the damp foreground illuminating and challenging the muted firmament.

Her frustration at not being able to open the large picture window was because she couldn't hear the first sounds of the morning. No birdsong. The fixed window was the downside of the house. Trapped inside, Kate detected not even the slightest breeze causing a leaf to quiver. Within her mind an idea was forming … that an artist had captured his subject, perfected his composition and laid down his brush.

The outside held close the uneasy calm in the house and within herself. A rabbit ventured on to the lawn: a brave movement, coming out into the open, exploring its need for sustenance. The creature moved, paused, its nose searching. Disturbed by something unseen by Kate, it sprang into action, scuttling for cover. I will *not* do that, Kate thought; nothing in this silent world will stop my resolve. I shall shower, dress, phone Dom, buy food, eat. Explore upstairs. In daylight. There can be no ghosts in daylight. I shall disperse my stupid fears and make room for rational thought before deciding on whether or not to go back to Warwick.

By the time Kate had showered, new brushstrokes had been applied to the sky's perspective – the grey had transformed into strands of silver merging with a pale blue haze, growing in strength minute by minute and banishing the earlier opacity.

Following her fruitless first attempt at calling Dom, Kate got through the rest of her list, beginning with successful shopping in Burnham Market – which was why, laden with carrier bags, and being dependent on the Coast Hopper for transport, she postponed trying him again until later. As she sat on the bus she made up her mind to adjust her order of to-do tasks and explore upstairs before phoning him. By achieving that first, and hopefully finding nothing untoward in The Void, she could entertain Dom with her tale of nonsense and not just talk about Mark. She would walk along in front of the Boathouse, get some sea air and sit on the far bench where there was generally a good signal. Once she'd unburdened herself to Dom she might walk to the pub, grab a drink, chat to Margret to make amends for her brusqueness last night and come back to the house to cook a cosy supper. Great plans.

A quick lunch; Kate actually found she had little appetite for food. The day couldn't progress until she had been upstairs to take a proper look at the empty flat. *Oh, get on with it you stupid woman*, she said to herself, knowing that the sooner she poked about in the corners in daylight to prove that there was nothing sinister, the sooner she could bring up the subject with Margret and laugh about what female imaginings can do.

Kate wished she had left the wardrobe pulled out to save her exerting the effort again needed to uncover enough space to squeeze through. Having done this, she sprinted up the short flight of stairs and stopped abruptly at the top.

The first thing she noticed was his long dark hair which just touched pale, bony shoulders. He was painfully thin with shoulder blades protruding from his naked back above flared jeans and a well-worn brown leather belt. The concentration of his whole being filled the room as he stood before the canvas positioned on the easel. The second thing she noticed was her total lack of fear. It was as if it was the most natural thing in the world for him to be standing there.

'You did it then,' came the softly spoken voice.

4

A CHANGE OF VIEW

'I knew if I waited ...'

Kate turned, so slightly, to leave.

'Don't ...' he said. *'Please ...'*

Her instinct implored retreat; any other response would take her over a threshold from one life to another. She had never been as hesitant of anything as in that one short moment.

'Breathe, take a step forward and you won't turn back.'

Her feet were leaden. 'I ... can't.'

'Why?'

'I don't know.'

'I don't know much either, come and stand here next to me and share the view.'

Kate intended a step backwards; but somehow felt compelled to move to the huge window – a window similar to the one downstairs. Only this one was hinged open at each end, inviting warmth into the cool room. While keeping him at arm's length, ready to bolt, Kate tried to fix her eyes on the view. Something was different ... the stage of the tide?

'That wasn't so hard then?'

'No.'

His face turned towards her, willing her to look at him.

And so she did.

There was no element of choice.

In front of her stood possibly the most beautiful man Kate had ever seen, with a beauty that couldn't be defined – it came more from his tranquillity than his physical appearance. His features were strong, framed by dark eyebrows raised in appreciation of her turning towards him. His full lips held a serene smile. His long hair – deep dark brown – was swept back, held away from his eyes with a strip of material tied around his forehead like a bandana and knotted at the back of his head. He must have been about twenty-five, or a little older? A good ten years younger than herself, she surmised.

As a first impression he was perfect. Not for the first time she sensed danger – aware that perfection could never be sustained – as sooner or later he would surely show weakness, human faults. No man or woman could be without flaws. Kate wanted to freeze-frame everything … *let nothing change, let the illusion last.*

'How long have you been up here?' she said, forcing herself to break the spell, her held breath spilling out over the words.

'A while.'

'How long is that?'

'It's all so indistinct, so vague …'

'What do you mean?'

'Sometimes it seems I've been waiting eons …'

He looked out of the window.

'… and sometimes, only a few minutes.'

'Waiting for what?'

'For you to come upstairs.'

'You've been watching me, Mark, Joe?'

'They've gone now … that's why you've finally been able to come.'

'This doesn't make sense.'

'Does it matter?'

Wanting to back off returned, it tugged at her sleeve. She grappled for explanations: he's a stalker, a tramp, or worse – an absconder from prison wanting to do harm? *What sort of danger have you landed yourself in?*

'I won't hurt you.'

'How did you know I was thinking that?'

'Haven't got a clue … it was as if I heard you … or more like, I felt it … I think.'

'How can I believe you won't harm me?'

'Be cool, I'm a gentle soul – sadly lacking company, like you. Anyway, I'd hate to ruin the day and spoil the sunshine. How can anything bad happen on a day as mind-blowing as this.'

He pushed open the window further, letting it swing wide. Kate watched him as he leant right out with his arms apart to inhale deep breaths: breathing in slowly from his diaphragm before letting go of the breath as he relaxed his arms in preparation for the next intake. She watched the rise and fall of his shoulder blades, the lifting and lowering of his arms and then saw something that stunned her. It was a dazzling day outside! Midsummer. That was what was wrong with the view.

The season had changed.

As that consciousness dawned, her whole world shifted. There was nothing normal to cling on to any more. Playing for time, trying to make sense of things, Kate hesitantly explored the attic. Unlike her last visit, it was now full of light with smaller windows on each of the other three walls. The sun poured in, its shaft illuminating the two players on the stage.

The time-shift provided evidence everywhere: the bed of faded cushions, his jeans with the triangles of flowered material sewn into the seams to form the flare and, nearby, a record-player with its arm poised for action. Kate knelt down and examined the label on the large black disc waiting to be played: a Beatles LP, *Sgt Pepper's*, it had been one of her father's favourites.

She could see that her every move was being studied, and all the time there was that smile. Was this intruder smiling *at* her, *with* her or at some purpose soon to unfold? Or, was she the intruder? Kate grew light-headed and marginally nauseous, identifying the lingering smell as incense coming from half-burnt joss sticks, which were rammed into the remnants of well-used candles placed around the room amongst dirty ashtrays.

The struggle to come up with a logical answer continued. Maybe he was a travelling artist, going from place to place, trying to set the scene for a painting with all this sixties' stuff. This triggered a further idea; Kate went across to the canvases spotted on her previous visit to the attic and turned them around one at a time, handling their weight and awkwardness with some effort, in search of corroborating her guesswork.

When all the paintings were standing alongside each other she stepped back, disheartened, as all hope of the sixties' theory faded. All three were views from the window, all painted from exactly the same angle. However, each one was unlike its neighbour, in that it was transformed by the depiction of the weather or the time of day: the light, the height of the tide, the balance of the boats in the water all radically affected the end result. Each touched Kate in a unique way, eliciting a different emotion. They were not 'just paintings'. *They're amazingly good! Magnificent works of art painted by a beautiful man!*

'These must be worth a fortune,' she said.

He turned his back on her and walked towards the easel. As he approached the canvas, Kate appreciated the truth as he hesitated to begin. That intensity she'd witnessed when she'd first seen him, came from what he'd been about to create. It had been the intensity required to feed the first movement an artist makes when they put their mark on a blank canvas; the origin of commitment, born out of fear. Fear of the unknown. *We were both stepping over a precipice when our worlds collided*, she reasoned.

Kate – who still believed she could cut and run at this point, backtrack and turn what was happening into an amusing story to tell friends – listened to herself shouting, 'This isn't real! My mind is working overtime! It's because I'm stressed out – yesterday was … I've created the perfect man to compensate. You – don't – exist. Go away!'

He didn't flinch; just picked up a paintbrush, the tip of which he stuck in his mouth, while his hands dealt with squeezing tubes of paint onto a plastic plate ready to mix them together.

'I am going back downstairs,' Kate continued. 'I'm going to turn on the television, listen to the news and tune myself back into the real world.' And, under her breath, 'You don't exist.'

'I've never been called perfect before,' came his reply.

She sighed, 'That's why you *can't* exist – nobody's perfect.' Along with the time-shift witnessed outside, something also altered inside Kate. Despite this notion of impossibility, a new irrationality found her wanting a piece of this perfection, real or imagined; the hippie environment and its promise had begun to reel her in.

He dropped the plate to the floor, took the paintbrush from his mouth as if it was a cigarette holder, blew out imaginary smoke and threw the brush onto the plate. Kate moved towards him, took hold of both his hands and scrutinised his long fingers on which, she discovered, he wore a number of rings. Not able to look up directly into his eyes, she stared down at his bare feet.

'Who *are* you?' she said.

'Sye.'

'Sye?'

'Simon Hilliard on my birth certificate. Sye to those close to me.'

'To me you will be Simon, as we've just met ... and hardly that.'

He laughed at her.

They were still holding hands. Kate was mesmerised by the rings; some were cheap and gaudy, plastic and angular, whilst others were exotic in design, romantic copies of eastern trinkets. It seemed odd for a man to wear such things – then again everything was out of the ordinary; those small objects were no different. His hands took charge and led her to the cushions where he knelt and guided her down to the floor to sit opposite him. He studied Kate's face as if attempting to drink in her physical essence before trying to reach in and steal her innermost thoughts; she felt awkward and self-conscious.

'I'm also full of questions,' he said eagerly.

Like an excited child, waiting for an adult to explain the world, thought Kate.

'I don't know why, or how, I'm in this place – or why I've such a need for you to share it with me.'

The anxiety inside showed in her hands which were holding his much too tightly. 'You *must* remember how you got here?' She let go. A look of dejection crossed his face as the physical contact broke. Once more Kate saw the child in him; perceiving that he hadn't learnt to hide his emotions, as adults do.

He took hold of her hands again, saying, 'I haven't held anyone's hands for a long time. You're full of warmth and I can tell you've stashed away so much love because there's no one to give it to.'

Kate bridled at this, the conversation had leapt a mile in intimacy. 'That's nothing to do with you and not true anyway!' She left him abruptly, went over to the paintings and turned them back against the wall. 'I suggest you try and paint something different. They may be great paintings but isn't it about time for something new?'

Anger erupted from Sye. 'DON'T TOUCH THEM AGAIN!'

Her words had found their mark and hurt him. She'd meant them to, although she was shaken by the ferocity of his response. But he'd deserved it – the truth he'd spoken had touched her core. He's right though, she conceded reluctantly, I've so much love inside, pushed down deep. I wanted to use it up on Mark, give it to him freely. Instead, there were always obstacles in the way and when I landed awkwardly he was never there to pick me up – always occupied elsewhere, not even looking in my direction.

'It's the wrong brand, this love of yours,' said Sye, still sitting cross-legged amongst his cushions. His anger had vanished as quickly as it had arrived. 'Imagine it, like it's all bottled up and waiting for the cork to be pulled. Maybe the answer is simple – that it merely doesn't suit Mark's palate – or maybe the fizz vanished long ago without a trace.'

'There you are, you're doing it again, having an uninvited conversation with my mind. I'm not staying around any longer to give you that pleasure!' She went to the top of the stairs, intending to leave.

Showing no wound from her words this time, Sye got up and moved towards the empty canvas. He loaded his paintbrush with some vibrant crimson paint and made his first mark, quite casually without any of the previous hesitation.

He smiled at Kate. 'Come back soon. Please. Come in daylight, there'll be plenty of that – with my windows on the world up here. Don't come at night, or someone might see the torchlight.'

Kate took a last look at him, now immersed in his painting – seemingly oblivious to her existence. She left without speaking again and on reaching the bottom of the stairs struggled once more to shift the wardrobe back into place … to close the door resolutely between his world and her own.

5

REAL TIME

Angela Haughton was bored. At seventy-four years of age she doubted she would ever reconcile herself with those things her body forbade her to do: digging the garden, clearing out the shed, climbing up ladders to cut the hedge. Since being forced to live her life teetering from chair to chair – far removed from her childhood stepping-stones games – she recalled these former chores as one who'd conquered mountains in the past must look back and wish they could relive the experience. And driving; how she longed to pop to the shops alone, without her doting husband. Bliss!

'Hi Ange,' came a voice from the front garden. 'It's Sadie, can I come in?' The key turned in the lock. Before Angela could summon a response, the girl was in and fighting off the two spaniels barking fiercely at one end of their quivering bodies while showing their approval at the other. 'You'd think they'd be used to me – shut up you two!'

The dogs took over the sofa, opposite Angela's electronic wonder of a chair – the all-singing, all-dancing massage monster which could even tip her up and out like a dumper truck. Sadie kicked off her shoes and pushed the dogs off what they thought to be their rightful territory. She sat down with no grace at all and stretched out long legs, flexing bare feet against the arm rests once there was no more available space. Those endless legs emerged from her much hated maroon school skirt which, in Angela's opinion, was hitched to an indecorous length.

Sadie admired the black paint on her toenails. 'I *love* your sofa! It's *so snuggy* – not like Mum's posh leather thing – *Take your feet off it, don't eat on it* and –' Sadie made a sad face, 'no doubt one day it'll be *Don't cuddle up with a boyfriend on it. As if …'*

Angela had a good idea who this last comment referred to.

'What's new?' Sadie demanded.

'Not much. I'm sick of all the soaps, it's the same story over and over.'

'What?' said Sadie while texting on her mobile.

'Meet, love, fall out, hate, murder or – more often – commit multiple murders until inevitably, like a genie from a lamp, something positive emerges in some shape or form. All living happily ever after, until they appear on another soap that is.'

'Oh I know, everyday stories of everyday life,' Sadie said wisely, as if she was listening after all.

Angela struggled to understand how the youth of the day could have two conversations going on – one in real time and one in text time.

'Put that silly thing down and talk to me – you can't do both at once, either be here or not be here. I don't want to be in limbo with you, thank you very much!'

'What's limbo?'

'Somewhere in between.'

'In between what?'

'Never you mind, the answer to that's much too complex for four o'clock in the afternoon.'

'Except for the murder bit,' said Sadie, switching back to the previous conversation. *Like they do*, thought Angela, pleased with the agility of her brain even though her body was giving up the fight.

Sadie picked up the *Radio Times* from the coffee table and flicked through it. 'It's like our lives see, we all go through this stuff – except the murder bit.'

'Some people do,' replied Angela.

'Do you think soaps like that give people ideas, about murders, I mean?'

'Goodness me, Sadie, what's happened to you today? Deep thinking at the end of a hard day at school, whatever next!'

'Well it's … because of Drama.'

'Are we back to the soaps?'

'Nope, it's like, we've got this new *D-D-G* drama teacher – he's real cool. He says that we're all so good at talking in his class that he's going to start a Debating Club so we can talk about useful things and EXPRESS OUR OPINIONS MORE PURPOSEFULLY … or p'r'aps it's usefully, something-fully anyways.'

To Angela's annoyance, the educational points were enunciated very precisely, in such a way that you might speak to a child. It was disappointing; Sadie was usually the one person who didn't treat her as though her mind had been lost along with everything else.

'I'm not brain dead yet, young lady!'

'I know that, silly, it's me, I was trying to remember it all and get it right, it's my brain that's useless, not yours.'

'The one thing that didn't make sense to me was d-d-g, whatever that means.'

'Drop dead gorgeous, of course.'

'I see,' said Angela but couldn't for the life of her really see why this generation were so lazy that they felt the need to incessantly use abbreviations and turn life into a code breaking event.

'Anyways, I thought, if I join … I'll be coming out of school the same time as Joe after football on Thursdays when he comes to see you before his dad picks him up. We could walk back together.' Sixteen going on eighteen, Sadie tucked her head down and feverishly worked her thumbs around the keypad of her phone. Angela saw the blush spreading before the curtain formed by the girl's jet-black hair hid it from sight.

Sadie's thumbs took a rest. 'He'll be here soon, won't he?'

'Sorry to disappoint you, he rang earlier and said he's dropped out of the football team – goodness knows what Mark's going to say. I've hardly seen Joe since his holiday. When he got back he came to see us, for as short a time as possible, to collect some shopping.'

'Oh.'

'He rang his grandfather yesterday and asked for a lift after school. I think they're plotting something together. John won't be long, you can ask him yourself – you may well be able to discover more than me.'

Angela's deliberate use of her husband's proper name, John, was lost on Sadie who'd no understanding of the importance of correct appellations. 'I'd like to wait and see Batty, but I've got loads of homework and Mum says if I get everything done in the evenings this week she'll take me to see a film on Friday for a belated birthday treat, *and* I can take a friend – I'd have asked Joe, if he'd been here.'

Sadie threw in this last piece of information nonchalantly although Angela knew that if that had happened, it would have been a big deal for her neighbour's daughter. She'd flinched at the use of Batty, an affectionate name for her husband only used by family; on the other hand she didn't mind Ange as this was the girl's own invention. It caused a nice feeling of rebellion in Angela when considering the shock her own mother would have suffered, knowing that her baptismal name had been shortened in such a rough manner by one so young. Her mother was of another time, a generation of manners with hats and gloves worn without argument on chaperoned visits to town. Angela thought of herself as being at the centre point of a pendulum swinging from the *correctness* of the world her mother lived in to the *casualness* of Sadie's. Belonging a little to both worlds, she could never quite figure out which was the better existence. Had she been the lucky one? Living through so many changes – many of which she'd failed to appreciate with a careless blink of the eye. She often asked herself, can you ever value time enough? The answer, she found, was – probably not; particularly now she had acres and acres of it to fill.

'I've got an idea,' said Sadie, surfing over the wave of the last conversation and landing back on a previously trodden shore. 'How about I come in each day when I get back from school and you can help me with this debating thingy. We have to prepare something each week – read it in the paper like, and talk about it. If I tell you what it is, you can do the reading bit and tell me what I need to know. We can talk about it for, say ... ten minutes every day and that'll help it stick in my brain. It'll work two ways, we'll both get something out of it. It'll exercise *your* brain so you don't turn into a really old person and I'll get your great knowledge and wisdom. I shall be the best bit of your day!'

This happened to be the longest speech Sadie had ever made and it gave Angela a glimmer of hope with regard to debating skills. Before any reply could be formed, Sadie was up and off with the dogs at her ankles. Angela watched those long, long legs as they attempted to negotiate getting out of the front door without her yapping companions escaping.

'And … if I'm here every day, one day Joe might turn up too!' Sadie shouted. The door shut with a clatter. Angela reached for the TV remote. The door reopened. 'And Ange, if it's *your* lucky day, I'll take you for a spin in that wheelchair you've never been in!'

The door slammed again and Angela winced at the thought of the glass panels shattering. Next came the sound of the key turning the lock – good girl for remembering, she thought. The reference to that wheelchair struck a different chord. 'No she won't!' she told the room. 'No one is *ever* going to get me in that thing!'

Angela felt enlivened by Sadie, a daily visit to look forward to would be a bonus. It was uplifting to think that she could still affect the world and somehow pass a nugget of wisdom from one end of the pendulum swing to the other.

Unfortunately her sense of well-being did not last long. Imprisonment had turned her into a philosopher, except she'd no one with whom to share any new-found understanding as Batty paid no attention to that sort of thing. He was a practical man, always trying to get her to be more positive through activity, rigorous in his intention to ensure all those tedious physiotherapy exercises were completed every day since that damn fall. Did divine retribution exist after all? Her husband would describe this notion as "rubbish" while she would counter by pointing out he wasn't the one sitting in a chair with hours and hours to ponder. Was it true, she would often wonder, that it's the good who die young? This belief had subliminally been growing inside since Mark's first wife had been killed in that terrible accident. If ever a soul existed who could be classified as good, that had been Francesca – in *thought, word and deed*, together with that unforgettable voice which had sung its way through such a short life.

Her own, long life, had been different.

Almighty God, our heavenly Father, we have sinned against you, through our own fault, in thought, word and deed, by what we have done, and by what we have left undone.

The words learnt at the age of fifteen in Holy Communion class would not fade and not quite allow themselves to be shaken off even after much neglect. Such ruminating brought about the conclusion that it was about time to balance the books and undo some of the wrongs she'd committed. In spite of a lifetime of trying to reject God and His great work, He had started to figure more regularly in her musings – what harm could there be in ensuring that she lived by His creed before popping her clogs.

Life was a balance sheet, Angela concluded – helping Sadie could therefore be slipped on to the plus side of her own personal life-account. That left Kate, Joe and Mark where she'd so often chalked up figures in the negative column; there was much to rectify.

* * *

Joe stared inside the fridge looking for something to inspire his negligible culinary skills as his father, late back from a staff meeting, exploded into the kitchen. Joe braced himself.

'I couldn't believe my eyes when I read this!' Mark shouted. He was holding the letter Joe had left for him at school.

'You'd want that from the other boys ... a letter of resignation.'

'Can't you see? It's different, I'm your dad, why couldn't you *speak* to me first?'

'Couldn't.' Joe closed the fridge door and pulled the cuffs of his sweatshirt further down over his wrists.

'How do you think I feel, my son dropping out of the team at this stage in the school year? I have to build it up after last year's leavers.'

'Not my problem.'

'You're my star player.'

Joe was trapped – his father blocked his exit from the kitchen – unless he bolted outside, and it wouldn't be much fun to be stuck out there in the pouring rain. No choice then, time to get real. 'That's it; I'm your son ... your star player. They all know they've no chance. All that extra coaching you give me. I'm not cool with it any more, get it!'

'No I don't *get it*. But you *get it* – you get a lot more attention than most of that lot get from their parents!'

'Only if I'm playing football.'

'What's that meant to mean?'

He turned his back and murmured, 'Have you got all day?'

'What did you say?' said Mark as he forcibly made Joe face him.

'You got all day? To listen – yeah, right.'

'Go on, I'm listening now.'

'No you're not!' Joe shouted. 'You don't want to know what I want ... or feel ... about ...' he searched for the right words and glared at his father, '... anything like. It's not worth ...'

Mark let go and reeled backwards as if he'd been kicked in the stomach. Joe watched him wrestle with what to do next. Having often enraged his father to the point of reaching a precipice, this time it was different; he'd pushed him right over. He feared the comeback; unknown territory.

'Look ... neither of us has eaten ... we'll get a take-away,' said Mark quietly.

The idea of sitting down to eat together after this was a joke, thought Joe.

'Let's calm down, take half-time so to speak, and get some food inside us. Then we can kick a ball about in the garden. When we've done all that we can have a good man to man chat.'

Sometimes Joe couldn't believe the stuff his father came out with. It's another joke, he's just wanting time to prepare his defence on this new playing field.

'Fuck off!' said Joe as he slammed the door behind him.

6

STEPS TAKEN

Two weeks after first encountering Sye, Kate still remained undecided on the direction her life would take. Her mind had processed the meeting as a dream, or even a nightmare, and she persuaded herself of the impossibility of Sye's existence being anywhere other than in her own overactive imagination. To counter one world she refused to face, she allowed the real world to take over and control her thoughts, while the unexplained experience lay below the surface – like a shoot held underground before it breaks through the earth to find the answer as to what it would become.

Kate never felt directly threatened with the wardrobe jammed hard into its space, but began to invent plenty of reasons not to spend long periods of time in the living room contemplating the view. Those fourteen days had been spent as if she'd been waiting for the outcome of a medical test, putting uneasy thoughts as far away as possible. Denial of all things *above* forced her to get on with why she was there alone in the first place, knowing she couldn't keep putting off the decision about her marriage – it wasn't fair on Mark. This desire to organise her thoughts manifested itself in countless hikes along the beach. As she walked, the voice that occupied her head whispered like the sand which often nearly blinded her on the more merciless east-wind days. Sometimes the sand spun around her feet, just above the ground, and at other times it would be driven higher by the wind and blast at her hair before trying to etch the patterns of the changing tide on her face. Some days the sand yielded to her sinking feet, demanding a considerable effort to make the next small step, whilst there were other days when hard sea-rippled ridges could be felt right through the soles of her walking boots. The best walks were enjoyed when the sun shone timidly at first, growing in confidence by small degrees, to illuminate the scene strewn with motionless pools left behind by the sea. On days like these Kate would walk barefoot, ignoring the chill on the virgin surface of shimmering coastline – her footprints making their claim – and only then could she lift her face to the sky with a buoyant sense of self-belief and exhilaration. But, more often than not she would have to wrap her body in all the protective clothing she could manage, cowering as she braved the empty beach.

So often the elements defeated her in the end – there is only so much pain a person can take before retreating.

Despite all this introspection, actual communication with the outside world did take place. Kate often went for her walk in the morning before catching the bus to Burnham Market in the afternoon to wander around the shops and galleries. Her favourite pastime was scouring the second-hand bookshop for a bargain amongst the packed shelves of once loved volumes. She had taken to eating a small meal at the pub in the evenings, often with one of her book-finds for company, to spin out time away from the house. Kate would choose one of Phil's starters instead of a main course as most days she'd have grazed on treats found in one of the local delicatessens, still behaving like a tourist rather than a resident. She usually stayed until Margret and Phil closed up, following which this unlikely group of companions would end up in Phil's flat: the young trendy chef, the thirty-something high-flyer and the pensioner who was not anywhere near ready to admit that yet. They relished the ease of the disorganised muddle Phil lived in, bound by a mutual need for the comfort provided by their evolving friendship.

'You're certainly a good advert for my food, coming here each night – I wish you'd eat more though, you're not having enough to keep a gnat alive, let alone make me any profit. Good job it's out of season, otherwise I'd have to make you eat in the kitchen,' teased Phil. 'Can't I persuade you to eat a full three course meal one of these days?'

Kate frowned. 'And sit for longer at the table? There's a limit to how much of my own company I can take.'

'I can sympathise with that,' interjected Margret. 'Why do you think I'm so keen to work here and put up with Phil every evening?'

Phil poured them all a large glass of his favourite Spanish wine. 'I presumed it was because of my handsome good looks and rate of pay!'

'Hold on with that wine,' said Margret, laughing. 'I'll fall off my bike …'

Kate took her first gulp. 'You'd better not do that, I'm relying on you and your bike to chaperone my walk home – you know, in case smugglers' ghosts are waiting to pounce.' It ought to have been humorous banter except as soon as the words were spoken Kate had to acknowledge what was hiding in the recesses of her mind; the thought was quickly pushed into its box and the lid shut.

Margret summoned up a broad Norfolk accent, 'You couldn't be more right, there be lots of ghosts in these here parts.'

Kate considered grasping this as an opportunity to unburden herself but fear of ridicule held her back. She was thankful the topic was dropped as the conversation took on a different direction. Each of them recounted stories from their lives to date – filling in the blank spaces, bit by bit. That is Phil and Kate did, while Margret merely seemed happy to listen. Phil often chose to describe his past travels which had begun in France, followed by Spain and Greece. He'd tell them how he worked his way around the tourist trails, in both good and bad kitchens, hoping to learn his trade from those who used ingredients with flair and skills passed down through generations.

On this particular night he opened up even more. 'It was while I was working in Corfu, stagnating in one of those All Inclusive hotels, that I met Grace. She was on a sort of gap year, waitressing in the restaurant with a friend who chose to stay put with a bronzed Greek picked up on a beach. Grace was stunning – planning to conquer the world! She made me realise I was treading water.'

'You met in the sea?' asked Kate facetiously, as the full effect of the wine took hold.

'Very funny … no, I wasn't *learning* anything any more,' he said. 'I'd become trapped in a cycle of earning, clubbing and drinking – when shifts allowed.'

'Seems like heaven to me,' said Margret.

'Believe me it gets tedious after a while. Grace snapped me out of it and we set off on an education of travel, cooking, sex and booze in Italy.'

'Sounds like the swinging sixties,' said Margret, morosely.

'Not long after we'd got there, she wanted to travel further afield so we worked and saved until we could afford to get ourselves to India – she wanted a different experience altogether. We got that alright.'

His audience waited for him to continue. He didn't.

Kate pitched in: 'What happened to gorgeous Grace then? Did her *amazing* loveliness catch the eye of another?' Words straight away regretted. 'I'm sorry, I don't mean to be a bitch, it slipped out – the wine.'

'It's ok,' he said. 'You're right about amazing loveliness, but it wasn't beauty like you see on the front covers of magazines, all make-up and stuff … when I said stunning I meant on the inside really. It was her spirit that attracted me, led and moulded me until …'

'So – ' said Margret, sitting bolt upright and folding her arms, 'what happened to her?'

'Go on, Phil,' said Kate, sensing the pivotal point of the story.

'We'd worked hard, loads of overtime … saved everything we could to get there and then … our lives … forked. You see, when we reached India, I couldn't stand the poverty everywhere we went, being a tourist and not being able to do anything – standing by and watching. It overwhelmed me and I needed to escape. Grace on the other hand witnessed all that deprivation and wanted to stay. She tried her best to persuade me to stay too. You see, I couldn't … I panicked, was ashamed of myself – my inability to actually *do* something. She's working for Save the Children out there as we speak.' He paused, picked up his glass, vaguely registered that it was empty and replaced it on the table.

'Then I heard from Dad saying he wanted to retire. Would I be interested in running the pub? It was still privately owned, you see. I used it as an excuse to get away from India, to run and hide myself out here. I tried to persuade her to come with me, get married and start a family: we were sitting on our hotel balcony with a massive panorama of Delhi all around – on a night when all the aromas and sounds of the city rose from the streets below. Curry and chaos …'

Kate was transported, her senses aroused. She could tell that Margret felt the same.

'I could promise her so much except the one thing she wanted. In the end I didn't stand a chance. All those children – they won easily.'

'You never know, perhaps one day in the future,' Kate said – fatuous words, she thought, but what else could she say?

'The likelihood of that is zero. I love it here, it's home. I love getting up each morning and going for my run, making my own plans and seeing them through. Grace taught me that you see. Taught me that you need a strong sense of direction in life – unfortunately ours followed different tracks. She'd have nothing to do out here, she's moved on from waiting tables. I get a postcard from time to time. Not often.'

On her way home with Margret pushing the bike, using its meagre lamplight to guide them in the dark, Kate returned to those words "sense of direction". They'd stung her and seemed to have affected Margret too, who walked mutely alongside. Kate suggested that she stayed the night in Joe's room rather than going home alone so late, hopeful of the chance to bring up the subject of the attic again. It remained an unrequited intention – stuffed back into the box of ghostly matters.

'No thanks. Prefer my own bed. I think I'm up to pedalling.' Kate doubted the truth of that and watched the back wheel of the bike wobble away as it tried to cope with its owner's cycling proficiency much impaired by wine.

The second Kate walked in through the front door, the change was apparent. Over the last two weeks she'd acted out of character, letting things go. With no one to pick up after or care for, the usually ordered kitchen had gradually turned into a dump – a term often used by Kate to describe Joe's bedroom back home. But in this strangely disorientating moment her walking boots stood by the front door neatly stored, not left lying randomly where she'd pulled them off that morning. The kitchen table had been cleared with no sign of her solitary breakfast anywhere. Her abandoned newspaper had been carefully folded and the coat left thrown over the back of the armchair had disappeared – probably efficiently stowed in the dratted wardrobe. Kate felt unsteady, her mouth dry, and there was a small nag of pain in her right temple – the wine taking its revenge. Alcohol equals dehydration so replace the water, she reminded herself. She took a large tumbler from the cupboard next to the spotless Belfast sink and filled it from the tap.

Turning back to face the kitchen she hoped to see that it had all been an intoxicated delusion. The disturbing orderliness remained, refusing to be shaken off. In need of an explanation, she guessed it must have been Margret who'd come in that afternoon and tidied up with some helpful motive in mind. It had been almost six o'clock when Kate had arrived back from Burnham Market and she'd gone straight to the pub from the bus, desperate for any human contact and the warmth of the fire after a cold, solitary day. Now, longing for the company of others for a different reason, she gingerly pushed open her bedroom door and saw that the duvet which she'd kicked off onto the floor had been moved. It lay on the bed, obediently in place.

A memory jolted her: *it couldn't be Margret.* Earlier both Phil and Margret had been discussing their successful trip that day to King's Lynn to buy new additions for the B&B guestroom they were preparing at the pub. There had to be another explanation. It must be Mark, perhaps he'd come back to sort things out with her and tidied the place up to get her in a good mood. He must be upstairs, having parked away from the house in order to catch her off guard. Kate tried to compose herself, glanced in the oval mirror on the kitchen wall, ran her fingers through her hair and frowned at the rather flushed reflection staring back. What on earth was she going to say to him?

Expecting to find Mark sitting on the sofa with his feet up on the stool as he regularly did, she was surprised at her sense of loss at not seeing him there – a notion usurped by the need to face the truth. She had to accept it. *So he's a poltergeist now and a tidy one at that!* The box opened – the lid shot up and everything escaped and tumbled out into her mind.

Shaking from head to foot, Kate ran down the stairs where she barricaded herself into her bedroom with the back of the wooden chair, knowing that it would make little difference. If Sye could command the house to tidy itself, what else could he do? Still shaking, Kate sat on the bed and considered making a bolt for it to wake up Phil in the pub or Margret at home. The thought of wandering about the village alone at that late hour put her off ... and would they believe her anyway?

That night all her demons were let loose, an array of thoughts danced, collided and entwined with any sense of lucidity lost. Having eventually climbed into bed she was too hot, too cold, too confused. *Too scared.* And there was nowhere to go. When she did manage to get to sleep, she dreamt of being with Margret again, but this time she was standing beside her at the water's edge – a solid darkness pressing in on them. They seemed to stand there for hours, full of anticipation for some unknown happening. The water in the channel conveyed the impression that it was waiting too, with a low mist hovering just above its smooth surface while the night decided whether to surrender to a new dawn. At last, with the very first glimmer of daylight, a V-shaped ripple disturbed the high tide, forming a point at the bow of a silent, gliding, vessel, sailed by smuggler ghosts, no doubt.

7

A LEAP

Just before daybreak, with so little sleep during that long night, Kate stumbled out of the house and down the lane to watch the sunrise over the narrow strip of water left at low tide. It was the complete opposite of her dream of high tide sapping at her feet, this was real life – this shallow water. You can drown in either, she thought.

On her return Kate emptied the wardrobe of coats, shoes, umbrellas and a sand-scuffed set of boules. That task completed, she tugged at the long drawer at its base to discover it was full of large books, mainly art related, which she took out and piled up on the stairs. At the bottom of the drawer was a stash of well-thumbed comics, these she left in place, untouched. Now that the weight of the wardrobe had been lightened, it shifted more easily than before, relinquishing its role as keeper of secrets with much less effort on her part.

Kate started to climb the next flight of stairs; half way up she sat down on the middle step looking towards the back of the wardrobe, hugging her knees and sharing the space with her fear. It occurred to her that this step was like a home base in a game of tag. She recalled an old-fashioned nursery song her mother would sing about sitting halfway up the stairs and it being a midway point between the "nursery" and the "town". Her child-brain thought of the nursery as embodying everything safe and secure, a place where one lived life protected for ever – the complete opposite of the town which held everything that was unfamiliar and frightening. As an adult she was still only beginning to accept the fact that life was never that black and white. Her mother's song rang in her ears, but Kate felt a long way from a place of safety; she had no refuge below, and above lay something quite terrifying, yet compelling.

With her nightmares out and living in the daylight, Kate had invented so many worst-case scenarios that she'd lost count. What was equally bad was that she had no one she could talk to about what was going on. Sitting at the kitchen table after breakfast she'd made a list: Mark – Dom – Phil – Joe – Batty – Margret – Angela. Each was crossed out, one by one. When she arrived at the end of the list she looked at the lack of women confidantes she had in her life, compared to men. What did that say about her? Mark had made it to the top of the list – it threw her that she'd automatically put him there, despite everything. Again Kate contemplated locking up and leaving, but on this occasion her thoughts were of getting the next flight she could to Nice, to talk to her parents. Yet she had to concede that even when they'd lived in England she'd never run to them for support and she wasn't going to start because of all this ... how would she begin to explain? Anyway they would be the last people on earth to believe in anything spiritual, unless it was in a bottle. There was no alternative; there remained only one *being* she could talk to.

Kate stood up to stretch her legs, now numb from sitting,

and climbed the remaining stairs to the attic. At the top she took a tentative pace forward and peered into the uninviting room, unable to decide whether it was courage or stupidity that had got her there. Huge relief – the attic was empty! Nothing: bare floorboards, no paintings, no cushions and, what was most important, no person. It *had* all been her imagination after all.

A wave of emotional strength galvanised her to move towards the window – rapidly followed by a sickening sensation of something being not quite right. As before it was the view that challenged reality. Checking her watch, to make sure she hadn't actually been sitting on the stairs for hours, she found there had been no lost time on its face. The position of the sun and the height of the tide were all wrong and didn't relate in any way to that which she'd seen earlier.

As she looked back into the room, this time she couldn't pretend it was her imagination. All her senses were assailed, triggered by the smell of candlewax, mixed with that sweet fragrance of joss sticks. There was the slightest hint of meandering music which steadily grew louder and louder until some mournful Indian instrument flooded the attic with its sound. The painting on the easel fought with the sound for dominance, its surface covered in clashing psychedelic colours, boldly applied to the canvas in a smeared, circular motion. Contrasting with the view from the window, the picture screamed a dare to the observer: *reject all natural beauty for the turmoil of this canvas!* She winced at the level of sound filling the room as the voice of George Harrison came from the LP spinning on the turntable. And amongst all this, cross-legged on the floor, centre stage, sat Sye.

'Sorry, I'll turn it down,' he shouted. 'There's usually no

one to complain so I tend to lose myself in it.' He lowered the volume, taking his time, watching Kate.

'And the weed no doubt,' added Kate wryly, when the sound had become tolerable.

'You mean the hash?' said Sye. 'It's my muse, it turns off all those boring colours outside and switches on beautiful concoctions in my mind; it turns me on.'

George Harrison's words were about the space that grew between people. Right on the mark, thought Kate. She was a good few years older than this man, but even greater was the time and space between their existences.

'It's not something that I've used to get through life,' she said, pushing back recollection of some of the props she'd needed at University. She mitigated her past behaviour by reminding herself that she too had been younger then.

'Except you're not getting through life, are you? You're quite stuck. Try some hash to head off a crash!' he said, laughing at his own humour. He picked up what Kate saw as a rather ghastly orange-flowered retro cushion and threw it at her. Despite its design, she caught it and hugged it to her body. The softness of the cushion comforted her for an instant, before she quickly threw it to the floor as she would have had it been on fire; moments ago it hadn't existed, now it did. Sye lay back on the cushions, relaxed and at ease. She could observe him well like this. With his hair falling away from his face, strong contours were emphasised, the hollows of his cheeks defining chiselled features. His eyes were shut and she realised that as she'd avoided matching his gaze on their previous encounter, she'd no idea what colour lay beneath those closed lids.

'Stop staring at me and come and sit – you make me feel

forced to stand and welcome you and it's more comfortable down here.'

Kate didn't move. Sye sat up and opened his eyes. A growing desire to see what colour they were, made her step closer. It was a shock – his eyes pierced her; they were an electric blue. Dark hair and blue eyes, a striking combination.

'Look, I'm sorry … about the tidying thing … it's not like me at all … look around you; it was an aberration, it won't happen again.' He laughed at himself, and stopped abruptly. 'I was pissed off waiting, if you want to know. I waited long enough in the first place for you to get rid of Joe and Mark – thought I'd have to do something spectacular to achieve that but you did it all by yourself. Well done!'

'Don't be patronising,' Kate spat out. She was still standing, looking down at Sye, conscious that while she remained on her feet, above him, she had a chance of getting back in control. With his legs still crossed he rolled over on the cushions and collected one to hide behind to use for mock protection.

'Sorry, sorry,' he said, pretending fear. 'I know I'm a shit. But, scout's honour, I didn't intervene. What happened between you and Mark was all your own work.' Sye casually leant over to the record player, picked up the arm and lifted it off. He then grabbed the *Sgt Pepper* LP and threw it so that it landed almost on top of the record sleeve next to her feet. The faces on the iconic cover peered out from around the edge of the disc.

'I can't believe you came downstairs and went through my personal things. What right have you got to think you could tidy up my life?'

'No right at all, but I have got some kind of … *superpower.*

Look at me!' he shouted as he jumped up onto his feet and thrust out his chest whilst flexing his biceps. His eyes were alight, his laughter demonstrating how impressed he was with himself.

Kate unleashed her sharp tongue: 'You do think a lot of yourself, don't you?' She kicked at the cushions and moved back to the window, forcing those eyes of his to bore into her back, not her soul. Kate determined not to let him in.

Silence.

A long cold silence.

It was as if all the colour had been drained from the room. She turned around, this time deliberately slowly, hoping that her tempestuous words had broken what surely *must* be a dream and that like a stilled miniature snow dome, everything would have fallen gently back into place.

Yet Sye was still there, hunched up on his cushions, hugging his knees as she had done on her safety step. He was rocking; it was barely observable, a small repetitive movement which Kate found invaded her own body consciousness, mimicking her own heart rhythm. For those few seconds they were held together in time, like conjoined twins whose bodies were tuned to each other's life-flow pattern. He lifted his head and there were tears held in his eyes, not spilling over. Against her better judgement, Kate moved towards him and knelt down opposite, uncertain whether his reaction was caused by the weed, the circumstance in which he existed or her sharp words. Conceivably all three, she surmised. Still, what *was* the truth of this situation and this indefinable young man?

It struck Kate that he had stolen her thoughts: 'I wanted to attract your attention ...' Sye said, ' ... somehow. I could feel your mind fighting my very existence. I was fading in every way imaginable. I could tell you were pushing me out and filling your mind with others, mostly Mark …' He wiped his eyes with the back of his hands. 'He must wait, he has to. I come first, *you have to understand that*.'

She didn't.

'Otherwise it's hopeless. *Again*. I didn't go through your things, I didn't go downstairs, I had no need to. I can do things with my mind. I'm not very good at it … it's getting easier. I practised on little things at first. You didn't notice the zip on your make-up bag done up, a spoon left on the draining board put back in the drawer, a sock hidden in a walking boot. When you were out I sort of … did it in my head. And it worked, it brought you back, didn't it?' His broad smile was one of triumph.

'I was right then. A tidy poltergeist, that's what you are!'

'I'm *much* more than that,' he snapped back, his mood bouncing backwards and forwards like a tennis ball across a net. His look was intense, those striking blue eyes wounding her as much as her careless words had wounded him.

Kate needed to do something to stop herself returning his stare while she tried to fathom what he really was. She picked up a joss stick and softly blew out the flame. The scented smoke hung on in a long strand, like a stray shard of mist between them. The aroma enjoyed its freedom until it was consumed amongst the stale smell of the neglected ashtrays. If it was a warning, Kate chose to ignore it; instead she acknowledged to herself he had somehow manipulated her to move from her secure step for ever.

'So what now?' she asked.

His eyes lit up. 'I don't know. I need you … to visit me.

To validate my existence; already having someone to talk to has transformed everything. Believe me, I don't know what's going on but I do know getting you here was imperative – I've no doubts about that.'

'But you're not like me.' Then the words rushed out of Kate's mouth before she was able to stop them: 'Are you dead?' What a question, never in her wildest dreams had she ever thought she would in all seriousness speak those three words in that order in one sentence.

'Yes.'

A simple answer.

Kate felt sick, the room tilted.

'I need some water,' she somehow succeeded in saying, desperate for something real to neutralise the unreality.

'Sorry, I think it's turned off up here,' said the man who was an apparition, poltergeist or some other kind of spirit. Kate's mind was still trying to settle on a known concept. 'Have some of this.' Sye picked up a half-used joint, lit it and passed it over. She was sorely tempted. When she shook her head, he placed it in his mouth and took an intense drag, deliberately taking his time, watching her reaction.

'I said *yes* because I know I'm *not alive*,' he eventually said. 'I also know I'm lost, somewhere between what you call reality and something else; the next thing – God knows what that is, I don't.'

'Can't you tell me why you're in my life, my space? We have nothing to do with each other, there's no link between us.'

'There's a possible one, maybe …'

'Explain.'

'We were both rummaging about in our past trying to

make sense of our present.'

Kate picked up the record and put it back in its sleeve, the faces on the cover mocking her.

'None of this makes sense,' she said.

'Don't you think I've asked myself every conceivable question about all this?' He waved his hands aimlessly. The joint fell from his fingers onto the bare floorboards. It lay there, lifeless without the breath needed to inhale its promise.

A notion struck Kate. 'Can your thoughts control *me*?' Fear came back making her whole body feel cold, detached from her racing mind. 'If you can think yourself into another time and space *and* move things around, what can you do with me?'

'I can't control you, not directly, physically or mentally, the stuff around you is different.'

'How do you know you can't control me?' The fear shivered over her skin again, taking possession. 'Have you tried?'

'I've tried with the people walking along the embankment out there. They weren't very co-operative at all, wouldn't let me into their heads. I thought I'd succeeded with making a dog leap into that fresh water channel beyond the reeds, then it retrieved a stick thrown in by some kid who'd been out of sight. Big disappointment on my part. What do you mean *another time*, what are you talking about?' Her earlier comment had just found its mark.

'It's obvious isn't it?'

'No.'

The fear forced Kate's words into a shrill rant. 'Look at you, your long hair and hippie clothes, your music – this whole damn place oozes the sixties and I've seen the turn of the millennium!'

'*What!*'

'I think your psychic leap has missed a few decades,' she replied.

You wouldn't have supposed a ghost could actually turn white, Kate thought as she watched him take in her words. She bent down and picked up the joint from the floor. When she looked up he had gone. The room was completely empty. And in her hand – a slowly vanishing trace of colourless dust.

8

WAITING

That Sye had shown himself to be as vulnerable as Kate made all the difference to her. A shared connection *had* been found – a mutual fear of the unknown and a strong desire for answers. Kate's new understanding was a revelation. Sye's *need* of her presence – to somehow enable either the continuation of, or a change to, his manifestation – equalled her craving to solve this unearthly mystery. No more steps in life could be taken until a resolution for both of them had been found. It was for this reason that the wardrobe had not been pushed back into place, but left awkwardly, to permit clear access to their joint pathway. There was no doubt in her mind that another encounter in the attic would happen soon. Her revelation about the time difference had unnerved him and she acknowledged that he needed space to get used to the realisation that they each belonged to a different era.

To ease her own adjustment to this state of affairs, Kate conceived a word to describe the physical and emotional place she'd stumbled across: *Timescape*. It was comforting to have a specific label for her unique experience. Two weeks later, still waiting for Sye's reappearance, she stood looking out of the window in the attic and wrote the newly crafted word in the dust clinging to the glass, savouring the way it captured within itself the word *escape*. It would be such a pleasure to share it with Sye. While tracing the letters repeatedly, she stretched out its sound tunefully, playing with different notes, in the hope it would conjure him up. Apparently he wasn't that impressed. Kate hadn't expected him to take so long – surely, as he'd already adapted to a whole change in being, this one leap shouldn't have freaked him out so much.

On every daily visit to the bleak, uninhabited, room there was nothing. Not a whiff of incense or a note of music. Disappointment grew and filled the hollow – it remained a very silent emptiness. When all this began it would have been a relief if Sye had moved on, but that time was spent and that state of mind passed.

There had been no personal communication from Mark either. It was a whole month since the split, albeit at her request. He had been dutifully sending on all her post which was collected together each week and forwarded in a large brown envelope. Not ever was a note added. The envelope would be opened hungrily and sifted through with apprehensive anticipation, leaving Kate's emotions uncharacteristically disordered, as it became apparent that no sign of Mark had been slipped inside. What the package did communicate was the deep hurt and anger caused by their split; it was a physical punch in the stomach to see his handwriting on the envelopes. Like a child seeking out *some* sort of attention, good or bad, she just wanted anything from him – an angry rant or a hopeful plead, a caring enquiry or even a rambling letter of daily events suggesting that she was missed amongst them.

Why didn't he make any move at all?

The absence of contact shouted out at her. She could almost hear her ordinarily even-tempered husband telling her to 'bloody well hurry up' and sort out the direction their lives would take – together or apart? He had no idea that it wasn't that easy; any original purpose had become interwoven with what else was going on inside the four walls of The Old Pilot's House. Kate searched for Mark inside the brown envelopes in the same way as she searched for Sye upstairs – hopefully, needily, with fear and with regret that the wrong words may have been spoken at the wrong time to both men.

9

DIVULGENCE

The pub around the corner from McKinley Nichols filled up, as Friday evening refugees from the world of work dropped in. The mixed bag of clientele reflected its need for a makeover, it being neither genuinely traditional nor contemporary in its décor and suffering from neglect since the seventies.

Mark sat in the corner of the bar waiting for his companion. He felt guilty about taking over Dom as a confidante from Kate, but was convinced that their friend held the key to his understanding of what she'd been going through. These Friday night meet-ups in the pub had become a habit as it was the one evening he could have a decent drink. Not much could be imbibed on Saturday nights as he played football early every Sunday morning with the parents' team, usually spending the rest of the day preparing lessons for the next week or marking cover work for subjects well out of his area of expertise.

Dom arrived; he signalled his intention of going to the bar and did Mark want topping up. Replying with a thumbs-up, Mark then responded to a text which had come through from Joe: WNT B BACK 2NITE, STAYIN @ GRANS. That's a relief, he thought, as he keyed in a brief reply: OK SEE

YOU 2MORO. Dom lined up a new pint of bitter next to Mark's half-empty glass and sat down opposite.

'You look happy, good news?'

'Sort of, I don't have to worry about Joe tonight. He'll be well looked after as usual by my mum and dad – so no confrontation or total non-communication to steel myself for.'

'That good eh?'

'You could say so – I've hardly seen him since he left the football team, he vanishes most days after school and I'm always busy with meetings, or matches, anyway.'

'Don't you see him in the day, around school?'

'I think he's become an expert on avoiding me, can't bear anyone to see us together in school, I'm barred from even sharing the same air.'

'That's typical, of his age I mean.'

'Sometimes I see him with that girl who lives next door to my parents – that's a worry too. Just when I need to talk to him about all that sex stuff, we're not speaking at all. I wish Kate were here, she'd know how to handle it.'

'I don't think anyone knows the right way to deal with the idea of the next generation discovering sex. Did you talk about it in great detail with your parents? I know I didn't!'

'To be honest I can't remember.'

'There you are you see – no memorable conversations. Anyway aren't the schools meant to teach them how to put on a condom … *and* I believe you get a free pair of underpants these days if you have a chlamydia test!' Dom knocked back his beer.

'I'm uneasy about that girl though, she's not got a good reputation at school – got a bit of a mouth on her and she flirts with some of the other male teachers.'

'Because they let her, I bet – or wishful thinking on their part! It's what he needs, someone to bring him out of himself, spotty adolescence is the worst thing on earth, don't you remember?'

'Too long ago for that,' mumbled Mark.

'If you remembered, you'd be able to relate to what Joe's going through.'

'Oh God,' Mark sighed, 'I'm a rubbish parent, sometimes I think you'd make a better job of it than me.'

'It's easy when you're just an onlooker. I don't have to live with it.'

'And I'm an equally rubbish husband by all accounts too.'

'No … help, someone please!' Dom had a theatrically pained expression on his face. 'Not back to that … thought we sorted all that out last week.'

True, conceded Mark, he'd spent much of the last seven days struggling to digest their conversation. Whilst he'd known that Kate had been finding Joe's adolescence difficult, he'd failed to see the extent to which she'd taken everything so personally. What had hurt, was all she'd told Dom about how he and Joe had not let her in, about their "special bond". Mark was beginning to realise that this was what had blocked her from a close relationship with Joe, so when the difficult times arrived they'd had nothing to draw on. God, life was complicated – at least the goalposts stayed in the same place on a football pitch.

Dom pulled off his tie, carefully rolled it up and placed it in his jacket pocket. 'Each week we go over the same ground, sitting in the same place, in the same pub – if you've nothing better to do tonight we could go for a meal and go on to a club. It would make a change, wouldn't it?'

'It'd make a change but that's not to say it's a good idea. I live in hope that Kate and I *will* get back together, I don't want to blow it with her by picking up a replacement. Don't think that would go down too well.'

'You'd be so lucky!' Dom laughed.

'Did she ever talk to you about the baby thing?'

'No,' replied Dom unconvincingly.

'It wasn't what she wanted at first,' said Mark, determined to elucidate. 'When we first married, "Kate Nichols" was the full on career girl – but you know all about that, working with her.' Mark realised the two pints on an empty stomach were beginning to make him state the obvious. 'But she started off keen to mother Joe … it didn't work. My parents spoiled him thoroughly after Fran died and Kate wasn't willing to do that. He habitually went to Mum with a problem, not Kate. And I let it happen.'

From staring down and nursing his bitter, Mark looked up to see an expression on Dom's face he couldn't quite read and wondered if it was pity; it was good to feel that at least one other person cared enough to listen to his ramblings.

Mark gave an appreciative smile and continued. 'And then she threw in the baby idea, wanted a child that would be both of ours – it seemed right at the time. I know this will sound sort of wrong … but Fran and I were planning on having another kid, so, you see, as well as losing his mother along with one set of grandparents Joe also lost a brother or sister never born. I began to think that if Kate and I made up for that, if Joe could get involved with the baby, it'd help us bond as a real family and make up in some small way for what he'd lost out on. I didn't reckon on him hitting puberty though.'

'Listen to yourself – yes, it does sound weird,' said Dom. 'You said *yes* to a baby because you thought it would help Joe, not because you wanted to create another human being in its own right.'

Realising, far too late, that he'd scored an own goal, Mark drained his glass before replying. 'That's a place I don't want to go. Anyway the baby thing didn't happen. In the end she wouldn't even discuss IVF, accused me of … "having no space on the team for any other members" – the team being made up of purely Joe and me according to her.'

To Mark's embarrassment what he'd just said got to him; Joe and me – there didn't even seem to be that any more. *Sod it, I'm **not** going to cry in front of Dom.* Dom was quickly there with his handkerchief, Mark pushed it away.

Instead, to cover up his shame, he leant over and stole a serviette from the adjacent table and wiped his whole face with it to deal with the hot sweat which had swept over him. 'It's much too hot in here. It's the alcohol getting to me *and* not knowing if Kate's blown the final whistle, or half-time.'

Dom leant across the table and gripped Mark's wrists. 'Shit happens, *every day*, happening everywhere I'm afraid, people move on, things change.'

Mark was taken aback: when looking for consolation, stark reality had been served up instead. He felt claustrophobic under the intensity of Dom's gaze and unrelenting grip. Pulling away, he seized the menu lying on the table. 'Shall we order some food?' he suggested, thankful to be able to hide his discomfort behind a barrier of colour-enhanced grills.

'I agree, we need food,' said Dom as he snatched the menu and closed it. 'Or we'll both be under the table before we eat what's on it. But let's not stay here, my friend.' He playfully hit Mark over the head with what he obviously thought of as an offensive menu of pub grub. 'Let's go and get a curry.'

Later, between mouthfuls of Chicken Jalfrezi and a pretty decent red wine chosen by Dom, Mark asked how the business was going. Initially Dom remained remarkably quiet. Normally he would boast about this contract and that deal and the generous sums of money that these would yield, to the point that Mark would end up feeling totally inadequate on his teacher's salary. After some coaxing from Mark, Dom opened up.

'To be honest with you, the business is in critical free-fall without Kate. So you and I are much the same aren't we? Waiting for her. You see, I've spent a fruitless afternoon working on this peppermint tea ad.' He referred to his Blackberry. 'All I came up with was ... ah, here it is ... *Let the Tea take the Strain.*'

Mark looked blank, was he meant to applaud?

'I doubted the pun would work.' Dom deleted the item from his phone. 'Like you I'm nothing without her – if she'd been there she'd have persevered with copious research until it triggered a uniquely inspiring proposal.'

'As you say, it looks like we're both in need of my wife ...' said Mark, not used to such outpourings from Dom. 'It's like we're both on the losing team – we plainly have to face this together.'

Dom smiled in agreement and poured them both another large glass of wine. 'We should ...'

'What?'

'It doesn't matter ... forget it.'

Mark could see it was Dom's turn to sweat. 'You alright mate, you look a tad hot.'

'Too much spicy food.'

'I've followed your advice – about letting her have some time to herself, without any contact – some time to really miss me, I hope. It's got to come from her, if I push things, I shall blow it.'

'But it's been four weeks. I've put a lot of things on hold at the office. It's time she stopped messing us about.'

'Don't be too harsh, it doesn't suit you – I thought we were here to talk about my problems. You're a bit on edge aren't you?'

'You have to realise, I've never worked alone before,' said Dom.

'Before Kate, I had lots of time alone – you get used to it after a while.'

'You had Joe.'

'That's different.'

'You've always had someone, you've never been on your own – even now Joe *needs you* to be angry with.'

'What are you trying to say?'

'That he's angry and taking it out on the one person who won't leave him or let him down, the one person who he trusts enough to keep coming back for more. That person is you Mark, you can do it – you're more than strong enough – hang on in there for him.'

'I do love him you know.' What am I doing, thought Mark, talking about love with Dom. Where did that come from? It was easy to see why Kate could offload on to Dom about anything.

Aware that the plates on the table were beginning to

slowly shift from side to side as they would on board ship at sea, he pushed away the one passing in front of him, folded his arms and lay his head down to stop it happening; it was a strange thing, this sharing of feelings. Mark stayed there, contemplating the misery of going back to an empty house and listened to a muffled conversation between Dom and the waiter. He was vaguely conscious of the fact that Dom was beginning to slur his words and was struggling to punch in his correct credit card number. The wine had been good; they'd probably both suffer for it in the morning.

The next thing he knew was Dom shaking him out of his stupor while speaking on his mobile: 'That's right, we'll be outside … asap please.' Dom somehow helped him to his feet and steered him out of the door; the cold air outside immediately began to have a sobering effect on Mark. They held each other up.

Dom seemed to be on a different planet. 'Odd thing love … so many shapes and sizes … you don't choose it, it chooses you, don't you think?'

A taxi stopped. Mark got in the back.

Dom instructed the driver, climbed in, and almost falling on top of Mark somehow settled himself on the seat. He put his arm around Mark's shoulders. 'I think a club is a good move, it'll cheer us up.'

'I don't know – I said I'm not interested in pulling other women.'

'Nope,' said Dom.

The driver stopped outside Shines and they fell out of the car together. Mark allowed himself to be led towards the flashing lights surrounding the club's entrance where he was scrutinised by the bouncer who then vacantly nodded acquaintance to Dom.

'Oh God,' said Mark for the umpteenth time that evening – 'it'll probably be full of Sixth Form girls with skirts up to their crotch! This isn't a good idea.'

'Probably not,' said Dom. 'Sometimes you have to go for the bold choice in life.'

When they entered the club, Mark was way out of his comfort zone. The place was packed with both men and women – but not together. The loud pulsating music had worked its purpose seductively on couples enjoying the freedom of the atmosphere. He looked quizzically at his friend. Watching Dom hand over their coats to the cloakroom assistant with whom he easily bantered, Mark quickly gathered that he'd been there many times before.

'Listen,' said Mark, suddenly clear-headed. 'This is a mistake.' All he could think about was the taxi driver … a familiar face … a parent at the school? Dom, still smiling, stepped up very close to Mark and spoke loudly over the music.

'No, it's no mistake – my mistake's been living with all your and Kate's problems for far too long without sharing my own. It's simple – at last I am – *this is me, Mark.*' The music stopped.

'Well there were better ways you could have told me.' Mark spoke sharply into the hushed throng, exited the scene and went to find his coat. As he left the building, he had the notion that the bouncer was a former pupil – hell, he thought, paranoia was setting in!

Dom was there in front him as he reached the pavement, blocking his way. He clasped Mark's arms and pinned them to his sides.

'Hey, you're hurting me,' said Mark, wincing and trying to escape the grip. Dom immediately released the pressure, but not the hold. He looked directly at Mark and spoke clearly this time.

'Don't you realise, it's not just Kate that I've cared for …'

Mark's head was swimming; was he catching the drift of Dom's words right? In the next second all doubt had gone. Dom tenderly moved his hands from Mark's arms up to his shoulders and kissed him, once, on the lips. Mark froze.

'It's been a long journey to get to this …' said Dom, who turned and walked back into the club with each step marking his dejection.

Mark made no attempt to follow and stood there vaguely registering the total non-reaction of the bouncer – a scene most likely witnessed to the point of boredom so many times before that he had undoubtedly lost count.

10

CONFESSION

Dom woke up in the car park near Brancaster beach, a few miles from Kate's house. He'd got lost, cutting cross-country from King's Lynn, and had taken the wrong direction on reaching the coast road. Seeing the turning to the beach he'd remembered being there before with Kate and Mark a couple of years ago, having driven out to see them on holiday with the pretence of discussing some problem that had cropped up at work. That day was a good memory and couldn't be resisted.

He looked at his watch: 3.30 in the afternoon. The realisation sunk in that he must have been asleep for four hours. Everything had been on the wrong track since last night, including his body clock. Not that he could remember much after that clumsy moment with Mark; not that he wanted to remember. Recalling going back into the club and continuing to drink till the early hours, there emerged a distant memory of someone putting him in a taxi. Whoever it was must have found his business card for an address because that's where he'd woken up the first time – in the doorway of McKinley Nichols. The nice policeman had roused him; he vaguely recollected a search for the key and needing help to unlock the front door.

The next conscious thing was waking up in that wonky swivel chair in Kate's office, wondering why he'd ignored his own room and searched out hers at the other end of the corridor. His drunken self must have been looking for her – it made good sense to him: he *had* to be the one to get to Kate first, to explain what had happened. Dom was afraid that Mark might use this as a trigger to get in touch with her, an excuse to go out there. Time was on his side however: in the pub Mark had gone on about there being a meal in Warwick on Saturday night, for Angela's birthday or something. Through the blur of his hangover, Dom had reasoned that there was a window of opportunity if he left for Norfolk straight away.

Now parked up, and sitting behind the steering wheel of his metallic BMW, he peered out. Fresh air beckoned; a very necessary requirement before facing Kate. Leaving the car, he soon found his way through a narrow gap of sand between the sea defence of large rocks. Remembering wide stretches of glistening sand-flats with the sea hardly visible on the horizon, it was bewildering to be standing on a confined apology of a beach with high tide charging at him. Deservedly, he thought. There was nowhere else to go; he needed to feel the potency of the sea-breeze on his face and clambered up onto the rocks, realising that his best work suit would soon be visiting the dry cleaners. From this vantage point, precariously balanced, he essentially had the uninterrupted view of a complete circular vista, apart from the golf club buildings which perched there braving the elements. Everything was grey: the sea, the sky and all that sort of mush inside his head.

When it started to rain he warily climbed down across

the rocks and went back to the car, still with little coherent thought emerging. He'd wanted to rehearse what he would say to Kate, instead he would be improvising.

It was late afternoon when Dom arrived at The Old Pilot's House and he was disappointed to get no answer from his effort with the door knocker. He looked through the kitchen window. No Kate. He walked through the small front garden to the back, where he found a rusting outside staircase and a couple of bedroom windows to peer into. Nothing. It was pouring; she couldn't be out on a walk in this weather surely? Remembering the pub up on the main road, Dom figured that respite there would be a good course of action while he waited for Kate.

When he got to the pub it was closed. Luckily a side door was open and he heard a woman singing along to the radio.

Dom stood on the threshold and observed a small kitchen. 'Excuse me, what time do you open?'

'Not till six …' said the voice from behind an open fridge door.

A young man came into the kitchen, dipping his head to avoid the archway, through from what must have been the bar. Dom's heart sank as he was scrutinised from head to foot. He hoped they would take pity and not be put off by his unkempt state – surely he looked more like a stray puppy than a predatory wolf.

The man picked up a large metal tray, and hands from behind the fridge door began to pass out some bags of meat which were placed into the container. Getting no further response, Dom went to leave.

The man cleared his throat, 'Mind you, if you're looking

for a bed for the night, then we're open any time.'

Dom was rather taken aback by this, until the woman, who looked old enough to be the mother, came out from the fridge. 'What he means is that we've spent all day setting up our new Bed and Breakfast room, so now it's up there empty with no one to christen it tonight.' She passed him a flyer from a pile on the work-surface. 'Look, here's a picture of the room, and the prices, there's more information on the back. Don't you think it looks impressive? I did it all myself on the computer, with Phil's expert tuition of course.'

Phil reached up to a hook next to the fridge and retrieved a small key attached to a much larger red and white lifebelt key-ring. 'We'll let you have it for a cheap rate if you like and you can tell us how comfortable it seems – and what we've forgotten. It's been hard to think of everything, hasn't it Margret?'

'We've got most things covered,' she replied. 'Those little soaps, shampoos, like a proper hotel, sewing kits, toothbrush, toothpaste …'

Dom stepped further into the kitchen, glad to be in the dry. 'Sounds perfect to me,' he said. 'It's very trusting of you, I don't usually look like this – got caught in the rain on the beach.' He realised how implausible that sounded, standing there in his suit.

'No problem. So, as you've probably gathered, I'm Phil and this …'

'… is Margret,' said the woman looking down at the bottom of Dom's muddy trouser-legs. 'From the look of you, if you don't mind me saying, you're some breed of salesman out of your depth here in our rural backwater. I suggest if you're selling to farmers, you buy yourself some boots from the Boathouse shop tomorrow or, if you're after that smart lot in Burnham Market, you're going to really have to clean up your act.'

He looked down at his favourite sand-muddied alligator shoes and had to concede she was right – although he wasn't too happy about being judged as a passing salesman. The offer of a bed for the night wasn't so bad, what with being cold, wet and hungry and also ever more doubtful as to whether Kate would put him up at the house once he had accomplished what he'd set out to do and confessed all.

'Look we can't let you come through the kitchen, go to the bar entrance and I'll let you in there,' said Phil.

Meekly, Dom did as he was told, finding he was more than ready to sit down and rest his weary bones on a comfortable armchair in front of a hospitable open fire.

* * *

When Kate turned up at the pub that evening at half past six she didn't immediately notice Dom's comatose body.

She was staring at the blackboard looking at the *Specials* and overheard Margret say to Phil, 'We'll have to wake him. It won't be long before we start first bookings. He hasn't even seen the room.'

Phil paused as he expertly sliced lemons at the bar. 'It was a mistake to let him have it … he didn't say anything about where his car was or his overnight bag. I hope we're not going to have any trouble.'

Kate followed their gaze; a pair of legs stretched out from the high-backed armchair. Despite the mud, she recognised the shoes … 'Dom!'

'You know him?' asked Phil.

'A little.'

'Good, can you wake him and persuade him to go up to his room. He literally came in, took one look at the fire and fell asleep.'

Kate sat on the arm of the chair and realised in a rush how good it was to see Dom – and then started to panic about why he was there. What had happened back in Warwick? She prodded him lightly.

Dom came round, regained focus and beamed at her in recognition. His smile quickly vanished.

Kate took his change of expression to mean that her first anxious thought had some foundation. 'Upstairs, now!' she said. 'I presume he's in the B&B?'

'Yes, and don't let him throw up or anything. He looks incredibly pale,' said Margret.

Dom dragged himself out of the chair and started to smooth down his badly creased suit before allowing Kate to show him the way.

'I'll sort him out, don't worry,' replied Kate – burning curiosity scaled the stairs behind them.

'You do realise they think you're my boyfriend,' she told Dom when they reached his room. She expected a pithy retort to come back at her; it didn't.

He was desperate to have a shower, but she flatly refused to let him until he'd explained his reason for being there.

Her first question was: 'Is Mark ok?'

'I think so.'

'What does that mean?'

'We had a skinful last night.'

'Oh, I thought you meant … is Joe alright?'

'I think so.'

'Has something happened to Angela … or Batty?'

Dom shook his head and looked at the small complimentary bottle of red wine on the table. Kate knew it tempted him and was surprised that he didn't make any move to open it. Instead he sat on the edge of the bed looking ill at ease, behaving as though they were on an awkward date rather than being established friends.

'Out with it, what's brought you here?' Kate offered the long-suffering smile she'd often used on Dom at work, and waited; he seemed exceedingly reluctant to get started on whatever was troubling him.

'Is it work?' she prompted.

'Look, can I have that shower? I feel like something the cat brought in. Give me some time to … orientate myself. I'm starving, can we order some food and eat up here? Is it any good? Go and get a menu, there's a good girl – I've missed you solving all my problems – pamper me, *please*, pretty please.'

Dom was reverting back to his usual self and, having established that nothing untoward had happened to those back home, Kate gave in and took pity on him.

While he showered she went to get a menu from downstairs and caught Phil and Margret in a conspiratorial conversation; at her approach they busied themselves behind the bar. Returning to Dom, she went to knock on the door of the en-suite to see how long he'd be. The shower was still running; he was talking to himself, apparently practising some kind of speech.

The meal was excellent. Kate had wanted to impress Dom with Phil's culinary prowess so she'd ordered the best the bistro had to offer. She was rewarded for her pains by the way Dom cleared his plate using the homemade bread to wipe up the residue sauce from his wild mushroom and venison stroganoff. He licked the tips of his fingers with delight to ensure nothing had been missed and sat there waiting for dessert in the brand new white dressing-gown carefully chosen by Margret for B&B customers; yes, the Dom she knew was back again.

Whilst eating, the conversation was light, out of necessity. Margret had insisted on serving them upstairs, hovering about as much as possible on each visit. By the end of the meal he seemed relaxed by the good food and wine and had even managed to persuade Margret to leave a bottle of brandy upstairs with them.

'That was magnificent,' said Dom, pronouncing his verdict. 'Your chef friend is wasted out here you know.'

'He's been quite a discovery – and not just for the food.'

'I see. Are you going to tell Mark?'

Kate laughed. 'No, you've got the wrong end of the stick, Phil's a friend that's all, honestly, he's much too young for me anyway – although, now you've mentioned it …'

'Don't you dare tell Mark I gave you the idea, he wouldn't thank me for that along with everything else. Anyway I'm the one who's jealous.'

'What do you mean?'

'It would have been alright if Phil had become your lover, but a friend – I feel usurped.' Dom got up and grabbed the box of tissues next to the bed, affecting tears.

'Don't be – you're my number one friend.' She jumped up and kissed him on the cheek. 'Or number two if I can still count Mark – that's still a good rating, don't you think?'

Dom rubbed his cheek where she'd kissed him. A new seriousness took over his face. 'Do you think a good friendship survives anything that's thrown at it?' The game he'd been playing was over and anxiety had entered his eyes; he wasn't looking straight at her any more, his gaze had shifted to over her shoulder.

'Well … most things, I hope. Come to think about it though, there must be something that would cause a problem – you haven't killed my mother, have you?' said Kate, still attempting to keep things in playful mode.

'No I'm being serious, but if it was something unforgiveable, would past history hold a friendship together or would all trust be lost?'

'You're talking in riddles. Dom, if you've got something to say – give.'

Dom was holding tight to his brandy glass. He swilled it round slowly several times before finally saying: 'I kissed Mark.' He knocked back the brandy.

Kate took her time to react and poured herself the brandy she'd refused earlier. This was one response she wanted to get right.

She took his hand and sat down with him on the blanket box at the end of the bed. 'Oh Dom, you idiot – whatever did Mark *do?*'

Dom kept hold of her hand, but still didn't look at her. 'He stood there. Blanked me. I didn't mean to, didn't plan to, it just happened. Look, don't think Mark did anything to lead me on. It came out the blue, we'd been drinking – I lost it.'

'Poor Mark.'

'What do you mean?'

'He won't know how to handle this, it's completely off the compass for him.'

'And you, do you know how to handle this? I'm all at sea without a paddle – excuse the cliché, but it's exactly how I feel.' He looked at her now, searching her face for disappointment or, worse still, contempt.

Kate made certain that neither were there. 'I must admit this is all new to me,' she said. 'Not been here before – we'll have to make it up as we go along. You'd be amazed to know how good I'm getting at that.'

'You're not surprised?'

She was relieved he hadn't picked up on her careless throw-away comment. 'What? Which – that you kissed Mark or that you're gay?'

'That I'm gay.'

'I've known ever since that party at Uni when I tried it on with you.'

'You did? I don't remember that.'

'Thanks for the compliment – sadly at the time you were too drunk to notice and too interested in Tom Banks.'

'I don't remember any of this.'

'At the time I was rather glad you didn't. I thought I'd made a real fool of myself. I was so relieved the next day when you didn't remember.' Her memory of that evening was seared on her psyche and had affected her ability to make the first move in a relationship right up until she'd met Mark. It was the one part of her never shared before with Dom.

'I've made up for that, haven't I? I've by far won the "making a fool of myself" competition.'

'I hoped it would make you feel better knowing that you're not the sole person around here that's done so.'

'So you're not angry?'

'Why on earth should I be angry that you're gay? Or do you mean because of Mark?'

'I mean because I tried it on with Mark as soon as you weren't around.'

'It seems you gave it a few weeks and you've told me you'd been drinking.'

'Yes – but it was out of order, my best friend's husband.'

'Leave it, forget it. You're right, he's going to struggle with this – as I said, it's totally out of his usual experience – you know, with all his macho sports life.'

'You'd be surprised what goes on in the men's changing rooms. There's many a footballer or rugby player that hasn't come out.'

'Not in Mark's mind. So don't tell him that or he really will lose his bearings!' Kate was laughing, not at Dom, but at her own husband.

'So what do we do?'

'We wait and see. Let's see what, in fact, Mark does – how he reacts.'

'You know what that will be, don't you?'

'I suspect you're going to tell me.' Kate patted Dom's knee as she would a small child, not the broad hunk of a man many a girl at University had tried hard to impress to no avail.

'He'll use it as a reason to come out here. I told him to let you be, give you space. I don't suppose you realised how much he's champing at the bit to get in touch.'

Kate's relief on hearing this statement was immense. The reason for his long silence. Of course, it was obvious, she could see that now, he couldn't have kept it up without someone to help strengthen his resolve. But this relief in itself was unsettling; she thought her feelings for Mark were in decline and here they were, surfacing again. Where would she put those feelings if she continued to slip from one era to another? There was no viable answer to this – her two worlds ran like parallel tracks, destined never to join together.

Dom poured himself another large brandy. 'He'll probably come tomorrow. That's why I rushed over here to see you. For you to hopefully absolve me first, so I knew where I stood.'

'So now you know. Look I need to get some sleep and I've got a lot of … things to do tomorrow if Mark's going to turn up.' She could see Dom didn't believe her. 'I mean I need some time to think about what I'm going to say to him.'

'We'll all be fascinated to know what that is,' said Dom quietly.

'Get a good night's rest and leave early, before he comes,' Kate urged. 'You don't want to risk passing him as you leave the village. It won't help matters if he thinks that you've been here. If he turns up I'll let you know what he says.'

'Don't wait too long to do that. Isn't it time for you to come back anyway, not just to work things out with Mark … I need you too … we need to sort the business out.'

'You're quite capable of holding the fort, a bit longer won't make much difference.'

'*Yes it will!* You don't realise what's going on with you stuck out here with the seagulls. The recession's beginning to bite. I'm going to lose the peppermint tea contract and others are slow to come in. Bigger companies are tendering lower prices and without your flair I'm not getting anywhere. You need to know – if you don't come back soon – I'm seriously thinking of winding up the business.'

This time Kate was wrong-footed. Until the point she had sent Mark away at the end of their holiday she'd been in control of life in the real world. Suddenly everything that was happening either in Warwick or Norfolk was moving beyond her influence. It was like watching a film at the cinema and seeing herself on the screen, with no ability to change the direction of the plot or camera focus and with scenes taking place randomly without a script.

'Look I can't get into that,' she said. 'It's too late and I'm far too exhausted to discuss it tonight, don't do anything rash and *don't* drink all that brandy when I've gone.' She hugged Dom, more tightly than usual, located her coat, bag and torch and left before he could offer to walk her home.

'It was an awful shame that Tom Banks wasn't interested in me, it wasn't for the want of trying,' Dom muttered as they parted.

11

HOOKED

Compulsion overwhelmed Kate. As she ran down the lane to the house, the torch gave an almost non-existent glimmer, letting her down when she needed it most. Somehow, her old life crashing in, in the form of Dom – and Mark's possible arrival – had kick-started a sense of urgency; all she could think about was the necessity to persuade Sye to come back.

Getting into bed, she set the alarm on her mobile for what she reckoned would be half an hour before daybreak – it was all guesswork and Kate hoped the timing was correct. Right at the start he'd said "come in daylight"; she wasn't going to miss any of it and aimed to be up there waiting in the attic as dawn broke.

She woke earlier than planned and lay in bed for a while with her mind running over her conversation with Dom, before her thoughts were broken by the cheery alarm from her phone – a ringtone chosen in another place, another time. She dressed in the dark, pulled back the curtains and waited for the first sliver of daylight.

It was not long before she was able to see enough to make her way up both flights of stairs. Standing in the empty attic, it was time to be proactive. She flung open all the windows to let in the dawn chorus, needing all the help she could get. 'Come on Sye,' she urged out loud. 'Please be listening, please come, please forgive my insensitivity last time.'

The state of nothingness continued.

Outside even the bird cries were muted and there was quietness in the view, no noisy colours … only the channel of grey slipping in from the horizon between the salt marsh and the embankment. Nonetheless it was still "awesome", as Joe would say. Kate looked helplessly across to where she knew the land gave way to the sea – where, hiding beyond the dunes was a secret shore, out of reach for the idle and those who'd seek to exploit it; the ultimate pleasure of stepping out onto the solitary sea-glazed sand always had to be earned.

'Beautiful isn't it? As long as you see beyond the mud-flats and know what can be found out there,' said Sye from behind her, breaking the silence with his uncanny habit of echoing her thoughts. Kate carried on staring out, not wanting to face him until she could gauge his mood. Was he still angry? For him, was their last conversation seconds ago or half a life-time? Or did the hours pass for him as they did for her with the clock sanely ticking?

'I've been up here looking for you so many times,' she said. 'I thought …'

'That I'd gone? No, I just needed to get control. Of myself, I mean. I was at the mercy of this *thing* and that wasn't a good place to be. I wanted to control time, make it wait for *me*. Make *you* wait for me. Congratulations! You passed the test!'

'What test?'

'I wanted you to *need* to see me – for your desperation to match mine.'

Kate blushed – she was glad not to have turned around.

'The reason I *need* you, as you say, is because I have to work out what's going on here and until I do that I can't begin to get to grips with the real world.' Her hands clung onto the edge of the window-sill to keep herself fixed there, knuckles white with the struggle.

'Don't spoil it – let's just concentrate on what you call *here*.'

Kate let go of the sill and faced the room.

The record player confirmed the shift; its turntable needing a disc to play.

'The real world will wait for you,' Sye said.

Kate was reminded of her childhood fear. Where *did* everyday life go when she went to sleep in her dreams, and would it still be there when she woke up?

He spoke again, 'You can get back, it's me that can't.'

She decided that she couldn't do other than trust him, having been the one who'd kept choosing to climb those stairs and the one who had willed him back into her life only minutes ago. 'It's all getting too complicated out there … what with Mark coming,' she said quietly to herself.

Sye heard every word. 'You mean you chose to visit me rather than be with him – I'm flattered.' He leant out of the window, and called, 'She's up here with me Mark!'

Kate clutched at his shirt to pull him back in, her fingers brushing against his skin. It was as warm and as human as Mark's would have been had he been standing there. Yet she was cold. Her feet were freezing and the usually visible veins in her pale hands almost non-existent. Too many questions. No answers.

She shut the window. 'He isn't here yet … I mean, I'm expecting him, well I think I am … I had to see you first.'

'So you *did* choose me over him – you're taking the risk that he'll arrive while you're up here.'

'It wasn't choice, it was compulsion. As I said, I *had* to.'

'Sounds more like an addiction to me,' said Sye, leaving her for the comfort of his bed of cushions. His tone was triumphant.

'Like *you* have,' Kate retorted, aware that he was bringing out the sharpness in her again; she must stop this if they were ever going to move on from the back and forth of scoring points. She sat down where she stood and leant against the wall beneath the window.

He changed his tone and spoke softly, 'Call it what you like, it's cool. Why does this whole thing have to have a label? *Relax* – let's live in the now, forget the past and not worry about the future.'

'People say we should learn from the past.'

'People say a lot of things. It's what happens in this little bit of time that matters. You've got a world out there full of problems and *me* here – we can just *be* here. No outside influences. No real time. We can talk, feel the music – give in to it all, let it flow over us and if we do that we'll soon uncover what's brought us together across these years.'

Kate was lulled by his mellifluous voice and the easiness of following his lead, a blessed relief from trying to lead others.

He was sifting through his record collection, pulling out and putting back rejected LPs into their sleeves – as ever, it was the familiar, brightly coloured Beatles' cover that he paused over. 'I can never decide who my real hero is,' he said. 'John or George? I suppose that John is the true poet, don't you think? I mean he says so much that I feel – the soundtrack to my life, he says it like it is and yet George gets the rights to my soul.'

He slid the record sleeve across the floor to her. Kate knew that he was speaking from within his own time. He had no knowledge of what came next, *this* was where he'd stopped existing in the regular sense of the word. She studied the record cover: his heroes, dressed in their day-glo military styled uniforms, posing in front of a sea of faces. Cardboard cut-outs of Marilyn Monroe, Bob Dylan and Fred Astaire stood amongst so many who now qualified for ghost status or were heading that way.

It was clear to Kate that this wasn't the moment to fill him in on the tragedy of John Lennon's death at the hands of Mark David Chapman on the steps of the Dakota building. Instead she only told him part of the story. Of how the Beatles' fame had lived on and how she had even seen Lennon's song-writing displayed in the British Museum, written on scraps of paper or, in one case, on his son's birthday card. Sye seemed to love hearing all this abridged *future*, wanting more and more – at first. Seeing her editing skills were about to struggle with the added untimely death of George Harrison, Kate decided it was time to change the subject before she exposed Sye to too much sorrow all in one go. She wanted to protect him and not snuff out his youthful enthusiasm – it would be akin to telling a child that Father Christmas wasn't real, just as the sack of presents was opened. To Sye, the Beatles were together, alive and well and as young as him.

He must have sensed her hesitation. 'Look, I don't want to know any more – about your world, your stupid times – this is *my* time, *my* here and now, and if you're with me you must be wherever I am. I thought I'd gone, it was all so dark in my head, no – in my soul, in my … psyche, oh I don't know.' He ran both hands through his hair and kept them there plainly trying to hold his mind together. 'What I do know is that I've got this extra time, either for good or bad behaviour. I expect it's the latter, I didn't do much of the good, I don't think.'

He came across to her and snatched back the record sleeve. 'Don't mess with my memories, Kate. Don't take away anything more from me – you're meant to make everything better – so play things my way.'

'It's alright,' she said. 'I won't spoil your game.' It was happening again, every time Kate was feeling sympathetic towards him, beginning to relax, his mood would change; she struggled to keep up.

'It's not a game – absolutely not a game – it's more like limbo, somewhere between heaven and hell if you believe all that,' he said.

'And do you believe in *all that*?'

'I don't know – I didn't know when I was alive before and I'm not much the wiser since I did this dying thing.'

'In what way?'

'It's like I know there must be *something,* otherwise what the hell is going on with me? Excuse the pun! This can't be hell can it?'

Kate couldn't answer his question.

He did. 'It can't be hell because you're here with me and you're not dead.'

Kate was glad about that.

'Enough of the metaphysical. Let's make us a little closer to heaven.' Sye stood and picked up a half-empty bottle of beer which was standing stranded in the middle of the floor. With the bottle in one hand, he started to search around for something under the cushions before retrieving a dimpled glass tankard, into which he poured the beer with a flourish. He tossed the bottle behind him; it landed noisily, rolled across the floor and came to a halt at the top of the stairs. Kate was surprised he didn't drink out of the bottle like Mark or Joe. Little things change, she thought, not just the big things.

He brought the glass over to her. 'Want some?' he asked, grinning.

She shook her head. 'Too early.'

'I forgot it was morning … hold it a minute while I make us more comfortable.' He handed her the glass and set about reorganising the array of cushions, punching them back into shape before considering the best spot to place each one. 'I don't think too much about time, it doesn't affect me any more – except waiting for you … and avoiding the dark.'

Kate handed the beer mug back; she was aware of him scrutinising her face.

'Ta,' he said. 'You look tired. Have you been up all night? Come here, relax, you little old lady!' He sat down and patted the cushion next to him.

'Thank you very much for that! In my world there's many a woman with a toy boy.' Kate hoped he didn't understand the term; it had somehow slipped into the conversation though she had no plans for their relationship to go in that direction. Life was complicated enough as it was.

As always he appeared to tap into her thoughts, unnerving Kate every time: 'I'm not going to try anything on, honestly. I want you to see that nothing out there matters in here. All those thoughts that are chewing up your brain can just fly out of that window, join the birds, land on that far-off beach and be spirited away by the tide. We're all washed away by the tide in the end you know. You can *free* yourself up here; see the world from a different perspective.'

Kate's response was to join him on the cushions where she started to drink eagerly from the mug – it reminded her that in such haste that day, she'd had no breakfast and no early morning cup of coffee. Sye placed his chosen disc on the record player and lined the needle up with the track he wanted. This time it was John Lennon's voice which dominated the room. Kate recognised the lyrics which she'd often danced to as a young child, holding her mother's hands. Now, as then, she likened herself to the girl described in the lyrics, existing within a montage of fanciful scenes which could change on a whim. Kate gave in to the cushions, and as she listened, something changed inside, muddying rationality. She began to see there was no boundary to enclose her. Any disbelief in what was happening dropped away as they lay side by side, staring up at the ceiling, not touching.

Kate vaguely asked herself if the beer she'd consumed was real or imagined. But found she didn't care that there wasn't an answer. Her thoughts coasted here and there – was she in his time, or did he infiltrate hers? Or both – somewhere in between – or perhaps together they made a new sort of time. An image of Mark materialised and floated away on purple clouds. It would be good to opt out for a while, to have some peace. Sye didn't seem to want anything other than for her to be "cool", chilled out, relaxed. It was tempting and Kate found herself in that instance, as Eve must have been, not questioning the serpent but innocently thinking that no harm would come of her actions.

Sye got up and began to move lazily around the room lighting his joss-sticks, watching her all the time. The fragrance filled her nostrils and tranquilised her mind even further. He was dressed in his flared jeans with some kind of faded kaftan shirt over the top – Mark wouldn't have been seen dead in something like that; she could hear him saying it. Sye carried it off somehow, it was of his generation.

He lit up a joint, not bothering to offer it this time and began to dance, to sway – she was high anyway, hypnotised by the power of the music, the incense and his moving this way and that. The girl in the song ended her haunting journey. Kate was aware of Sye flipping the disc and John Lennon was usurped by George accompanied by the increasingly familiar sitar strains which played on and on …

Kate tried to comprehend one single track continuing forever … time had fallen away and was without end. Her eyes closed as the cushions supported her lethargic body. She could hear Sye's gentle drags as he smoked and sensed that the intoxicating wafts were reaching her. Although she didn't consciously inhale they still seemed to fill her being, lift her further away from any former life and place her firmly inside the fantasy of it all. The attic – and the cushions which held her – had become her real world, a sanctuary. Normality was a dream or a land the other side of the wardrobe, somewhere she didn't want to be any more. She fell asleep dreaming of the White Witch, with Aslan bound to the Stone Table … about to die.

Kate woke with a start; a split-second of fear, promptly banished by recollection.

Sye was painting.

'What do you think?' he said as he continued to swirl gold paint across the canvas, cancelling all previous effort.

She clambered onto her feet – her throat dry, it seemed a long time since she'd actually spoken.

'It's ... different,' she said, glad to have not lost the power of speech. 'It's a bit ... retro. I know I said to try something different. I meant, stick to what you have a real gift for, those wonderful landscapes – but paint *a different view.*' She made towards the paintings which were leaning against the wall as usual, with his talent hidden from view. 'I just love the way you capture even the smallest changes to give each painting its own distinct atmosphere.'

'Leave them,' he said tersely, abandoning his efforts and moving across the room to the small window opposite. 'Leave them alone. *Please.* It's time for you to go.' He pointed with his paintbrush, 'I think you've got a visitor.'

Kate peered down onto the short gravel driveway – there was no one there. It shocked her that it was dusk.

'Go on, go. He's there in your time.'

She followed his instruction, knowing instinctively that Mark was near, but when she reached the top of the stairs to leave, Sye ran over to her, kicking the beer bottle across the room like a football.

'One thing ...' He held her arm to stop her progress down the stairs. '... you *were* happy today, weren't you. You were happy, right?'

'Yes,' said Kate, remembering her earlier serenity. In fact right there and then, with that touch of Sye's hand – there was a flow of being between the two of them beyond description or any previous experience. She was much warmer now, perhaps she should stay.

Could Mark really be there? She was doubting her previous instinct.

'Yes, he is,' replied Sye. 'When you're with him, remember that feeling you had with me.' He let go and went back to his painting.

There was that hollowness again; the same sensation experienced when she'd previously sought him out, only to find nothing there. The desire to stay was strong.

'You can't stay, you have to go.'

Kate descended the stairs reluctantly and pushed the wardrobe back into its place. On reaching the kitchen she unbolted the door, with care this time, and opened it. Mark was sitting outside in the car with music blaring; staring out – in a world of his own.

12

UNDERCURRENTS

On first sight of Kate standing framed by the front door a question formed in Mark's mind: *How do you greet an estranged wife, with a handshake, a hug, a kiss on the cheek?* Kate resolved the dilemma by moving back into the kitchen to busy herself with the kettle.

'Coffee? Tea? Or something stronger?'

So that was his answer, no physical greeting at all after those weeks apart; just a gaping crevasse where once there had been an invisible thread. Mark hadn't been prepared for how the awkwardness of the situation would affect his body – a similar experience, he suspected, to what Joe must have suffered when he'd hit that recent growth spurt, with ungainly limbs wondering how to navigate the space around him.

'*Please* sit down,' said Kate, 'you're making me feel weird.'

'Let's go upstairs,' suggested Mark, not waiting for a response and treading carefully to find his way between the books piled haphazardly on the staircase. He picked one at random and carried it up with him. 'What's with all these?'

She followed closely behind.

'Nothing ... I ... intend to read them.'

'What, all of them! You are settling in for the long haul!'

Kate ignored his comment and sat down on the sofa, that all engulfing sofa on which, in past years, they had snuggled up, yielding to its comfort. He sat on the footstool in front of her, hugging the book he'd picked up, and thought how unsettled she looked, her mind in faraway mode. A bit shifty really. Not like her.

Her distraction was disconcerting. When he'd got out of the car after sitting waiting for half an hour she'd stood there at the door smiling a false sort of smile. As soon as she'd spoken, he'd felt like an uninvited intruder – she didn't seem to be functioning as normal, whatever normal meant these days. He'd even begun to wonder if she was hiding someone. *Please, not a lover.* Which is why he'd suggested sitting upstairs – to be certain no one else *was* there. But the minute they'd reached the first floor he'd begun searching for an excuse to go back downstairs to take a look in the bedrooms.

'Don't be silly,' said Kate. Mark guiltily thought she was referring to his suspicions, before she added, 'I wanted to take a good look at the books and choose one to read … they were in the wardrobe drawer, that's all there is to it.'

'I didn't know you were that interested in art, not this sort anyway,' he said, thumbing through images of Turner's landscapes, trying hard to hold back the foreboding of doom which had taken control of him.

'I am … out here. It's all about landscapes … out here.'

'I've been wondering how you've been filling your time.'

'Walking and … there's lots of galleries … I've been looking around. What's wrong with a new interest, anyway?'

A defensive response if ever there was one, thought Mark.

'I suppose if you're cycling from gallery to gallery, you must be worn out with all that exertion … and the walking of course,' he said sarcastically.

'I take the bus. I haven't got around to organising a bike. Anyway, the galleries, they … they'll give me inspiration for Agency pitches if you want to know!'

'You're planning on coming back then … to work at least?' Remembering what had triggered his visit, he found he didn't want to talk about Dom – all that didn't seem to matter now. He was more interested in what was going on in Kate's mind and in this life she was making without him. Things were miles worse than when he'd left in September; it no longer seemed to be just about them, her mind was unquestionably elsewhere. He could do with time to work out the score; perhaps stay on for the next couple of days – it was half-term after all.

'Let's go up to the pub for supper,' he suggested. 'You obviously like the food. I saw from the credit card statement that you've been eating there most days.'

'I'm glad to know you're still taking an interest in what I'm doing!' Kate said, somewhat harshly he thought; after all this separation had been her call, even though he had to concede that he'd played a big role in pushing her in the direction taken.

'That's not fair! I didn't deserve that.' He knew he was about to make further accusations and somehow managed to pull back. What proof had he got, other than imaginings anyway? 'Come on, let's go and eat, unless you've got something in the fridge,' he said, hoping that this would put a stop to the spiral of recrimination.

Kate didn't respond.

Mark left her and went downstairs with the intention of investigating the fridge. That done, he took the opportunity to check things out and soundlessly pushed open each bedroom door to take a look.

'Kate,' he called from the foot of the stairs. 'Kate, you know there's nothing in the fridge, let's go up the road to the pub.'

No reply.

Mark went back up and found her still sitting as he'd left her, looking wretched. He took her hands and pulled her up. She submitted to this movement like a rag doll and followed his lead down the stairs and out into the cold early evening air.

'You need to lock up,' he said as Kate started to follow him. 'God I hope you're taking care out here by yourself.' She smiled wanly and went back to lock the door.

They sat next to each other in the small alcove, usually reserved for loving couples, watching Phil move around behind the bar getting ready for his evening customers. Mark noticed him wink at Kate twice. The first time was when they thought he was looking down at the menu. Their connection shut him out. She offered to organise the drinks with the excuse that she knew the menu off by heart and had already made a choice. Instead of going up to the bar, as any ordinary customer would, she slipped behind it with a manner of familiarity and spoke to Phil, out of Mark's earshot. That had brought about the second wink coupled with a reassuring hand on her arm, a fleeting touch. Kate came back and perched on the edge of her chair in such a way that at any moment she might happen to find another excuse to return to the bar.

'Let's order,' she said, brightening up with that false smile again. All Mark saw was a pathetic attempt to hide guilt.

'I'm not so hungry now,' he replied churlishly. 'This is all gourmet rubbish – I wanted something normal, not this stupid pretentious ...'

'I'm sure Phil will accommodate.'

'Oh I'm *sure* he will.' Everything had got more complicated. Mark felt angry and uncomfortable. As well as having to put up with all that shared intimacy behind the bar, that woman who let them The Old Pilot's House kept looking across while setting up other tables, acting as though she knew something he didn't. If she hadn't been willing to extend Kate's stay, none of this would have happened. So *she* wasn't one of his favourite people either, together with winking Phil who must be verging on being ten years younger than himself. No contest then!

'What made you come here today?' said Kate. 'I know it's half-term, but you've usually got all that work to do ...'

The perfect invitation to talk about Dom. It was then his anger took over. No way was he in the mood to tell her about that shattering incident – not while feeling incensed about everything else which was so obviously fouled up! Mark had an overwhelming urge to walk out. So he did.

* * *

Kate stood staring in the direction of Mark's dramatic exit. What on earth had changed between leaving the house just ten minutes ago and his flight? She'd been successful in warning Phil not to mention Dom's visit ... *and* given Mark the chance to talk about what had happened back in Warwick.

'That was quick.' Margret was at her elbow.

'He's gone … I think he must have changed his mind … I must have said something.'

'Get after him – it's clearly what he wants – you to *want* him. Isn't that why he came all this way out here to see you?'

'It wasn't the only reason.'

'Look he'll be gone if you don't get a move on,' said Margret, propelling Kate towards the door.

'Since when have you been an expert on men?'

'Never have been – I just know some things can't be undone when you leave them too long. Don't let this be one of them.'

'But I'm not sure that I want …'

'You won't know unless you try.'

* * *

Margret watched Kate stand on the corner staring down the road; she'd been watching Kate a great deal of late. Her friend's dejected body language told her that the car, heard in the distance, speeding out of the village was Mark's. She continued to watch as Kate crossed the road to head down the lane towards the creek.

Margret returned to the warmth of the pub and grabbed the coat Kate had left behind. 'Give me a minute,' she said to Phil. 'Kate's forgotten this.'

He responded with an acknowledging wink as he answered the phone to take a booking.

When Margret reached the entrance to the small beach which served as a car park for the staithe, she became anxious as there was no one to be seen. The moon gave light to the evening, catching the tips of the sailing boat masts, lined up along the edge of the road. She heard a slight sound from behind and turned to see that Kate was sitting at the far end of the long bench always filled on summer days with ice-creamed children, dog-walking grandparents or those more serious coastal path walkers checking for a stone in their shoe. Kate was crying, very quietly. Margret reached inside the pocket of Kate's coat and found a packet of paper tissues; she handed them to Kate and put the coat around her shoulders.

'Sorry.' Kate sniffed as she pulled out a tissue from the pack and began to mop up.

'What for?' asked Margret.

'For … causing a scene.'

'What, in front of me and Phil – what are friends for anyway?'

'I seem to be messing up everyone's life … back there with Mark … I don't know what I did wrong! And I was *so* hungry, I haven't eaten all day.' Kate smiled ruefully.

'Something must have upset him, rushing off like that.'

'Perhaps it was because I had something else on my mind when he arrived – it was so strange being with him after all these weeks. I needed time to adjust … I thought I'd covered it up. By the time we got to the pub I'd relaxed a bit – he was ok when we arrived – then he flipped. Like a switch had been turned on.' Kate wiped her eyes again with the tissue.

'You weren't expecting him then?' Margret asked.

'Sort of. Dom had warned me,' replied Kate. 'I thought he'd come to tell me something, confide in me – but he didn't. I gave him the opportunity and it seemed to have the opposite effect on him, he didn't pick up on it at all, just left me with my mouth open halfway through a sentence. I'm so confused.'

'Don't you think that's what he wanted? You left *him* confused at the end of your holiday, so it's your turn to suffer. What he wants is for you to make the effort to go after him. That's how I see it. I mean, more than running the short distance down the lane – it's time to go home, Kate.'

Margret gave her a moment to let that sink in before continuing. 'You need to know something … I've been thinking of making some alterations this winter to the house anyway … sort out the attic into a proper flat so I've got two properties to let … or I might make the one you're in bigger. There's an internal staircase behind that awful wardrobe. I could get more rent for it in the summer and retire from some of my pub work.' She waited for a reaction. It came quickly.

'No! You can't!'

'Oh yes I can … I can do what I like with my own property you know.'

'No! I mean you can't … not yet … because …' Margret could see Kate trying to calm herself in an attempt to sound less frantic, '… I'm in it, and I'm not ready yet. I need more time to … to get my head straight.'

'Don't you think you've had time enough for that?' Margret asked as kindly as possible. She got up to leave – Kate's initial response to her announcement had been as expected and it was time to get back. Her suspicions had been confirmed; it *had* been Kate she'd spied staring out of the attic window as dawn broke that morning. The desire to know what Kate had found up there would have to wait. One step at a time; enough had been said, for today. She shivered and it wasn't because the heat of the pub had left to make room for the cold to infiltrate her bones; it was the fear that after all this time she might have to confront her own past.

What if Kate had learned something about that former life?

What if all she'd hidden away from others during the last four decades could destroy her life all over again?

It was time to end the conversation, for the time being. 'I've got to get back, Phil will be getting in a state if that fortieth birthday party start arriving and I'm not there to help. Come with me, it's warm there – we'll get you something to eat before you go back to the house.'

* * *

Kate floundered on the wave she'd been riding. Sprinkled with sunlight it should have swept the beach, alluringly bringing with it Sye and all he had to offer. Instead the wave had broken before it reached the shore and come to nothing.

It wasn't only the impending eviction which had shaken her. A new thought had emerged – one that had wormed its way into her consciousness – that Mark's behaviour earlier had something to do with Dom's kiss.

What if Mark had enjoyed that kiss? Had liked it, had discovered a new depth of feeling for Dom?

Knowledge of her husband told her it would be the least likely thing to happen, though these days nothing would surprise her. In the last few years had she missed something shifting between all three of them while she had been so wrapped up in her own problems? It explained his sudden departure.

What if this evening had made him realise that he felt nothing for her and everything for Dom after all?

The more she thought about Mark and Dom, the more

she convinced herself that the knock-on effect of her chosen separation from everything in Warwick had thrown the two men together in a way she had never anticipated. Was Mark now on his way back there, intending to tell Dom of his new awareness? Both her worlds were on a collision course. If there was a choice, which would I save? *Can I save either?*

Kate wished she could fully confide in Margret, to be guided through these treacherous waters. It was not an option, not while Margret herself represented part of that threat.

On reaching the brightly-lit pub, Kate was conscious of a crowd of people entering at the same time, all laughing and joking. *Could life ever be that easy again?*

13

REGRETS

It had been an emotional day so far. To stop thinking about her conversation with Batty over breakfast, Angela tuned her mind to exploring what could be done with a million pounds *if* she won the lottery. The interesting moral question was how much she would spend on the family and how much would be given to others. Sadie had pleasantly surprised her when they'd discussed the topic the other week by arriving with a long list of charities to support if she was the lucky recipient of such a prize – before spoiling it with talk of tattoos and copious body piercings. Angela shuddered at the thought.

Their discussion sessions, designed to help Sadie shine in her Debating Club, hadn't led to the girl's greater knowledge of political facts and global news, as Angela had hoped. The debates in question turned out to be focused more on personal views of ethical issues, tricky at the best of times. From what Angela understood, the first few weeks were a warm-up to heavier debates on such things as abortion and animal rights, but so far they'd only dealt with: *The accomplishment I am most proud of, I think my parents' generation had it tough/easy* and last week, the million dollar question. When Sadie first announced this subject, Angela changed the word dollar to pound and had straight away "gone off on one" (as Sadie would say) about the Americanisation of the English language and the terrible shame of it.

Angela knew she often wandered off the point; sometimes the irrelevances triggered were appreciated by Sadie and sometimes she would simply tune back into her mobile phone. The session regarding their parents' lifestyles had ended up with the two trawling through Angela's collection of faded black and white family photos. This held Sadie's interest for longer than usual until, inevitably, she'd beamed into another conversation with the aid of that pushy little pink phone.

'Why don't you switch it off while we look at these?'

'Sorry,' said Sadie. 'What did you say?'

Angela reached across, prised the phone away and shook it at its owner.

'It's *Emmy*, *it's important*,' countered Sadie, grabbing it back protectively, still oblivious to the idea that having a 'third person' in the room could cause offence. Angela gave in, suspecting that she was far more tolerant than Sadie's mother would be. Any tolerance was rooted in the fact that she delighted in the time this young person was happy to spend with her. To have half of Sadie's attention was a good enough start and more than often caused Angela to work even harder at introducing noteworthy tales and humorous anecdotes from the past in an attempt to entice her away from that frantic tap, tap, tapping.

'Look at this, I was about your age here,' said Angela handing Sadie a photograph depicting a lazy family Sunday afternoon in a back garden strewn with deckchairs and tennis racquets.

Sadie studied the photograph. '*Your* mum and dad had more time for family – and friends – mine live life at top speed and moan at me when I can't keep up. *They* think I'm not working hard enough. *I* think their problem is that they can't get off the treadmill.' She scrunched up her nose, made her hands into tiny paws and squeaked … 'They're like little hungry hamsters, chasing, chasing … and getting nowhere.'

Angela laughed, 'I know you don't see it now, but the good thing is, one day you'll have a bigger and brighter cage and a more exciting treadmill because of your parents' hard work.'

Sadie handed the photo back. 'Very funny, but they're missing out on the way. Even I can see that – they don't. Although your lot didn't have so much, like I said, they'd more time for family – you can tell from these pictures and your stories.'

It was during moments such as these that Angela could glimpse a more mature Sadie on the brink of womanhood.

'I think your parents come out as the winners,' Sadie announced.

'No you're wrong, there was too much suffering – two world wars.'

'In between all that though, they had time for each other, stuck it out together. But those awful clothes … and your *hair*! How did you survive without hair-straighteners?' She pointed to another picture of Angela frowning at the sun from under a rather frizzy fringe.

'Oh Sadie, trust you to bring it back to appearance – thank goodness women didn't have tattoos in my day. Promise me you'll never do that, you'll look like a sailor!'

'Well, I can't … I can't promise …' said Sadie, as she

tugged down her waistband and shared with Angela the little dove perched on her right hip.

The conversation leading to the little dove revelation had taken place a couple of weeks ago, a topic now put aside to make way for a new debate: *The one thing I wish I could go back and change would be ...* Angela didn't have to think for long or search her soul for an answer. However, *this* answer wasn't something that could be shared with Sadie. The truthful response would have to be substituted with another aspect of her life – such as, 'I wouldn't have gone for a walk the day I broke my hip' or 'I would have become an astronaut and not a secretary'. Knowing what the one big issue was, and that she couldn't talk about it, somehow took the edge of her usual eager anticipation for conversation with Sadie that afternoon.

At breakfast Angela had brought the subject up with Batty. 'If you could go back in your life and alter something you did, change something for the better, what would it have been?'

Batty had peered over the top of his newspaper, his glasses balanced right on the end of his nose in an attempt to focus. 'I'd have travelled to Australia to watch England win the Ashes.'

'No, that's somewhere you wished you'd gone. My question is ... it has to be something you would *undo*, change, *do* differently.'

'I'll need time to think about that. For goodness sake let me read the paper and organise my bets if you want me to win all that money you were talking about the other week.'

'We've moved on from the million pound conversation – I need help with this one today.'

'Later,' came the voice from behind the newspaper.

When Batty had finished cleaning up the kitchen after breakfast, he came into the sitting room and sat himself down on the sofa opposite Angela. He looked at her intently. 'I wouldn't have spent all those years on the allotment. I'd have spent more time with you. Taken you by the hand and travelled to far off exotic places, not just stayed around here and watched my beans grow.'

Angela saw real regret in his eyes and sadly noticed how their blueness had become almost grey at the edge, matching his hair.

He got up and perched on the arm of her chair, his familiar hand taking hers, and the roughness of his skin confirming days spent tending his plot. 'I've left it too late, haven't I?'

Angela heard the catch in his voice as he spoke. She could never bear to see her husband cry, and responded in her accustomed way when discussing a problem with him: she found an optimistic aspect. 'Look on the bright side, we've had all those gorgeous vegetables, look how healthy we are … apart from my damn hip. You've supplied our "Five a Day" for as long as I can remember and that's why we've still got each other. All that travel would have worn us out!'

Batty beamed, as a grateful response, lifted and kissed her hand and brushed his lips on her forehead. 'Best put on my gardening shoes then and get on with it if that's the case – got a lot to get cleared today before the winter sets in. Thought I'd have a bonfire later.'

Settling down to read, she was glad to have pleased him with her reply; her temporary contentment came from knowing that he could now enjoy his morning on the allotment.

But Angela's thoughts crept back to her own regrets – her attempts to hold back the floodgate with the problems of the fictional characters in the novel she was reading failed.

Batty arrived back from the allotment in good spirits, smelling of smoked wood and the flavours of autumn. He left his muddy shoes at the open garden door and Angela had sat looking at them for some time. Those once trendy trainers rejected by Joe as being "uncool" had been eagerly accepted by Batty as perfect for the garden – even with their luminous green flash along the side. Batty loved them; because they'd been Joe's. They shared many similarities in temperament as well as shoe size, Angela mused.

While he went to clean himself up, she decided that her own thoughts on the subject of the day couldn't be shared with him, not after witnessing all that regret which had come to the surface earlier. It would be too painful. She struggled to pull herself up onto her walking frame and moved with difficulty to the large picture mirror on the wall. Facing up to her reflection, which would for ever be unfamiliar to the younger, fitter, self which still existed somewhere inside, she spoke to an imaginary Kate. 'I *should* have taken a much bigger step back from Joe when you came along. I *should* have given your relationship room to thrive and turned that child around and sent him back whenever he landed on my doorstep with his problems. I'm *so* sorry.'

How she envied the Catholic in the confessional – longing as she did for absolution.

By the time Sadie arrived, Angela had retreated from any

uncomfortable thoughts in an afternoon nap. Batty had left without disturbing her to go to the betting shop and Sadie's noisy entrance woke Angela with a start. The dogs announced this intrusion and tried to round up their visitor to increase the pace of her journey down the hallway. Angela felt drained from sleep; not in any way revived – or ready for conversation.

It was immediately noticeable that Sadie didn't seem to be up to much either. Angela knew that something was wrong; with not a lot else to do with her time these days, the signals emanating from others were easily picked up. Sadie ignored the dogs and paced the room, not diving onto the sofa as usual. She hadn't asked Angela how her day had been or where Batty was, the questions habitually posed and all part of their ritual before launching into a new debate. Sadie was quiet. And so was her mobile.

'So what are we talking about today? Remind me,' asked Angela, pretending to be vague in order to galvanise the girl into a response. Sadie hunched her shoulders and attempted to hide further behind her curtain of hair.

Angela tried again, 'That's not like you, not like you at all, it's not often you're lost for words.'

'I have been thinking … about what I'd do differently like.'

At first Angela thought this preparation to discuss the topic was progress – then she suspected that the exercise had not been a happy one. Had the question uncovered unwanted demons for Sadie, as it had for her?

'Spit it out,' said Angela, not unkindly. She braced herself for anything, whilst wondering where this was leading and sensing that it didn't look like she'd have to divulge *her* regrets to Sadie, not yet anyway.

'P'raps if …' Sadie got out her phone.

'Put it away, Sadie.'

'… if I'd told Joe how much I liked him.'

'Go on,' said Angela, *I can help her with this.* Despite her age, and consequent distance from the experience of young love, the scars of her own first infatuation still existed under the skin.

'I suppose because we're sort of neighbours, me living next door to you like – I started off as his friend and I hoped he'd begin to see me as more than that but there's … nothing now. I don't think he's ever thought of me as a girlfriend, more like, well – just your next door neighbour who happens to go to his school.'

'Give it time, if it's going to blossom it will, if it doesn't you'll …'

'I know it won't happen!' snapped Sadie, tucking her hair behind her ears and exposing mascara left smudged under her eyes.

'Why not?'

'He doesn't want me even as a friend. He's got new mates, new interests. He ignored me this afternoon when I asked him if he was walking back to see you.'

'Do you think there's another girl he likes?' said Angela.

'Why ask that? What do you know?' Sadie's eyes threw accusation at Angela.

'Nothing, I'm sorry, I presumed that's what you were talking about …'

Sadie's pale, pinched face screwed up even more tightly. 'Well I wasn't – I hadn't thought of that.'

Angela remonstrated with herself for handling this badly

and made another stab at it. 'Tell me about his new friends,' she suggested.

'You don't want to know.'

Angela waited for her to go on.

'They do stuff.'

'What do you mean?'

'They're …' Sadie chewed the edge of one of her nails. 'Oh I don't know, I don't never go near them … the others say they do drugs and …'

Angela was fully alert now. 'Do you know that, for a fact?'

'It's talk – gossip like. He often rushes out of school, not talking to no one. We all hang about, outside the gates, and he always did too. But now he goes quick, regular like … secretive though, looking over his shoulder … all worried like.'

'What do the others think he's up to?'

'That he's meeting that lot. Half of them have been excluded so they meet down at that boarded-up hospital site – they know ways in.'

'I hope you keep well away.'

'I do, honest, we've all been warned about being suspended if we're caught down there.'

'So what can I do to help? There must be something.'

'I don't know, *please don't tell his dad*. What with him being a teacher there. Joe'll work out that it came from me – it'll ruin everything, even more, and if his new friends get that I'm involved … you don't upset *them*, honest.' She looked frightened.

Angela assured Sadie that whatever happened she'd guarantee it wouldn't involve her. It had taken some courage to confide all this in the first place and Angela wasn't about to make life even more miserable by creating further difficulties at school.

She patted Sadie's hand. 'Let's just keep an eye on things, see how things go. Why don't you give the dogs a run outside for me and when you've done that make me a nice cup of tea.'

When Sadie left that day Angela hoped that the old adage, "a problem shared is a problem halved", had at least worked a little. One thing she was convinced of … it was time to formulate a plan.

It wasn't until tucked up in bed that night that Angela changed her mind about her initial idea. She was going to ask Batty to say to Joe that they had some jobs around the house that required the two of them to do. It would've provided the opportunity to observe the boy, to see how he looked *and* open him up with a little gentle conversation as she'd always done. *But hold on a minute*, she remonstrated with herself; these plans were counter to everything promised to that reflection in the mirror. Here she was standing in as parent again. Old habits die hard.

There was a better way: Sadie was right about not informing Mark – however there was no reason not to tell Kate. She hadn't promised that.

Before dropping off to sleep, Angela resolved to write to Kate. It was what was needed to get her away from Norfolk *and* to help her start building a relationship with Joe while getting him through this problem, as any real mother would do. In order to achieve that Kate would have to come back to Mark. Angela had a clear vision – it *was* time to change, but not until she'd got everyone re-established on the straight and narrow.

14

AN INVITATION

Angela became adept at dodging Batty as he went in and out of the house on his errands – shopping, collecting books for her from the library or visiting the betting shop (an activity which, much to her concern, was becoming more frequent these days). Every time the dogs leapt up at the sound of the car in the drive, she would slip the drafts of her letter to Kate inside the travel section of the Sunday newspaper and add it to the pile which Batty never bothered to look at on the table next to her. Consequently it took a number of days, with much editing and occasional changes of heart, before she was able to make a carefully handwritten final copy.

Dear Kate,

Before I go any further, please don't tell Batty I've written. He's often told me off about my interfering ways and anyway what I'm going to tell you about Joe would break his heart.

I'm so sorry that you and Mark are having problems and even more apologetic that on reflection I may have been the cause of what has gone amiss since you became part of our family.

The truth is you are so needed by us all, even though it must feel differently to you. Mark is like a ghost. When he walks into our house, he's completely lost his spark or any enthusiasm for life. He seems so confused and unable to express himself. All I know is that he and Joe are hardly speaking now and it's more than just the usual 'teenage thing'. Joe's not right – and it's not because of you staying on in Norfolk.

You see something more unsettling has been brought to my attention. I know you're thinking "interfering old bat – here we go!" I wouldn't blame you. You would have been right in the past, but I've come to realise that it's not my place to solve all Joe's problems – it's yours and Mark's together, you are both his parents now. So why am I telling you first? There are two reasons. One is, that to be honest if I was to tell Mark in his present mood he would, I know, make a mess of it. It's going to need a woman's approach, a mother's touch. Secondly there is a school connection to Joe's problem and that could complicate things even further. I'm hoping that Joe can be sorted out before life goes too wrong for him and that's why I am just sharing suspicions not facts. If we wait for something to actually 'happen' it may be too late – sorry to sound so dramatic!

You may not know that I have a new friend who is sixteen years old! It's remarkable how well we can communicate across the generations – so refreshing and invigorating. Sadie's extremely fond of Joe and, like me, has his best interests at heart – I think she wishes he would take care of her heart if you get my drift. *The other day she confided in me that she thinks that Joe is going off the rails with what you and I would call 'a bad lot' – they sound like they are 'real mingers', as she would say, such an ugly word but it suits them. He's dropped the football team by the way and slopes off after school to goodness knows where most days, ignoring all his usual friends.*

I see so much less of him and when he does come here he won't look Batty in the eye and avoids talking to me about anything he is doing. It's as though he has had a complete personality change. He never even takes his coat off – as if he's got no intention of stopping. He just stands there tugging his cuffs down over his wrists. There's something about him that I can't quite sort out in my mind … furtive would be a good description. Sadie was so upset the other day – she suspects his new friends are into drugs – oh I hope not Kate – something bad is going on – he looks dreadful.

Kate, we need your help with Joe. I realise I have played the substitute mother for far too long. I'm so sorry Kate (I know I've already said it – I mean it) – I hope one day you will forgive me. I'm also sorry to be putting all this on you when you've so much else on your mind. Think about it Kate, this can be something that brings you and Mark back together – working together as parents to support Joe. Please don't leave it too long before you come home. You are missed.

With sincere friendship,

Angela

Once written and secured in its envelope, Sadie was more than willing to post the letter. Angela then began her wait for a response, with fingers crossed that it wouldn't be in the form of a phone call when Batty was in earshot.

15

NIGHTMARE

After walking out on Kate in the pub, Mark had driven back to Warwick burning with anger and confusion. It seemed to him that autumn was destined to be the time when bad things happened and he took his torment out on the car, risking speed camera after speed camera, not caring any more. Halfway home he pulled out onto a roundabout narrowly missing a lorry and visualised Fran in her last moments as she grasped the fact that the tractor was an unavoidable object. Shaken, he sought refuge in the next layby, switched off the engine and tried to regain control of his stomach which was having an out of body experience.

Closing his eyes, Mark gave rein to memories of Fran and that horrendous day; from the beginning when he'd had the news of the accident to when he'd sat for so many lonely nights at Joe's bedside wondering what to do with all his numbing grief and rising panic about bringing up a small boy alone. Thank God for his parents – without them those incessant grey days would never have been survived.

And here he was again with autumn once more being the bringer of gloom and doom. Not like before, with one titanic strike – sudden and shocking. This time it was a series of body blows, culminating in this loss of control: of his car back there on the road, of his own emotions *and* his sense. When he considered the very real possibility of losing Kate to someone else he felt gutted; when he looked at himself he saw the most stupid man on the planet. Losing Fran was a random event that couldn't have been avoided, but this time he'd played a big part in causing the wreckage. Last time when life had fallen apart, there'd been Joe to force him to hold things together. And this time? Was there still further to fall or had he hit rock bottom? Only one way to find out, he told himself as he started up the car.

When Mark arrived back in Warwick, despite the late hour he called in to see his parents. All they wanted to talk about centred on whether or not Kate was coming back; Angela, in particular, interrogated him in an attempt to find out if they'd got over their "problems". The thought of pouring it all out horrified him, so he clammed up – like Joe.

The next couple of days of half-term were spent catching up on school work, and trying to haul himself out of the miseries by attempting practical jobs around the house in the hope of taking his mind off darker thoughts. This didn't work – it forced him to think about all that would need to be done to get the house up to scratch if they did irrevocably split up and had to sell.

It was a relief to get to Wednesday when he was in charge of the Duke of Edinburgh Award trip to the Lake District. He counted the kids onto the coach, counted them getting off at the service station and counted them onto the coach again; this tedious repetition continued ad infinitum until they arrived back on the Saturday. While watching the tents go up and the tents come down, ticking health and safety checklists, recording accomplishments, heading off arguments and clandestine adolescent encounters – Mark made up his mind to get Kate back, somehow.

On the Saturday evening, by the time the song-drunk teenagers had been seen off the coach for the last time and handed back to their parents, the kit sorted, and colleagues – who hadn't a life to rush back to – thanked with a drink at the pub, it was close to midnight when he reached home. In a state of near exhaustion he turned his car into the tree-lined drive which swept around the semi-circular lawn in front of the old school now converted into luxury flats. The imposing building stood there, illuminated by ground lights set in the lawn, looking like the backdrop to a stage set ready for curtain up. Although now framed by the cream-rendered, new-build houses on either side – one of which he owned – the whole place still had its foot in the past. The rich seasonal shades of fallen leaves covering the lawns were picked out as his headlights gave even more light to the scene. It was a great place to live, a quiet cul-de-sac where nature co-existed happily with the human race. The whole set-up was more upmarket than he'd been used to, before Kate, but when they'd first got together they each had a house to sell so they'd been able to buy their dream. *Some dream that turned out to be …*

His train of thought was broken by the realisation that the lights were *on* in his house – Joe was staying at a mate's for a few days, it couldn't be him. Mark pulled up outside his next-door neighbours' house and switched the headlights off; if his house was being broken into he wasn't going marching in and getting himself killed into the bargain. Next door still had their lights on – he saw Steve's round face at the window and reckoned that the two of them together might make a better job of sorting this one out. Steve's front door opened; Mark could tell by the expression on his face that he wasn't pleased.

'About time, it's a good job you're back *at last*, we were going to call the police!'

'Right, sorry mate,' said Mark. 'I mean, let's get on with it, before they get at Kate's jewellery.'

'Is that a good idea what with Joe being there – do you want him and half your pupils pulled in?'

'What?'

'They've been at it since lunchtime. I don't think it started as a party as such, there was Joe and a few lads, and a couple of girls I think. I thought you must have ok'd it. They were out in the garden and it all seemed harmless – then it got dark and the volume went up.' Steve melodramatically paused at this point before continuing. 'Keith from the Schoolhouse went over and complained about the noise and got a mouthful of bad language. He was going to call the police earlier, I put him off – saying you would be back soon – that was half an hour ago.'

Mark didn't want to hear any more but there was more to come. Steve pulled him around the side of the house to the fence by the back garden. 'I think it's getting nasty now,' he said in a low voice, 'there's something brewing out there. Suzy didn't want me to go and intervene – you have to watch yourself with kids these days, if you know what I mean.'

Raised voices could be heard; trouble wasn't just brewing, it was about to boil over. 'I know that voice,' Mark groaned, 'I've heard it often enough at school, usually in fights, egging others on.'

He saw red; the school bully was about to seriously damage someone in *his* backgarden – while probably drinking *his* beer! Without any more hesitation he marched in through the front door and – stopped; it was carnage. The place was packed with kids from school, drunk, and high on drugs as well, he assumed. Bodies were swarming over each other in the living room and spilling out into the hallway. One girl, who he'd considered to be one of the better behaved at school, was throwing up on the stairs. It didn't surprise him that she'd given up on the downstairs toilet – the door was surrounded by girls trying to talk whoever had locked themselves in to 'come out and face up!' Mark didn't stop to sort that one out, hoping whoever it was stayed put – those girls were on a mission.

He walked through the kitchen, across a floor covered in broken glass and swimming in beer. Joe was nowhere to be seen. As the party-goers recognised their PE teacher they melted into the background as he pushed his way through to the garden. Mark found a crowd of four lads about to set on each other, lads who were all quite capable of inflicting harm on others without thought or regret. One of them had a knife – one of *his* kitchen knives! Joe was sitting on his childhood swing, completely out of it, about to slide off; the girl he knew as Sadie stood next to him trying to keep the swing steady.

Mark marched over to Knife-boy and squared up in front of him, very glad that he had kept up his personal fitness in the school gym after work each night. *Pay off time,* thought Mark, *I'm more than prepared to smash these heads together!*

'Get out of my house NOW!' he shouted.

Knife-boy stared back with indolent mean eyes. The hand

holding the knife twitched.

'I said GET OUT OF MY BLOODY HOUSE NOW!'

Mark drew breath. 'And drop that knife before you even think about using it.' There was a flash of defiance as the knife was thrust towards him – the music stopped, Knife-Boy stopped, everyone held their breath. Joe looked up with a confused expression on his face. To Mark it was all happening in slow motion. He was acutely aware of everything around him: Sadie getting out her mobile and keying in some numbers, Joe slumping forward and falling off the swing, Steve's head bobbing up and down above the fence.

All the time Mark watched the face in front of him ooze with hostility. But Mark wasn't a fool. 'And if you don't move fast, it's your mother I'll be seeing tomorrow – and she's a *real* ballbreaker isn't she?' The lad ran – and with him, one by one, the rest of the crowd.

Mark couldn't look at his son. Instead he went back in to inspect the mess. The worst thing was the carpets, the rest could be sorted – all except Joe; dealing with Joe was another matter altogether.

Sadie coughed to get Mark's attention. 'Can I stay, Mr Haughton? If we get Joe to bed, I'll help you clear up.'

'What I can't understand is how Joe thought he'd get away with it, what with me coming home tonight.'

'It didn't start out like this, it wasn't meant to be a party, he only invited a few at lunchtime. They turned up and kept letting their mates in, I picked it up on Facebook, thought someone had to watch Joe's back so I came round – it was like everyone was off their head – I couldn't do nothing, it was well bad.'

Together they tried to get Joe up the stairs. On the way

his vomit joined that already deposited on the same step
– evidently one step too far, every time, reasoned Mark as
he got his son onto the bed. Although Joe smelt disgusting,
some colour looked to be coming back since he'd been
sick. Mark left Sadie attempting to clean him up, which she
seemed more than keen to do.

He wandered about trying to take it all in. When he looked
at the kitchen floor, he tried to weigh up whether to pick the
glass out of the beer or to attempt to clean everything up in
one go. Sadie appeared downstairs and came to the rescue.

'Have you got a garden brush and a mop, that'll soon sort
it?'

He dutifully found what was needed and together they
cleared the floor, while the toxic odour of alcohol mixed with
the vomit wafting from the stairs refused to budge. Following
this mopping up operation, Mark had had enough.

'Let's sort the rest out in the morning – it's been a very
long day.'

'You go to bed, Mr Haughton, I'll do a bit more. Can I
sleep on Joe's floor tonight? I can keep an eye on him – if he
throws up I'll wake you if I can't cope.' Mark was confident
she could handle most things if she set her mind to it and
acquiesced; he'd no energy left to argue.

The next morning when sleep had released him from one
nightmare back to the reality of another, Mark was amazed
to see how hard Sadie had worked. The kitchen had been
put back in some form of order, although the smell of
beer continued to loiter. He opened the back door and all
the windows onto a bright day; the sun found its way into
the house – along with the birdsong. The vomit had gone

from the stairs and the stain worked on. Most of the house had been tidied, albeit with much in the wrong place – and although it had not been vacuumed, Mark had a feeling that Sadie would be putting that right once she'd woken up. How he'd misjudged that girl – *I'm an expert at getting things wrong it seems*. Sadie came downstairs at ten in a positive mood which halted Mark's despondency.

'Good job I stayed sober, anyways I *hate* the taste,' she said when Mark thanked her for her efforts.

'Would you like me to cook you some bacon and eggs?' Mark suggested. 'It'll help get rid of the smell in the kitchen.'

'Cool – I'm *starving*! I'll carry on cleaning up – where do you keep your vacuum thingy?'

'You'll wake Joe with the noise,' said Mark, evoking Kate's reproachful voice – *You always put his needs first.*

'I don't think anything will wake him up. Anyways if he remembers what happened he'll just pretend to be asleep – I would if I were him.' She grinned at Mark.

'He's going to have to face me some time,' replied Mark, hoping that he would be able to control his temper when the time came.

'He'll be well scared. I'm a bit scared of you at school you know. Not today though. You know when you first came to Castle High and made *everyone* do PE I hated it see, felt *real* stupid being useless at it all in front of my mates. Right now, though, it's different, I feel real sorry for you, coming back like that. I was well impressed though – that Mic Spears, I hate him! You were well cool.'

'I'm not all bad then?'

'Well …'

Mark braced himself for further appraisal. Professional

development sessions with the Head had never been as frank as this.

'You *have* to talk to Joe.'

'We agree on that then.'

'No,' she said, 'not about the party … about … the other stuff.'

'And what would that be?' asked Mark cautiously.

'It's like … before he lost consciousness … before you got back … like before I got him round and took him outside, he let it all out at me, probably won't remember today though.'

'Go on.'

'He went on about when you came down so hard on all the wasters – all that PE stuff every morning – New Frontier I think you and the Head called it. They weren't impressed, no one was. Lots of them took it out on Joe – that's why he had to get in with them see. So, like, after holding out for a long time he gave in and dropped the football team. I reckon that was their idea – he had to show them he wasn't on your side any more. Who knows what else they made him do.'

'Made him? How?'

'You saw them last night – by the way, I think the bacon's burning.'

Mark's thoughts of breakfast were far away; he reckoned he'd been gobsmacked enough, yet it still kept coming at him.

Joe appeared at the top of the stairs looking very unsteady and deathly white. 'Come down you muppet,' said Sadie, 'it's ok, there's not much damage.' Mark looked sadly at Kate's cream carpets – there was no way his home insurance covered teenage parties.

'Bet you smelt the bacon,' added Sadie as Joe staggered

into the kitchen.

'Shit, no!' said Joe. 'Need water.'

Still trying to digest what Sadie had been saying about Joe, Mark wasn't ready to cross-question him. He looked at his son properly; it was something he hadn't done for a long time. There was the face he thought he'd known so well – pale and drawn with eyes looking down at the floor. His stooped shoulders reflected a body that was unfit and ill at ease with itself as he shuffled across the kitchen. This was something more than a hangover and so much more than the result of not playing football regularly for a few weeks. He looked at what Joe was wearing: his underpants and that awful sweatshirt with the sleeves which had been stretched to his fingertips and a thumb hole worked into the cuff. Mark's eyes locked on the cuffs pulled over Joe's hands – he couldn't remember the last time he'd seen him wearing anything with his arms uncovered.

Sadie grabbed Joe, rescuing them all. 'I think you could do with getting out in the fresh …' She stopped herself, ' … sad though, I sound like Mum. Don't tell her.'

'Put some trousers on him first,' said Mark.

Sadie tugged Joe out of the room and upstairs before Mark could say anything more. She needn't have worried. Despite wanting to let rip, he had received and accepted the message – from Sadie of all people – that much of all this was his fault. A few minutes later they reappeared with Joe clothed, but still protesting about their search for fresh air. *She'll go far*, Mark thought, as they walked off down the road holding hands.

Mark shovelled the burnt bacon into the bin. What to do next was the question? He powered up his computer to see if it had been damaged. Someone had been into it. Joe's Facebook page stared back at him from the screen – it had been left logged in. Full of guilt, Mark began to trawl through what looked like a lot of puerile language including the ill-fated invite to a few "mates". He followed the links. He soon saw in front of him conversations he could barely understand with those he'd never heard of. Amongst the slang he deciphered that this was some type of support group for those who handled what life threw at them in the same way that Joe did. Yes, thought Mark, *autumn lets me down every time.*

He kept his emotions in check while he retraced his steps back to Joe's original home page, logged off and reset his own password. He clicked on shut down and sat staring at the screen. Only then did Mark give in as tears were released for the first time since that day he had driven down to Cornwall to identify the bodies. Many, many times he questioned how he had driven so far without crashing, so blinded he'd been by crying, so exhausted by the gut-wrenching horror of it all. On arrival at the hospital he'd sat in the car trying to gain control and had woken with a start to gather that he'd fallen asleep for two hours, regardless of his desperate need to see Joe. Ashamed of how he'd given in to events, and guilty of leaving Joe alone for far too long, he'd walked stoically through the automatic doors which closed behind, shutting him inside the unfamiliar corridors of desolation. As he found his way to the children's ward, Mark swore to be strong for his son and to never let him see the weakness of those tears, ever.

16

CAT AND MOUSE

Since the evening of Mark's visit, the conversation on the ice-cream bench with Margret had prowled around in Kate's consciousness. She had to know what lay behind Margret's future plans for that unfathomable attic space now thought of as Sye's. This need to know, once roused, was wide awake and desired more information to feed it. *Why had Margret only just begun to talk about making these changes?* Nothing had been said when she'd asked to extend her stay back in September, and nothing had been touched on during their late night chats with Phil. By concentrating on this impending disruption of her double life, the idea of any new shift in relationship between Mark and Dom was banished to the furthest recesses of her mind.

Kate told herself that a direct approach would be the best way to deal with Margret and began to make plans. A sixth sense told her not to lay these thoughts open to Sye but to only have them when away from the house. She was sure that he couldn't connect to what she was thinking if she was outside, and had tested this theory by walking around the village whilst weighing up the pros and cons of absconding from everything and going to Nice to see her parents. During her next encounter with Sye, there was no suggestion of him having picked this up. Consequently any thoughts about Margret needed to stay safely out of doors.

Every day Kate continued to visit Sye, wanting to stay for as many daylight hours as possible, but knowing that part of her time needed to be spent getting out of the house to keep up an appearance of normality. She stood by her resolution not to express to him her fears about any possible change, because she couldn't bear anything to break the spell. His amazing ability to lift her out of the real world and into the sanctuary of another level of being, always caused her worries to fade into insignificance. If she was ever tense, he would presume it related to Mark and rapidly change the subject, preaching the "peace and love" creed of the swinging sixties while perpetually playing the *same* hypnotic track from the *same* Beatles' album, the sitar always there, trapped in the groove.

When she wasn't with Sye, anxiety about Margret's intervention endeavoured to take over, so Kate forced herself to become adept at thinking of other things when alone in her part of the building. It transpired that those seconds of exhaustion, just before sleep, were the most precarious as she was concerned that her dreams might follow her anxieties and somehow enable Sye to uncover the truth about the threat Margret posed to their attic life. It was a state of mind for Kate which did not encourage sleep. The solution to this, she found, was to lie there mentally retracing her afternoon and evening pursuits or conversations in the pub. Those parts of the day where she allowed her brain to function naturally could provide enough diversion of thought to draw on when alone in her bed.

On the first Monday that the village was relieved of half-term holidaymakers, Kate took action on the problem of Margret by getting up early and setting off to Fisherman's Cottage before breakfast. As expected, she could see that the small jetty ahead of her was now devoid of children with buckets and watchful parents, despite the tide being at its peak level for successful crabbing.

While making her preparations to leave, in order to ensure Sye's ignorance of her plan, Kate had concentrated her thoughts on the need to get some food in from Burnham Market and pay her rent that morning. She also filled her mind with thoughts of her next intended visit to the attic on her return from these chores. She'd smiled to herself; it was akin to speaking to Sye on the telephone or texting him a message. Immediately the smile disappeared and her eyes welled up at the recognition that at present she had much better communication with a ghost than she had when standing face to face with Mark. Denying the tears, an attempt was made to block that thought out; but its intrusion could not be avoided – a plain truth exposed. With everything so awry in real life with Mark – *it was all so much easier with Sye.* That she could sense Sye's pleasure at this consciousness shocked her – she was not the only one able to send messages.

Margret looked surprised to see Kate, answering the door in a long faded dressing gown with her hair wrapped up in a towel. The tactic of arriving on the doorstep at such an hour took away any chance Margret could have had to invent an excuse.

Kate held up her flask. 'I've made the best coffee, let's go for a walk, it's a glorious morning and I want to thank you for your help the other night when I lost it. I've got some one-day-old croissants I've brought back to life in the oven. How about breakfast on the beach?'

'I'm not going out that far so early in the morning. It may be bright out there now but I don't trust the weather at this time of year.' Margret stuck her nose out of the door, sniffed the air and retreated indoors without asking Kate in.

'Ok, I give in on the walk,' said Kate, slipping in through the door. 'Why don't we take it to the bench by the Boathouse – it's quiet down there today – and we can get the morning sun before your weather forecast takes over. You never know, I might be able to tempt you to change your mind about walking.'

'No – you – won't,' said Margret while hitching up her dressing gown to climb the stairs. 'Look, I'll come as far as the bench, that coffee sounded good. I'll get ready, it'll take me a few minutes, I need to dry off my hair before I go out there.'

Kate could hear Margret moving around upstairs as she dressed, followed by the buzz of the hairdryer. While waiting she wandered around the ground floor of the cottage – one narrow room wide and two rooms deep – and sat down on the edge of an enormous circular rattan chair with a highly decorated shell-like backrest; a completely incongruous throne, thought Kate. Apart from this, hard and unyielding beneath her, there were few signs of comfort or of a life being lived in the room. The flagstone floor, unloved and uneven, ran right the way through to the tiny kitchen. Kate surmised that it had not been layed to be trendy and that it was more likely to be the original floor put there to meet the basic needs of the first occupant of the property. The walls and mantelpiece over the fireplace housed no photographs of family, in fact no adornment at all – no paintings or treasured objects, no plants, flowers or books. It was a room devoid of purpose, as if Margret deliberately kept it like this to safeguard herself against a casual caller gaining insight into her life or background. This unsettled Kate further and fuelled disappointment, as she'd hoped this expedition into Margret's life might lead to an understanding as to why the wardrobe had first been placed in front of the stairs to the attic. Even in her own home Margret was evidently not the sort of person to give much away about herself, but perhaps there was a chance that conversation would prove more illuminating than this emptiness of a room.

It was startling to see Margret when she came downstairs with her hair loose and wearing large denim overalls. There appeared to be nothing of the woman with neat, pinned up, hair who rented out The Old Pilot's House, or the woman who worked every evening at Phil's in her black skirt, white shirt and dark green bistro tabard. Kate began to understand that there was much more to Margret than the face she ordinarily presented to the world.

Kate poured the coffee into the two plastic cups balanced on the wooden slats of the bench. 'Are you sure I can't persuade you to walk out to the beach?'

'I don't, ever,' replied Margret.

'What, in all the time you've lived here – never?'

'The whole way out? Not for a very long time.'

'When Mark and I came on our first holiday, we couldn't wait to get out there.'

'Most people feel like that,' said Margret, 'I was the same.'

'Have you always lived here on your own? It must have

been lonely – until Phil turned up anyway. Can't have been easy.'

'Well you'd know about that wouldn't you, with Mark not here.'

Kate tried in vain to redirect the conversation towards Margret: 'So what made you come here?'

'What makes anyone travel to another place? What made your parents go to Nice, for example?'

'That's easy – they'd given up on me ever providing them with the excitement and satisfaction of a grand wedding and a brood of babies, so they opted to spend all their pennies on themselves.' Kate knew there was bitterness in her voice.

'Don't you have any other family?'

'No, I'm the last of the line – hence my parents' immutable disappointment in me. You can't imagine what that's like.'

'Yes I can,' said Margret faintly.

Kate caught her words and wanted to clutch on to them, to turn the conversation back to Margret. Despite this, however, there was her own need to finish what she had started.

'I think I was a disappointment from day one. I wasn't a boy. Then they thought, good education, Oxbridge – they met at Cambridge you see – followed by a good go-getting husband or a rich intellectual and that brood of babies. Unfortunately they got none of that with me. They were totally unimpressed when I showed I hadn't the ability to get into either of their target universities. When I left the one place that would have me – they would never mention its name – and set up a business with Dom, they were impressed by him and got all excited with high hopes of a good marriage for me. Huh! That was a joke, bless him.'

'Phil and I thought you two seemed very close.'

'We are, like brother and sister. Anyway, I hit the last nail in the coffin when I turned up in Nice with Mark – poor, sporty and with a stepson in tow who would never be theirs. I was considered a total failure, through and through.'

'So they left before you met Mark?'

'Yes. They told me on my thirtieth birthday. They'd inherited bucket-loads from my grandmother. Retired the same week the money came through – upped and left a month later, leaving me to sort out the sale and clearance of their house. It was like they had died, too. I didn't get together with Mark for a couple of years after that so I was absolutely alone when they went – apart from Dom, he became my family, you see.'

'The infamous Dom seems to have been around for quite a while.'

'Oh, he's wonderful, you met him at a bad time.' Her growing worries about Dom and Mark stirred; further thoughts in that direction needed to be blocked off.

'Croissant?' she said.

'You know I'm trying to lose weight.'

'Sorry, forgot. Go on, have one – then we could try a short amble, to walk it off?'

'What about Mark's parents? I seem to remember they came on holiday with you when Joe was younger – you appeared to get on well with them.'

'Angela and Batty? Batty's fine, a bit of a maverick – in a quiet sort of way. Angela was very unsure of me at first. We're more or less ok nowadays … although, what I mean is, we were before all this happened. I shouldn't think she's much time for me now, not if Mark's cried on her shoulder.'

'Do you think he has?'

'I don't know, it depends if she gets him at a weak moment. On past form he'll go and stow it all away inside.'

Kate reflected on just how much that past form had led her to the surreal game she was now playing with the supernatural.

Margret prodded her in the ribs, 'Come on – tell me more about Angela.'

'Well, Angela *can* be an almighty control freak, and it was the one thing she couldn't control that disappointed her the most. You see it always comes down to the grandchildren – or lack of. The generation which gives you life *crave* the grandchildren.'

'We all want what we haven't got.'

'I suppose so.' Kate wondered what it was that Margret was still seeking all alone in Fisherman's Cottage.

'We were talking about your mother-in-law,' Margret reminded her.

'Sorry, yes, where was I? I think she hoped that I would rekindle a new life for Mark and Joe, after them being left so long without a wife or mother. You know, that I would write a brand new chapter for them. But the main thing is that, in Angela's eyes, I'll never live up to Fran.'

'So Fran was Mark's first wife?'

'Yes, Fran … or Francesca as she was known in her operatic circles … was killed in a car accident on a lane in Devon. Her parents died with her, Joe was only four then and miraculously walked away from it. I've always been told she loved to sing whilst driving – so I often visualise her driving along singing something like *Habanera* at the top of her voice – until that nanosecond when the tractor appeared on the bend and the singing stopped. The tractor was an immovable beast; the driver survived. He walked miles over fields carrying little Joe.'

'What a tragedy … so he never remembers his mother?'

'Oh yes he does, or he thinks he does, in an idealised way. Angela took care of that. Photos of her everywhere, recordings of her singing, stuff like that. Fran was young and had a dazzling career ahead of her. Angela and Batty adored her.'

'Where was Mark when it happened?'

'On a school trip. About to join them on holiday the next day.'

'Poor Mark.'

'Yes, everyone says that.' Kate was reminded as to why she didn't tell this story very often any more. She would get to this point and find that, while the listener was expressing sympathy for all concerned, all the wrong emotions would be churning inside her: jealousy and anger, together with a huge disappointment in herself for feeling that way. That's why she loved Dom – he knew it all, and she never had to go back over that particular bit of the past with him.

'Sounds like she was a very hard act to follow.'

'It wasn't until after Mark and I got married that it became apparent as to how Angela and Joe kept Fran's ghost alive. I'd naively thought six years was long enough to put the poor woman to rest. Mark seemed ok with it all, he didn't want to talk about it much, said he wanted to move on … and I thought that what with Joe being so young, he would be over it. *Enough of this* – let's go for that walk!'

'No, I said I wouldn't and I meant it. I've got an appointment anyway in Burnham and I need to get out of my scruffs and look the part.' Margret got up and threw the dregs of her coffee onto the grass.

'What part?'

'The part of someone who can afford exorbitant architect's fees!'

'Ah … you mean the cottage.'

'That's right.'

'It's definite then? How soon?'

'Yes, I've made up my mind. It will take a couple of weeks to get things rolling … at last.'

'But where will you put everything?'

'Some of the furniture, small bits and pieces, can fill up that room you've just been sitting in. Phil's said I can put the rest in that large shed at the back of the pub – the beds, the sofa and the like – except the wardrobe of course, it's time to get rid of that.'

Sure that Margret had left mention of the wardrobe until last to gauge a response, Kate chose to remain silent on the walk back and tossed the bag of croissants into the bin as they passed. Parting halfway between The Old Pilot's House and Fisherman's Cottage, Margret promised regular updates on the progress of her plans.

The inability to unearth anything at all about Margret's past was frustrating; all Kate had succeeded in doing was to worry herself even further. All the logistics of emptying the house, in order to begin work on it, had been planned and decided upon. And, to make things worse, she'd gone and given away much more of her own self than ever intended. *Why on earth did I let that happen?*

As she walked the last few yards, a chill wind made her button up her jacket. The breeze was picking up and rain threatened. It would be good to be indoors and seek out

Sye; the spectre of Fran, previously something she had just lived with, now triggered a strong desire for a tangible, more welcome member of the spirit world. The sound of her feet on the gravel drive as she hurried to the front door gave evidence to this eagerness. It was only on shutting the door that Kate caught a glimpse of Margret, standing behind the hedge fronting the main road, watching and waiting, a figure which then furtively moved away, clearly in fear of exposure.

The prospect of Margret hanging about necessitated Kate to leave the front door ajar, turn the radio up as loud as possible and wait a full hour before going up to the attic. An hour which passed with constant checking that no one was out there watching, while messaging Sye with thoughts of her impending arrival. By the time Kate felt confident she was not being observed, it was as if she had been pulled as taut as the strings on a cello – yet to no avail, as she remained as out of tune with the real world as she possibly could be.

17

PASSION

Kate sat on Sye's cushions, sobbing. He sat opposite, cross-legged, calm and peaceful.

'Look at the difference between your world and mine,' he said.

She couldn't speak – couldn't locate her voice – her face felt hot and blotchy.

'Relax, chill out, forget all that's upset you. Or tell me what's going on if you like. But don't worry, if you're not in a place to do that, it's cool.'

Unburdening to Margret earlier had released so many suppressed emotions. Even her previous soul searching expeditions on the beach hadn't uncovered the anger burning inside regarding her parents and all those guilty feelings about Fran. Now it cascaded through her brain, her body, her limbs – the whirlpool this time wasn't dragging her down into it, she was an integral part of the vortex, with swirling thoughts becoming more and more murky as the water got deeper. Dredging up her voice from the depths she carried on with her recollections as if Sye and Margret were one and the same being.

'You see … before I met Mark, I had so much drive … with McKinley Nichols that is … I had to prove to my parents that I could achieve *something* ... that I *was* a success.' Kate began to pull herself together and took a moment to slow her breathing. 'Dom and I were doing a great job with the Agency, although it tied me in knots. I *became* the business, working every hour God sent and thinking of nothing else. When I met Mark he gave me a new freedom and a new passion, to start with. He didn't introduce me to Joe until we had been together for about eight months – didn't want him upset if we split up.'

'How did Joe take to you?'

'Fine initially, and after we were married things were ok for the first couple of years. Then I came to see that it was all so easy because Joe was going to Angela – Mark's mother – with his problems. I eventually got it. How everything for Mark revolved around Joe. His son's demands come first – a real passion killer I can assure you.'

'Passion is a strange thing – without it we are nothing,' said Sye, smiling remotely into space. He got up and began to pace the room, from east to west, like a prisoner measuring out his cell. When he reached the far wall he stopped, leant against it, folded his arms and began again. 'But I'm not really talking about sex. I don't know about your world, but in my time it's free and easy – everyone's at it like rabbits – it's cheap, easy come, easy go. Pick them up, bed them and move on. They all just devalue passion. Passion is about wanting, desiring and devouring something you can't live without – it is life's breath and blood and flesh and vision ... passion is what we are here for.'

He came and stood behind her.

Kate knew he'd taken her words and tried to place her back in his world. She resisted, still reliving the past.   .

'But you don't understand. I poured out all that passion into wanting a baby. One of my own – one that *needed me as a mother*. That's where it all finally went wrong. The more needy I became, the more it seemed to me that Mark put Joe first – and the rest of the world for that matter. There was no time for *us*. So I took all that unused passion and turned back to my work and poured it out there again. I became obsessed by it all, like before, worse even. Then the more I worked, the less inclined *I* was to instigate anything that might lead us to make that baby … that beautiful baby. And so it went on – a diminishing cycle which left everything …'

Sye slowly spoke the words she couldn't find: 'barren … and empty – an empty space with all love and emotion poured out and flowing down the drain.' Kate flinched at this, Sye paused as if waiting for her to recover. Then he continued, '*That's why we had our connection, you must see that.* I have so much to give you; to teach you what passion means – it can happen outside of your present existence and what I can give you is *so much better than anything your paltry real world can pretend to give.*' He was still standing behind her, speaking as though addressing the nation now, building to his crescendo and resting his case with those last words.

Kate knew he was right. Without warning she faced an image of her husband holding out his hand for support; it was no good, he remained too far away. She was unsure whether it was he or she drowning, or both of them. The image disappeared, as quickly as it had arrived. The intensity coming from Sye obliterated the memory of any remaining connection to Mark.

A powerful case had been made for a life which could

be wholly stress-free, steeped in the simplicity of what love ought to be. She knew that in discovering Sye, she'd at last found what she had been seeking since childhood, someone who needed her as much as she needed them. It took no effort at all to close her mind to any knowledge that Sye was not human, as repeatedly George Harrison's voice drifted around the room. Random words beginning to make a new sense. They were floating into her and filling that empty space. She was no longer a barren, futile void; instead, she felt empowered with what seemed like a golden liquid coursing through her veins. Sye took her hands and pulled her up to join him; he found no resistance. Together they began to dance, circling each other, arms outstretched – unified in rhythm and time. The room appeared to be full of light, that golden glow extending from their inner beings. Even the Pharaohs would have envied the gilded richness of it all. She was spinning now, a whirling dervish, and as the view outside passed her eyes the whole world shimmered too, challenging the sun for brilliance.

And then it stopped, having slowed without her being conscious of the fact until the destination of stillness had been reached. It was as if she had just got off a fairground ride with feet unsteady, not joined in any way to her brain.

'You could be with me, like that – *all the time*. One little step and this could be your real world,' he said.

18

LOOKING EAST

During the next few sun-blessed days Kate rejected any thoughts of walking to the beach for one single space.

Four walls held her, and although the four windows enabled the whole of the surrounding landscape to be viewed, it was the sea prospect that drew her – as it drew Sye. He would only appear when she was standing staring out through the large window to the east, her back to the room – it had become the cue for his 'being' to materialise and then it would be as if he had been there all the time. In addition to abandoning freedom, Kate abandoned her friends, her own space below and any pretence of normality.

Nursing the discovery of just how soon Margret intended to disrupt everything, Kate lived her hours in Sye's gilded cage. Exhausted and exhilarated by their time together, even the habitual rhythms of day and night were lost with Kate sleeping for two or three hours when needed, waking each time as if she'd had a good night's sleep, with morning freshness and hope. They danced and talked and when they had finished talking they danced again – to the same intoxicating tune.

Sye showed few signs of tiredness. Kate would curl up in a foetal position, either lying next to him or with her head on his lap, secure in the feeling that he'd watch over her dreams until she uncurled to stretch her limbs. He would then pull her with care from the floor treating her as if made of fine sand – as though, if he pulled too carelessly, or too quickly, she'd crumble, trickle away and flow back into that old life. To acclimatise to the space again, he'd walk her so slowly from window to window with time existing purely as an irrelevant bystander.

It would only be momentarily that he would fade from Kate's presence. When this happened she would rush to the east window, full of loss, only to turn and find him behind her, with his reassuring smile. Sye liked to let in the sounds of birdlife and the gentle rattle of the sailboat masts. But were these sounds from his time or hers? Kate could never be sure. Whenever the outside crept into the attic, there was a sadness which pervaded his body; a body which could not walk out into the landscape he had painted with such sensitivity.

They would stand a while sharing the view, Sye behind her, his arms wrapped in ownership around her waist, his chin resting on her shoulder. In this way they would look as one out across to the marshes with their secret pathways and beyond to Scolt Head Island, the nature reserve which she longed to explore with him.

As soon as she welcomed back the energy that sleep had given they would begin to sway to the lilting music together, until their dance separated them, each to claim the space and fill it with their euphoria. Kate longed for their first kiss and ached to give her body to him, but this never happened; they had a spiritual connection, an emotional union not yet consummated physically. Once, when she had lifted her lips to his, he had placed his long fingers on her mouth and traced its outline with them, taking his time, his eyes giving away his yearning for her.

'Not yet,' he said, 'we both need to be part of the same world.'

'So what do we do with all this passion?'

'I keep trying to tell you – all we need to do is enjoy what we have, live in the moment and while we do that our connection will get stronger and stronger – you will see where we're going, soon, believe me.'

'Do you think our two lives ... I mean, the real time we both exist in ... can merge and become one?' she asked, pushing away any fear lurking nearby.

'We'll see.'

Sye had a fascination for the differences between their two worlds – 'now' and 'then' – or 'then' and 'now' – depending on whose point of view it was. He asked her to tell him what had happened after his demise – what had happened to humankind since he'd ceased to be part of a more corporal existence? She didn't know where to start, and when she tried he used it to prove the futility of her existence and the promise of his.

'Look,' he said, 'in the sixties we were going to change everything. Our parents had fought a war for a better life. It took my generation to question their view of what that was – we were going to be the "chosen ones" that moved on from war and made a difference. A world founded on living not killing. We were children of the universe, a youth revolution – it wasn't just music and haircuts – it was a powerful force and a beautiful one. "Make Love Not War" – we were going to come of age and take the world by storm with peace and love!'

'That's all gone now, we have mobile phones, Facebook and Twitter instead.'

'What's that?'

'Instant communication, where you can talk to anyone, anywhere all over the world – I wonder what would have happened if your lot had had access to that!'

Sye let out a long low whistle … 'Cool man, real cool.'

'So where did all the peace and love go?' asked Kate.

'In 1961, at the beginning, America had John Fitzgerald Kennedy as President, then the Beatles electrified us with their new sound – Beatlemania everyone called it …'

'… and then?'

'Kennedy was shot.' Sye grimly formed a gun with his fingers and shot himself in the head. 'Pow!' He stared straight ahead. 'At the beginning of the decade everything was new, exhilarating. We should have known that it was futile, we tried, we really tried. So, tell me, is the human race still intent on using the self-destruct button?'

Kate wanted to tell Sye that things had got better, that the world *had* moved on to become a more peaceful, caring place, that people had learned from the mistakes of the past. It was no use, the words couldn't be found – instead she was swamped by Sye's melancholic mood, drawn in and sucked down. 'John Lennon was shot too,' she said bluntly.

Sye's face crumpled.

Kate stepped towards him. 'I'm sorry, I wasn't going to tell you that.'

'There's no point holding back from me - not now!' he snapped, pushing her away.

Kate was confused, his sudden attack made her back away

from the edge of the ocean lapping her feet; the tensions of their first encounters rematerialised. Something badly made her want to hurt him. 'And George Harrison died at fifty-eight!'

Her words failed to have the effect she'd anticipated; Sye's mournful face transformed as if the channel had been changed on the television. 'Hah, he lived a lot longer than me. Had better luck than yours truly. Think about it – I shall get to meet them both at some point then. That's something to look forward to. They must be sitting on some heavenly cloud up there, writing some fab number one hits, singing and playing with the angels to perform to. Bet their hair's long now! Don't you see, they were the ones who stayed in India, embraced something better, found a state of mind to exist in beyond *your* destructive world. And now they're the lucky ones, the ones that got away!'

'I wouldn't know about that. *You're* so much better qualified to judge.'

'I get where they were at, that's why I keep playing and replaying that track – it's all about seeing beyond yourself as an individual to see that love, I mean *passion*, is about coming together under one magnificent banner, don't you see?'

And Kate *was* beginning to see – his preaching at last completely making sense. Nearly there now, she thought; it was as if his promised land existed just around a corner about to be turned. She felt ashamed of her doubts. Sye was winning her mind and would provide the tranquillity she'd been blindly searching for. The one barrier left was the buried thought of what Sye expected of her, or from her, in order to attain that complete state of being he promised. For the present, it stayed buried.

'So,' said Sye, 'The Fab Four – what happened to the other two?'

'Oh they're fine – multimillionaires or something. High up on The Rich List anyway; Paul's still singing and writing. Ringo? I don't know what he's up to.'

'Did the Beatles break up, before death did the job for them?'

'Oh yes, they played their last time together on a roof-top somewhere, can't remember where, I wasn't even born. It was an iconic moment. I saw some photographs of it – doing research. I wanted to use one of them for an ad campaign directed at Baby Boomers but had to abandon the project because of all the problems with copyright.'

'Baby Boomers?'

'They're what you would have been, had you lived.' Kate laughed, 'Come here, frown really hard – let me see what you would have looked like.'

Sye did as he was told and this time her fingers traced the lines on his face. Lines without a cause or reason, without a story behind them – without a life. Not growing older was so much sadder than growing old she thought. Kate put the palms of her hands over his eyes and lowered them, tenderly brushing his cheeks and stroking his strong jaw.

'You won't ever age. Will I?'

'You are quite ancient enough, *old* lady! You'll be picking up your pension soon! Let's stop living in my past and your future. It's now that matters, here in this room, in this … this … Timescape.'

'That's my word, you stole it!'

'You wrote it in the dust.'

'You watched me?'

'Yes, it was perfect. It describes this whole thing in one word.'

'Timescape.'

'I shall write a poem about it,' he said. 'Wait and see – I always was a better poet than artist.'

'What's happened to the painting you started, when we first met?

'Nothing, zilch, I've done nothing to it ... I'm a crap artist.'

'That's nonsense, I've seen ...'

Sye cut across her. '— I shall paint us in words. You'll need to wait ... I need the right life flow.'

'Life flow?'

'*Listen* to the song ... it's within, without; life, love ... it's cool ... I'll find the right words ... your words, mine, it doesn't matter who they belong to.'

'But it *was* my word,' Kate protested.

She could tell that Sye had lost interest in what she was saying. He'd moved to the window, leaning his forehead on the glass.

'Here, look at this.' He gestured for her to come to the window urgently. Kate obeyed.

'Look, she's watching, she often is. She's careful though, every time far enough away for me not to see her face. You wait, in a while she'll scramble down the embankment and head off across the mud-flats to avoid getting too close.'

But this time the figure of Margret didn't change direction; she strode towards them along the embankment staring at the house, carrying a camera.

'Get back from the window, she might see you,' said

Kate, confused as to whether or not their side of the window was in her time, or his. She turned to look at the room and everything from his time had gone. Except him. Nothing was logical any more.

Sye continued to peer out. 'There's something …'

'Get back, you idiot.' Kate tried to pull him away; he stayed put, refusing to budge, scrutinising the figure on the path.

He banged his forehead quietly on the window, twice.

She tried to reassure him, 'I'm confident she doesn't know anything about you. It's probably because I've been here so much, not out or at the pub, I bet she's wondering what I'm up to.'

Margret stopped to take a photograph of the house. Kate slipped back into the shadows. Sye didn't. 'I hope she hasn't seen you,' said Kate, 'she couldn't, could she? The camera will take the picture in her time, not yours, won't it?'

Margret carried on walking, stopped, paused, stared back out to sea and then carried on again.

Sye looked troubled. 'There's something haunting about that woman.'

'That's rich, coming from you,' Kate joked, trying to lighten the atmosphere.

He didn't respond immediately; a new idea seemed to be forming in his mind. 'Do you think body language stays the same, even though the frame changes out of all recognition over the years. I don't know you see, I've missed all that. I'm the same as … like before I …'

Something shifted in Sye that Kate couldn't quite determine. It was as if she was locked outside of the time he was in.

He carried on, 'I think she, that woman, loved this place

once, it's the way she looked up at the window, the way she looked out at the sea, she's part of this …'

Kate was consumed with an irrational jealousy directed at Margret who had broken into the spell that minutes ago had been hers. 'I have to tell you something … what she wants to do is to take this place apart and change everything. I think that's why she's got the camera – she's not looking at us, she's taking photos of the house.'

'What! She's going to pull the place down!'

'Not exactly – alter it, modernise it, build up here in the attic, take the roof off for all I know.'

'That's it then, I suppose,' said Sye in a matter of fact fashion.

Kate's heart almost stopped. 'What? Is it all going to end?'

'No – you're wrong there, it's the beginning, a new beginning which is going to happen a little quicker than I thought. Don't worry. It's cool, like I said before. Go and act as if everything is as it should be. Make something up about your absence. Say you've been ill. I've that poem to write. Go … don't hang about, go and meet her and talk as if nothing has changed in your life. Promise me?'

'Ok, I'll try.'

'Promise.'

'I'll do my best.'

'Promise.'

'Promise,' said Kate.

'And don't come back until I've written the poem.'

'How will I know? How long will it take?'

'You'll know when I've finished it – like you talk to me from downstairs, in your head, I can talk to you, as long as you are listening carefully. *Keep listening*, I'll tell you when

159

it's finished. Then I'll show you. *Keep listening.* Wait … be patient, it won't be long.'

19

ARRIVALS

The words permeated every move.

Keep listening ... Keep listening ... Keep listening ...

Even the blood pumping around Kate's body became attuned to the rhythm of those two words, as she retreated down the stairs and pushed back the wardrobe across the gap with a mighty shove, nearly dislocating her shoulder in the process. If Margret called in, the wardrobe had to be as she would expect to find it.

Keep listening ... Keep listening ...

Kate positioned herself at the kitchen table and stared at the week-old newspaper which had been left lying there.

Margret didn't bother to use the door knocker. She inserted her own key, opened the door and called out, 'Kate ... oh there you are!'

Keep listening ... Keep listening ...

'Sorry ... I've not been up to seeing anybody ... I've been ill ... bad headache ... drugged up with painkillers.' Although Kate started with the truth, the lie took root as she watched Margret's expression change from delight in seeing her, to concern.

Keep listening ...

In Kate's eyes, her lie looked huge and easily detectable

– in fact, everything downstairs came across as a distorted *Looking-Glass* world as she experienced a sensation equal to floating somewhere near the ceiling whilst watching her own body and voice act out the scene below. Her brain held within it a lack of clarity which had travelled back with her from that state of 'within-ness' to being definitely 'without'; it was as if those pulsating words from Sye were packed in cotton wool for safekeeping while stifling any sympathetic words coming from Margret.

'I suspected something wasn't right, I was worried about you … Phil was too.'

Kate tore away the cotton wool in her head, stood up and willed herself back to the present. While her hands went through the motion of folding the newspaper, she concentrated on recalling the reason which had made her leap from one world to the other – the sight of Margret walking along the ridge towards the house … Sye's reaction.

Keep listening …

'Have you been out to the beach?' she finally succeeded in saying. 'I thought you weren't a fan of walking out there.'

'You saw me on the embankment then?'

'Yes … I've just come down … from the living room … went to get the paper … it was too bright up there … thought it might set my headache off again … so I came down here.' Kate wondered if she sounded normal, she wasn't even convincing herself.

Margret picked up the newspaper, looked at the date and put it back on the table. She sat down opposite Kate, stared at her and smiled. 'I went as far as the first bench, on the turn in the path. I've been taking photos of this place from there, and some closer up. I've also got one from each side of the house. Can I take some in here? And upstairs? I want to get a good one of the large window …'

Kate tried to hide her consternation; *which large window?*

Margret continued, '… the one in the living room. I'm wondering about putting a balcony there, what do you think? It might work. I'm trying to put together a portfolio to take to the architect, you see.'

'Go ahead, help yourself,' replied Kate with relief on the one hand and dread on the other, but secure in the knowledge that the wardrobe was in place.

'You stay here; don't feel the need to come up with me if you're not well. You should take things easy, you still look wobbly to me.' Margret's concern came across as genuine to Kate, who watched as photographs of the kitchen were methodically acquired before one was taken from the bottom of the stairs looking up towards the wardrobe. On the way, Margret took her time and began to inspect the books still piled randomly up the staircase. It seemed to Kate that they tempted everyone as, like Mark, Margret selected one of them to tuck under her arm.

Kate did as she was told and stayed downstairs staring at the newspaper in front of her which boasted headlines reporting the disorder of life in the 21st century. None of it made any sense; the world she'd been immersed in over the past few days was her new reality. Sye had inculcated her with a world *his* generation had hoped to change, and then shown her a better place where the concept of "peace and love" was not a pipe dream. A Timescape located neither in 1968 *nor* now, but rather – a state of *being*, set in an idealised domain. Contemplating the personal and political misery spread across the newspaper, there was no more need to grapple with the choice – no alternative other than to join him. Like a promotional video, images recalling her recent days with Sye flashed in front of her eyes, image after image, infused with that seductive golden aura and those words … *Keep listening.*

She *was* listening; to Sye, and also – around the edges of her thoughts – to Margret who continued to pace around in the room above. Five minutes later she heard a noise at the top of the stairs which sounded like the wardrobe being moved. The images vanished. Kate leapt to her feet and stood at the foot of the stairs, to be greeted by Margret's rear view as she tugged at the bottom drawer of the wardrobe which appeared to be stuck fast. With much effort, nearly resulting in Margret losing her balance, the drawer allowed the intrusion and its challenger gave forth a satisfied sigh as she steadied herself and knelt down to peer inside.

When Margret returned to the kitchen, the hefty art book chosen earlier was dumped on the table along with a pile of comics with the title *Smash!* Kate began to spread them out, her hands agitated, sifting through as she took in the dates. Zig-zagged exclamations leapt out at her. The most recent was on the top – July1968 – where Batman and Robin, aiming punches in all directions, battled through their comic strip adventure.

An inexplicable compulsion shook Kate, a surge of resentment transformed into stabbing anger. 'Why are you taking the comics? Don't take them!' The voice was hers; the words were Sye's.

'I thought I'd got rid of these a long time ago,' replied Margret calmly.

Kate argued, 'If you rent the place out to another family

… with children … they'd want to read them … you *can't* throw them away.'

'They're ancient, today's children wouldn't be interested. I'll pop into the second-hand bookshop in Burnham, they'll welcome them with open arms.' Margret pulled out the drawer next to the sink, grabbed a couple of carrier bags and proceeded to fill them with the comics.

'I'll take them for you, I'm often there,' offered Kate, reining in the anger and trying a different approach.

'No thanks, I shall do it myself this afternoon. I won't stop for a cuppa, got to be off.' Margret slid the book under her arm, picked up the carrier bags and opened the front door. She crossed the threshold and stopped abruptly. 'Oh, stupid me, I nearly forgot … do you mind if I check the post-box? My architect's sent me some stuff I've been waiting for … when I rang I found out he'd posted it here by mistake instead of my place.'

She put down the bags and came back into the house.

'Between you and me he's a bit vague, that's why I want to take the photos to point out what I mean when I have my next meeting with him. I want to establish exactly what I want for this part of the house and then arrange for him to come over to see what's possible with turning the attic into a proper flat.'

Sye's antipathy continued to control her – Kate couldn't speak for fear of what she might say.

Margret gathered up the bags again and carried on, ignorant of any extended audience. 'He should have come this week but hasn't been able to as his partner's away and he's snowed under with work. It's a nuisance, this delay. It's the same firm Phil used for the pub alterations and they did a good job there so I hope it will be worth the wait. Sorry to prattle on, force of habit I'm afraid. When I'm on my own I save things up to say to people and then it all comes gushing out – not always in the right order – habit of a lifetime.'

The anger left Kate as suddenly as it had appeared but in its wake exploded an emotional chaos that seemed to be scrambling everything that Margret was saying. Kate wondered if this was what a person had to withstand just before a stroke.

Then relief. Rather than the physical collapse of her body, her brain switched to normal mode; she was back in control and aware that Margret was staring at her, waiting for a response.

'I said, are you sure you're ok, feeling better?'

Kate picked up her cardigan and put it on. 'I'm fine, I'll come up with you and see if there's any post for me. I doubt it though. With the way Mark left last time, I'll be very surprised if he's bothered to send anything on to me. I'll get the key.'

By the time Kate had found her key and made it up the path, Margret had already reached the rusty metal post-box fixed to the gate, pulled out her own set of keys and retrieved a thick brown envelope together with one other letter which she handed over to Kate.

'I expect mine's full of all the rules and regulations of things I can't do to the house – best be off then,' said Margret. Kate was sincere in her silent hope that plenty might be put in the way of any renovation and prayed for Listed Building status. She watched Margret walk down the main road towards Phil's and saw her form flatten against the hedge when the local bus pulled away having dropped off at the pub.

Kate opened her letter; the handwriting had given away that it came from Angela. After what had just happened inside her head, she reckoned it would be best not to read this missive in the house and sat down on the cold stone bench outside which offered no comfort at all as she digested the contents of the letter.

* * *

Margret took a quick look at the young woman who'd jumped off the bus but did not recognise her; the newcomer stood staring at the pub and then crossed the main road with little heed to the possibility of traffic. The two women met at the pub door; one put down her loaded carrier bags, while the other rested a bulky backpack on the ground between them.

'We don't do lunches out of season but we've got some nibbles at the bar,' Margret said. 'Phil should be opening up about now.'

'Oh, do you work here?' asked the visitor.

'Yes, but it's not time to start my shift yet, I've got …'

'Will you help me give Phil a surprise? He's not expecting me at all – he'll be quite shocked, I think. Would you go in and keep his attention away from the door? While you do that, I can slip into the bar after you.'

Margret was the one to be surprised – firstly by this request and secondly by the brilliant smile which complemented the well-tanned face waiting for an answer. Having made an intuitive guess at the young woman's identity, she nodded acquiescence, let herself into the pub and left the door ajar. Phil could be heard singing along to the radio in the kitchen

– which is where she joined him, feeling more than a little apprehensive as to how things would play out.

She held out her camera. 'Take a look at these photos will you, Phil.'

Their two heads were bent over the camera, viewing the first long distance picture of The Old Pilot's House taken that morning, when a voice called from the bar.

'Can I have two large glasses of retsina please?'

Phil almost knocked the camera out of Margret's hand; he froze for a moment and then slowly walked through to the bar as though he was being pulled by a magnet.

'We don't have any …' he began to say.

Without any hesitation, Margret followed up behind to see more. With a huge bear hug Phil picked his visitor up off the floor and carefully put her down again, before stepping back as if to verify she was real and not a mirage. Margret had to acknowledge that the lights in his eyes had never in truth been switched on at all – not until Grace walked in. Phil had always been full of banter, chatting happily, singing along like tonight in the kitchen, but his smile had never truly reached the corners of his eyes. That had been the one thing about him that he'd inherited from Old Phil.

Ill at ease at being the sole witness to their reunion, Margret slipped back into the kitchen with her camera and scanned through the images she'd taken: the different elevations – click, click, click, click – north, west, south, east. It was as expected. She clicked again – east, east, east. No, she had not been mistaken. What showed up on the screen made her past wounds ache.

* * *

Kate suffered the chill of her chosen pew as her head bent over Angela's handwriting; a voice from the real world was begging her to come home. She folded the letter, stuffed it into the back pocket of her jeans and went into the house.

On closing the door it started.

Keep listening, Keep listening, KEEP LISTENING. So much stronger than before. She ran upstairs to the wardrobe, pulled out her coat and wrapped around her neck the warm woollen scarf which Joe had given her as a birthday present one year. The words continued to get louder as she made for the outside door. Right after leaving the house, they stopped. Kate knew exactly what Sye wanted and set about presenting a semblance of everything being fine.

Her mind, however, was full of the contents of Angela's letter. She'd been able to tell from the postmark that it had been waiting to be found for a couple of weeks and could imagine the sender no doubt sitting at home wanting forgiveness and by now regretting the baring of her soul. What Angela wanted and what Kate sought from Sye did not fit together, like two warped jigsaw pieces from the same puzzle, destined never to slot into place. The letter had jolted Kate into recognising that to make any irreversible move towards Sye she had to put her house in order first.

Two things needed to be done right away: to catch the next bus to Burnham Market to get some shopping (hoping to be seen doing this 'normal' thing by Margret) and also, while there, to phone Angela, despite being at a loss at knowing what to say. As she reached the bus stop, Margret came out of the kitchen door of the pub and hurried over.

'Hello – off to Burnham?'

'Yes, I need to get some food in, now I'm feeling better.'

'You'll never guess who Phil's got in there?' said Margret, wide-eyed.

'What? A royal visit, down from Sandringham!' came the facetious reply. *Good, I sound like my old self*, thought Kate, pleased with her quick repartee.

Margret laughed at the suggestion. 'No such luck! Imagine – *Kate and William ate here!* No, it's *Grace!*'

'Grace who?'

'*Phil's Grace* – the one who stayed in India, I mean who *isn't* in India now, but *is* in the bar! It's a good job there's no customers. I don't think he'd notice them – go on, take a look!'

'No – not now, things to do.'

'Go on, you've got to see Phil, I've never known anyone change so fast. It's like he's a different person. Half an hour of being together has changed him out of all recognition!'

'I shouldn't think that's happened in half an hour Margret – I think that happened over a much longer period of time, starting from when they met in Greece. She's taken him back to that time and place, easily done, not rocket science … or even time travel. Is she planning on staying?'

'Don't ask me, how should I know? *Go and take a look*. It will be a while till the next bus anyway.' Her excitement was contagious and Kate, intrigued, started to see a parallel; if Grace's arrival signified a decision to journey in search of a better future, they would have much in common.

'I give in. I'm only going to put my head around the door and say "Hi" – it'll show Phil I'm ok.'

'Let me know what you think of her – I'm working tonight, so you can tell me then. You'll be in for your meal as usual, won't you.' It was a statement rather than a question and Margret didn't leave any time for an answer. She smiled at Kate and set off home. Under her arm was the large art book and her hands were full; one hand was still holding the camera and the other the bags full of comics.

20

DECISIONS

Phil and his visitor didn't hear the door open; Kate stood and took in the scene. They sat face to face on the bar stools both talking at once – Grace asking about the pub and Phil wanting to know all about her journey back to England, both eager to fill in the gaps since going their separate ways.

All Kate could see of Grace was the back of a faded green hoodie sporting a washed out symbol – an encircled figure with outstretched arms. When she let the door go it announced to the couple that they were no longer alone. As Grace turned, Kate encountered an open face, framed by light brown hair tied loosely in a ponytail. Her clothes reflected the uniform of a hardened backpacker – jeans, not designer-distressed, but worn-out by travel, together with equally weather-beaten walking boots. Every aspect of Grace was unassuming – but for her eyes, which were shining with the pleasure of seeing Phil.

To Kate, the couple existed within their own private spotlight. 'Sorry to intrude … I …' She stood there for what seemed far too long, lost for a reason as to why she'd gone into the pub, until saved by the recollection of her intention to phone Angela. 'Sorry, I mean … would you mind if I used your phone?'

'Of course you can – it's great to see you're ok. Look who's here!' Phil grasped Grace's hands and pulled his prize towards Kate, who waited to be introduced.

Grace let go and took Kate's hands instead. 'He's so hopeless, I'm Grace come back from …'

'Another life!' finished Phil.

'Something like that, you make it sound like I died.'

'Well it felt like …'

'Well I didn't. I promise you, I'm real flesh and blood, and now I'm here!'

Lost in space somewhere, Phil was still too busy grinning like one of those little smiley faces used on text messages – so Kate introduced herself: 'And I'm Kate, hopefully a good friend of Phil's.' Not wanting Grace to get the wrong idea, she carried on, 'Phil and Margret have both been such good friends to me and I suppose you'll be embarrassed to know we've heard all about you.'

Phil looked worried.

'Nice things of course,' she added hastily.

'Well I'm very pleased to hear that!' said Grace with an easy smile – and without any hesitation, she linked her arm through Phil's, claiming him as her own.

Whilst happy for Phil, the whole encounter had the effect of making Kate feel even more troubled by her own complicated relationships.

It was time to stop intruding on their reunion. 'Can I use the phone then?' she asked.

'Of course you can. Look, if you want some privacy, go up to the B&B, we've just had an extension put in, use that.'

'Thanks,' said Kate beating a retreat through the bar and up the stairs at the back. Sitting on the bed in the guestroom, she remembered how she'd sat there before listening to Dom's confession; light years ago.

Thoughts of Angela took over; her mother-in-law had undeniably put the ball in her court concerning Joe and Mark. It couldn't have been easy after all that time spent playing the role of being the one Joe turned to. Typical of Angela to leave it until it was too late. Perhaps it was deliberate. But then, Kate had to concede, Angela knew nothing of the promise given to Sye and nothing of her determination to share his world. Before that could be achieved issues needed fixing in Warwick, *before* – a small voice, lost inside, found the words – *before what exactly?* Kate blanked this doubt, ignored its existence and denied any uncertainty space to grow. It would all be fine, this new life – it was meant to be, and was going to be so much better than her tired worn-out one. Grace seemed to have made *her* choice between two lives – it was just the same. Kate picked up the receiver and dialled Angela's number; she curled up on the bed and waited for her mother-in-law to answer.

Much later that evening there was a gathering in the sitting room above the pub. Phil shared the sofa with Grace, his arm about her in a proprietorial fashion, while Margret claimed his armchair and cross-examined Grace, in the nicest possible way. Kate's day of trying to appear normal had exhausted her. She sat scrunched up on the floor, arms hugging her knees in front of the fire, with her mind often removed from the conversation of the others as she dipped back into the world she inhabited with Sye.

Grace was explaining herself. 'I missed Phil too much. I worked *so* hard at everything to shut him out. Sorry,' she said, resting her head on his shoulder. He grimaced a little and then smiled again. She continued, 'I decided to give it a year, I wanted to achieve something positive, working with all those children – which I did, to some extent. You see out there you never finish what you start, it goes on for ever – I hope I made a small difference.'

'Of course you did,' said Phil.

'But I missed you so much – I can't begin to say – Kate, Margret, haven't you ever felt like that?'

'Yes,' replied Margret. 'A very long time ago.'

Kate watched a log on the fire shift and collapse in two.

'Kate?' said Margret.

'Sorry,' said Grace. 'I know I'm going on ...'

'No, you're fine.' Phil reached out and nudged Kate with his foot. 'Hey you, talk to us.'

Kate swivelled around and surveyed the group. It was Sye who filled the room. The others? Distorted and insignificant.

'Great, she's back with us, come and sit up here.' Phil made a space between himself and Grace. Kate gave in and joined them.

'I'm not staying long ...'

'On the sofa or in Norfolk?' asked Margret.

'I have to sort things in Warwick.'

'Good, well done, excellent,' said Phil, 'you've obviously been pining for home.'

Margret leapt in, 'You can always come and visit us, use the B&B, and of course you can bring the family back for more holidays once the building work is finished.'

Kate hotched forward, away from Grace and Phil, and put her head in her hands; she wanted Margret to shut up, to stop making assumptions.

But Margret didn't stop. 'Cheer up, we'll have a leaving party before you go, just us four. We could go to Holkham Hall, take a picnic. What do you think Phil, if we pick a good day?'

Phil glared at Margret who in turn looked to Grace to support her enthusiasm. Grace looked down into her lap.

Kate sought to get out of the corner she was being pushed into, where explanations might be forced out into the open. 'Where can I hire a car around here?'

'I've got a number somewhere,' said Phil.

'I need to do what Grace did, achieve a few things … before I come back, for good.' Kate felt enlivened by her own words, *for good* was very definite.

No one spoke.

'I think I'll go to bed,' said Grace, 'and let you three alone.'

'It's alright Grace, please stay. It wasn't you earlier, it was me.' Kate realised how quickly Grace had established herself as part of the group; by sharing her own confidences so naturally she'd become one who could be entrusted with those of the others.

'Ok, if it's honestly alright with you,' said Grace.

'It is,' replied Kate, leaning back again and giving in to the comfort of the sofa before launching forth. She owed them all some form of the truth. 'When I get back to Warwick I'm going to talk to Dom about the business. I'm going to give it up. I know he's been thinking about it anyway. He needs to break away from me; our relationship has been like a marriage without the sex and he needs his freedom.' She waited a minute to let that sink in and then carried on. 'Next there's Joe, Angela is so anxious about what he's getting up to. That's what my letter was about, Margret. When I've found out what's up, Mark will have to face Joe's problems. He can deal with it – I'm not any good with Joe, he never listens to me.'

'That's not true,' said Margret, 'that first year you all came here you did everything together – tennis, kite flying, crabbing. I was amazed when you told me he wasn't your son.'

'It must have been back when we were both trying …'

Phil leaned forward and asked, 'And what about Mark? Is there any chance of you two getting back together?'

'No. I think when he came here last week he took one look at me and made the decision for both of us. It's too late now.'

Kate was aware of Phil's arm behind her reaching out to Grace. 'It's not going to be easy, being alone,' he said.

Margret leant forward and looked directly at Kate. 'And *where* are you going to live back here … the house won't be available for quite a while.'

Kate could hardly bear to meet Margret's eyes; the destroyer of paradise.

'There'll be something I can rent. I'll only need your place for a week or so when I get back, while I look for somewhere else, if that's ok with you. There's so much to let around here, it shouldn't be difficult to find something suitable. I won't be in Warwick for long and you're not ready to start the building work yet are you?'

Phil was up looking through the drawers of his desk behind the sofa. 'Here you are, Terry Nettles' number, he's got a garage over in Fakenham, I think he hires out a couple of cars. I'll take you over to pick one up if you'd like me to.'

'Thanks Phil. As I said, I don't intend to be away for long, a few days at the most. I want to get back as soon as possible.

I've spoken to Angela and I've persuaded her to let me stay in their spare room. I don't want to sleep in our house, with Mark. I'll go over and pick up some more clothes while he's at school.'

'Do you want me to start looking out for a place for you to rent,' offered Margret.

'Don't worry. When I've got the car I'll go to the Agent's in Burnham, before I leave for Warwick, and pick up some details. There'll be stuff on the internet too that I can look at when I get to the office.'

'This is silly,' said Phil. 'Why don't you book out the B&B over the winter months, I'll let you have it cheap. You're here most evenings anyway and you won't have to walk home in the dark each night.'

'Wonderful, but won't Grace need it?'

'I don't think so.' Phil looked at Grace.

'I can afford the full price,' said Kate. 'I've got my own savings. When my parents went to Nice and I sold the house for them they let me have the money. My inheritance, they said, in case they spent everything else! Perhaps it's time to use some of that.' The suggestion of hiring the comfortable B&B cheered her and she almost believed her own lie. It was all pretence; once back it would be time to enter the life Sye had planned for them, providing she could get access to the attic.

Kate tried again, 'Margret, if I take up Phil's offer of the B&B can I use one of the bedrooms at The Old Pilot's House to store some things, while you're having the work done.'

'I'm not sure …'

Grace jumped in: 'Aren't you're getting too far ahead, you've got a lot to think about and do before making firm plans – all things could change.'

Kate's instinct told her that it was Grace, out of all of them, who could see through her charade.

'It takes a lot of soul searching to give up one way of life for another,' Grace continued. 'When Phil left I was too full of my own self. I know that on the surface it looked like I was doing the noble thing giving up everything for the needy – yet I wasn't, not really. It was for my own glory in a way, I think. The knowledge of how much I had hurt Phil, how unhappy we both were, wouldn't go away. I was full of contradiction: on the one hand trying to help those children have a life and on the other hand destroying our life. In my darkest moments I even got it stuck in my head that I'd denied some imaginary child of our own the chance of life.' She looked at Phil before going on. 'I took such a long time to make my mind up because I didn't want to come back and let Phil down again. It had to be right this time and it was a hard thing to do because I wasn't sure what my reception would be at this end.'

Still standing behind the sofa, Phil placed his hands on Grace's shoulders. 'You needn't have worried,' he said.

She reached back and placed her hands on top of his. 'I know … I think I knew anyway.' It was as if no one else existed.

Time to leave, thought Kate. She leapt up, hugged everyone quickly, explaining that she had to pack, and left before the mood of revelation which hung in the room persuaded her to disclose far more than she wished.

* * *

Margret got to her feet slowly. 'She could have waited for

me.'

'I think she's got her mind on other things,' said Grace. 'Has she met some new man out here? It seems to me that she's somewhere else all the time we're talking to her.'

'No,' said Phil incredulously. 'She hasn't had the chance, don't you agree, Margret?'

'I have some suspicions,' said Margret, immediately wishing she hadn't shared her thoughts.

'Who?' asked Phil. 'Not some arty chap in Burnham Market? I know she's been doing the rounds of the galleries.'

'No, not there. Anyway, must go, I'll leave you two to catch up, I'll just make certain she's got home alright in the dark, my headlight will do the trick.'

'Grace,' said Phil, 'you have a treat in store one of these days – the sight of Margret's Mean Machine.'

'You've got a motor bike, you lucky thing!'

'No, not quite,' laughed Margret at she left the room and the comfort of Phil and Grace's happiness – a state which had always eluded her.

Except – she thought, endeavouring to reconstruct the memories – way back; at the beginning.

21

ANNOUNCEMENTS

Angela fought to put the phone back in its cradle on the small table next to where she was sitting but it seemed to have a mind of its own, falling out of her hand and coming to rest where her "ergonomically designed" grabbing stick couldn't reach. This miscreant object took its place amongst that day's countless frustrations – an interminable feature of life.

Still functioning with great efficiency was Angela's capacity for inner dialogue and the ability to communicate with the world; for this, a prayer of thanks was often offered out loud on her behalf by Batty, despite the fact that sometimes he wished for just a *little* more peace and quiet on occasions. Being able to express her thoughts with coherence enabled Angela to live with what she called the nuisance of physical helplessness. It was for this reason that the conversation on the phone with Kate that Thursday lunchtime had been so galling, as she'd had to search the recesses of her mind for rarely used words of supplication to reinforce those already written to her daughter-in-law. The effect of this concerted effort had, more than likely, given the impression that her physical handicap had started to infiltrate her brain.

Angela mulled over whether or not the indigestion rising

up inside her was the consequence of the kippers Batty had proudly presented at breakfast, or being obliged by circumstance to say the words which placed those she loved in the hands of Kate. While attempting to shift her body into a more comfortable position, she had to acknowledge that Kate had been right, a face to face conversation would be better than the tricky staccato dialogue just attempted.

She wondered if it had been wise to agree to Kate staying over for a few days: it would certainly put Mark's back up and the request had seemed an odd one to make. But after some thought she concluded that it would have been imprudent to have refused the spare room. Having been the one to have asked her to come back, to attempt to persuade Kate to stay with Mark would have stretched any goodwill gained to the limit. Being under the same roof as her daughter-in-law could provide an excellent opportunity to iron out past difficulties, smooth out the creases and encourage the rebuilding of the marriage. On top of this there was Joe and *his* problems to think of and … *where was Batty when he was needed to pick up that damn phone*!

'Batty!' she shouted. 'Come here, I need you …' adding silently '… as always.'

Angela waited until later to share her thoughts with Batty. She looked with affection across the room as he dozed in front of his favourite television programme – a game show he always intended to watch, an intention his eyelids rarely agreed with. Picking up the remote, she turned down the sound.

'What's going on?' came a muffled voice as Batty pulled himself back from oblivion; the drone of the TV sent him to sleep, but silence was guaranteed to wake him up.

'Talk to me Batty.'

'Haven't we done all the talking for today? It'll be time for bed soon.'

'I've been thinking while I watched you sleep – I'm bothered about Joe – and I've got some news to tell you … Kate's coming back at the weekend, she doesn't want Mark to know until we've had time to talk so … she's going to stay here.'

'That'll set the cat amongst the pigeons.' Batty was fully awake now and hunting around for his slippers with his feet; he'd kicked them under his chair as usual. 'What's Mark going to say about that?'

'He'll have to put up with it. Why he didn't see this coming, I don't know: he was too busy thinking about that damn football team and didn't see what was happening under his nose.'

'And what was that?'

'His family falling apart.'

'Men don't.'

'Don't what?'

'See things coming – they need their good wives to tell them,' said Batty as he picked up the newspaper that had slipped to the floor when he'd fallen asleep.

'Well *I'm* telling *you,* and *you're not listening* – it's Joe I'm fearful for.'

'That's a leap, I thought we were talking about Kate and Mark.'

'We *are,* you silly old fool! Nobody ever considers Joe's reaction to what's going on in his own home.'

Batty found the page with his sudoku puzzle and retrieved the pen Angela had bought him for Christmas from his shirt breast-pocket. 'You don't need to worry about him, he's fine – just a teenager, he's fine I say.' He pushed his glasses to the end of his nose to signal concentration and to terminate the conversation.

'What would you know; you don't see anything unless it's in that newspaper or on the television screen.'

'You'd be surprised ...' and with that Batty got up and retreated to the kitchen, to have a nip of brandy – the Dutch courage Angela accepted he needed every night before the exertion of getting her into bed. What did annoy her was his cheerful humming! How *could* he, when she was so troubled about everything, and why, of all tunes, that song from some Andrew Lloyd Webber musical. He knew she couldn't stand musicals or opera, not since Fran died.

When Batty returned, full of new vigour from what he thought of as his secret bottle kept out of reach from his wife, it was to receive new orders. Angela told him the grand plan – A Family Barbecue. She pointed out to him that it would be just like those past holidays in Norfolk when little Joe, round-faced and wide-eyed, would wade back with her and Mark across the creek at low tide from adventures on the salt marshes, their trousers rolled up to the knees, his small hand reaching to hers for support. Arriving back tired and hungry they would find Batty with the barbecue ready, play-acting that the fare about to be cooked had been foraged by the intrepid explorers – and Kate would crawl out from behind her book to join them.

To have a barbecue this weekend was a good plan. Angela continued to explain to Batty how they would keep it secret until everyone was gathered in the same place. They could invite Mark without saying that Kate was coming – or Joe.

No point spoiling the surprise! Oh, and she would invite Sadie to keep everyone amused and lighthearted. The family couldn't shout at each other in front of a visitor, could they? If they all ended up having a good time together it might put them back on the road to recovery ... and Kate could help sort Joe out ... and that would bring Kate and Mark back together again. Job done. Bingo!

Angela seriously thought about inviting that lovely man who worked with Kate – he was more like a brother than a business partner after all – but decided against it; there would be far too many squashed into their little bungalow if it rained.

Batty pressed the button on Angela's electric armchair to activate the tip-up, tip-out mode. She sat patiently while this process took place. Horrible contraption! Why did he always insist on using it when she was perfectly capable of getting out herself, albeit with a good degree of discomfort.

'So we need to make a list of food so you can organise the shopping,' she said while she rose in slow motion from her sitting position, ready to be launched.

Batty steadied the walking frame with one hand and his wife with the other while she transferred from one support to another. 'You must be mad, woman.'

'No, quite sane – I know my body is giving up, but you're stuck with my brain.'

'But it's late October ... it's far too cold for a barbecue!'

'Oh I've thought of that, they can all wear coats,' she said dismissively as she started the painful journey to her bedroom. 'It's not going to rain this weekend. You'd know that if you hadn't slept through the weather forecast.'

'But can you imagine the atmosphere ...'

Angela stopped halfway down the hall and refused to budge. 'Look, we can soon sort that out. Not knowing the others are coming will leave them with no time to brood over what to say – or think of an excuse not to come. It will be up to us to make it work. We'll give them a good time *and* provide the perfect opportunity for them all to see what they've been missing.'

'Come on love, let's get you to bed before your legs give up. You're going to regret this barbecue thing you know.'

'I've already regretted lots in the past few weeks. There's nothing to lose. If Kate comes here and spends most of the time avoiding Mark we'll never get to the bottom of Joe's troubles or mend anything. That boy needs protecting or he will implode!' She was beginning to get angry, but all those years of living with Batty had taught her *that* wouldn't work.

As he manoeuvred her into the bedroom and on to the little chair used to help her undress for bed, she changed tack and beamed the smile which she knew reminded Batty of the young girl he'd married, adding, 'What they all need is … a gentle prod.'

He didn't return her smile. 'That boy isn't a young lad leaping salt-water puddles on the beach any more. He's almost a grown man, wanting to take his own chances in life – his problem is that none of you will let him!'

Angela understood the point, but chose not to respond. With his usual care, Batty took off her shoes and socks and helped her out of her day clothes into a nightdress.

'I just know he's ok, he'll sort himself out, you'll see,' said Batty as he held out his arms for her to rise and to give support as she got into bed.

'What aren't you telling me?' she asked. 'You seem to

know an awful lot about Joe all of a sudden.'

Angela knew she'd been successful in cornering her husband when he kissed her goodnight on her forehead and gave in. 'We'll make a list in the morning of what we need,' he said.

'You'd best get it all tomorrow so we can put it away in the freezer before Kate arrives and gets wind of what we're up to.'

'Don't you think she'll manage to make an educated guess when I start preparing all that food?'

'Not if I get her to take me to the hairdressers – followed by a quick shopping trip. I'll get in that wheelchair for the sake of the family. Don't look so flabbergasted, I shall have to surrender eventually to the beast. I suppose this weekend is as good as any other time. It'll give you the opportunity you need – we can tell her Joe's coming if you like, but not mention Mark. It'll work better that way.'

'Whatever you say, Angela, I'm tired now,' said Batty.

Lying in bed Angela could hear her husband sigh heavily as he went to put the chain on the front door. The last instruction she'd given that day '… and don't forget Kate's bed will need making up,' had given rise to Batty grunting a reply she didn't quite catch, just the sentiment.

* * *

After leaving Phil's that night, Kate went home and straight up to the attic. This time she wanted Sye to listen to *her*. It was important to explain to him why she was going to Warwick and to justify the need to tie up all the loose ends of that other, unravelled life. A life to be found not decades away, or slipped into in an instance, but a life requiring a few hours of driving to reach its actuality.

She spoke out loud: 'Ok so it's night-time, but all of the others are back at the pub and the light from my torch is pathetic anyway. *I need you to listen*. I have to go back to Warwick … we all have our debts to pay and I need to sort mine before I can …'

Her words were interrupted by the shrill sound of what sounded like two cats fighting in the garden. She opened the window in the hope of disturbing them, but they'd vanished anyway, their battle over; all that could be heard in that still night was the almost inaudible fall of the waves on the distant shore.

Kate checked to see if Sye had appeared without a sound behind her, or was leaning idly in the corner or … perhaps had materialised to sit cross-legged on the floor with a serene smile on his face.

'Why does this conversation have to be all one way?' she asked.

She closed the window.

The stillness unnerved her.

'Why can't I conjure you up when I need you?'

The stillness engulfed her.

'I'M LISTENING OUT FOR YOU ALL THE TIME! WHY AREN'T YOU BLOODY WELL LISTENING OUT FOR ME?'

Silence.

A pallid full moon lit the space. It slipped in through the window and slid without fear along the floor to reach the three paintings leaning there, demanding she made them face its light.

Kate responded by turning the first canvas to look for a second time at a glorious dawn over the staithe with the creek stretching out towards the sea. Glorious from an artistic point of view but, at the same time, an opposite emotion could be drawn if you were one who depended on the sea for a living. As the sun rose it bled into the sky with wounds seeping into the shimmering waters slithering between the salt marsh on the one side and the embankment on the other. Despite its mesmerising beauty, before her eyes stood a sinister picture, full of foreboding, declaring a quiet awareness of what was to come. Kate couldn't quite grasp why it had this effect on her; she turned the next painting in the hope of escaping its mood.

The previous dark prophesy was realised. The storm had been painted from the same vantage point – but now hell had opened its vaults and let loose chaos. Whereas in the first painting there had been an equal balance between the sky, the tidal waters and the land, in this the marshes had been obliterated and the dividing line between sky and sea non-existent. The raging tide had reached the top of the embankment and the land it protected from an invasion of salt water seemed to tremble with fear. The masts of the boats were at dangerous angles to each other, at odds with the expected perspective of such a scene. Each brushstroke played its part in the depiction of nature turning on itself – destroying everything in its path. The artist had been skilful in the portrayal of fear *and* anger alongside each other, twisting wildly this way and that, in and out of the squall. These two emotions were held in the moment the brush hit the canvas, their passion captured years ago, to be passed on to today's viewer. Kate didn't dare to guess at the consequences of what happened next in the world of these paintings. It was as if the tragedy endemic in this picture leapt out from the past into the present, to where she stood, a voyeur, spying on another's pain.

It was a while before she could bring herself to look at the third and final painting. Again it was the same view; this time presenting the calm *after* the storm in which the late evening sun filtered through a silvery grey film with the promise of better times to come. The iridescent splinters of sunlight drew her in – but if the eye lingered on the compelling sky and avoided the rest, the aftermath of the sea's destruction would have been missed: the injured boats, broken masts and buoys left afloat without a purpose. High tide was receding, seeming content with all it had claimed: victim or victims, whether they were nature's creatures, manmade craft or even man himself. Despite the devastation shown, the artist should be praised for conveying this forlorn lack of hope in stark contrast with the splendour of the sky. This painting revealed both agony and ecstasy, beauty and the beast. The juxtaposition made the hopelessness unbearable.

A wave of misery flowed through her. It was a loss so great that Kate couldn't fathom why the extent of this suffering laid bare had not had such an overwhelming effect on her when she'd looked at these paintings previously. Mostly what had impressed her on first viewing was the artistic skill and, yes, her emotions had been touched, but *this* was something altogether different – pulling her apart from the inside. Was it that the moonlit atmosphere in the room made her more receptive to their content or had something fundamentally changed within her?

Unable to look any longer, she turned them back and spoke again to the absent Sye. 'If this is your work ... your experience ... if you felt this loss, you'll understand what I have to do. Raw misery lives in each of these paintings and this is what I am about to inflict on my family. I *can't* do that lightly to them. In my world, and theirs, the sun is preparing to retreat behind the clouds because a storm is coming. I can't leave everyone to drown. I *have* to limit the damage I'm about to cause and try to put the pieces of Joe's relationship with Mark back together, so they can support each other. You understand don't you?'

Kate followed her own reasoning – but there came no acknowledgement from Sye that he agreed with her. She wavered as she imagined Mark's pain of losing not only his first wife, but also his second.

Keep Listening!

It struck without warning; the recollection of how Mark had marched out of the pub with no explanation.

Keep Listening!

The concept of Dom and Mark planning a future together overpowered her; suddenly she was absolutely sure – any previous supposition converted to solid fact.

KEEP LISTENING!

Her resolve returned. 'I **will** come back Sye.'

The mantra ceased.

A draft of air, the scent of incense?

Intuition told Kate that Sye was there, standing behind her, his breath on her neck. She turned around. But if anything, the room seemed even emptier than before.

Leaving the attic to its loneliness that night, Kate was mindful that storms were lurking in whichever world she inhabited. At sea the tide was turning, to pitch its strength and passion at whatever stood in its path. In land-locked

Warwick, the shockwaves would replicate the effects of that storm years ago when the lightning had hit the metal boat masts – causing them to lurch and thrash before they fell to the mercy of the elements.

22

A MIXED MESSAGE

Wide awake in bed the night before facing reality in Warwick, Kate struggled to get warm. The hot water bottle was almost burning the skin on her cold feet, but they would absorb none of its heat. In the end she gathered up the duvet off Joe's bed, added it to her heap and felt the benefit.

Looking at the bedside travel clock with its luminous green hands she turned over on to her right side to be faced with the bright orange curtains. They were far too short for the window, an offence which left a cold dark strip at night and let in too much daylight at the break of day. Kate turned *again,* back on to her left – luminous green hands – back on to her right – annoying curtains, *again.* Trying dead centre, on her back, staring at the ceiling, she realised that the constant ticking of the clock added to the night's torture.

Next time her eyes opened it was 4.30; a fitful sleep had overtaken her, but not for long. Kate's instinct warned her that something had disturbed the little sleep so restlessly gained; she curled up, pulled the bedclothes around herself, *listening.* Nothing ... *Sye, is it you?* Kate waited for some sign or response, but there was no indication of him being either outside or inside her head. Not a wisp of thought came from him until ... at first like a weak pulse and then, like a heat-

193

wave, the entwined feelings of fear and anger shot through Kate, matching those that had assaulted her when looking at the paintings earlier. These emotions were not conjured up within her but were someone else's, seeking out a host, taking over. Kate fought to escape; tossing and turning. Impossible. She leapt out of bed to push the door to, piling anything she could in front of it – a chair, her suitcase – to keep out whatever wanted to get in. Attempting to shift the chest of drawers across the room, she appreciated the futility of it all. She fought the anguish inside her head while logic tried to argue that it was all just a remnant of a dream from which she'd woken. The cold dampness of her body, the sweat on the crumpled sheets and the rapid rise and fall of her chest all pointed to a nightmare.

Kate took some slow breaths and moistened her dry mouth with the glass of water beside the bed. The battle to control rational thinking continued. *Think outside the box … outside this room, this house, this village.* She forced her mind back in time and place, searching for those good times with Mark and Joe a few years ago, in their new home, when life had been so promising. Such thinking exposed deep sorrow at the recognition that those days of happiness could never be revisited; no time-slip could be conjured up to bring that about. Nonetheless the good news was that this emotion belonged to her and not to some external force. Her panic passed.

Pulling on her jeans and a jumper, Kate climbed back into bed, exhausted. She buried her head in the duvet in fear of being heard and wept for that time gone by. Clearly, when her marriage had hit difficulties she'd let the problems trickle through her fingers, instead of doing what she did at work which was to grasp challenges in a fist and fight to get things right. *How had she got it all so wrong?*

Two more hours of sleep were somehow claimed before her alarm ordered her to wake, pack and walk to the pub for the ample breakfast Phil had promised. 'Look, come early,' he'd suggested the night before. 'I'll cook all three of us a full English before we go to get your car. Grace, I bet it's a while since you had a decent breakfast and Kate, you look in need of fattening up – it'll set you up for the journey.'

When they arrived at the garage in Fakenham, the car wasn't ready. Phil's mate Terry turned out to be more like a contemporary of Old Phil's and a faded Teddy Boy to boot, with slicked-back, dyed-black hair who advised them that it would take a further half hour to check the car over and do the paperwork.

Kate persuaded Phil that she'd be fine waiting by herself so that he could continue on his planned Grand Tour with Grace, showing her the local area. Hugs all round were shared while silently Kate acknowledged her envy of the carefree day ahead of them.

'I owe you Phil – thanks for everything,' she said.

'No problem. *Our* pleasure,' said Phil. He slipped his hand around Grace's shoulder and propelled her towards a new life in Norfolk.

Kate hovered in Terry's makeshift waiting room; it reeked of engine oil which appeared to be smeared everywhere, including in his hair and on the dirty plastic chair. The wait provided her with a chance to get out Angela's letter and re-examine it. The contents confirmed all the reasons as to why this trip was so necessary, although the second reading made her feel less sympathetic to her mother-in-law. A cynical thought came to mind – was this pure manipulation by Mark's mother? But Kate rejected the thought: if what Angela said about Joe was true, she would definitely be needed to help sort him out, to at least get Mark to open his eyes and see what was going on before she left for good.

Additionally, there was Kate's need to confirm the reason for Mark's abrupt exit the other day. Had he simply given up on her or had he come to explain about his relationship with Dom and bottled out? So many questions … all so confusing. Her commitment to Sye remained … but to move on to that carefree life, answers had to be found and every effort made to make this final break-up with Mark as painless as possible for the sake of everyone involved. *If* he had strong feelings for Dom they might both walk away from the marriage having found what they were looking for – something they had failed to achieve as a couple. *If* she could help him sort Joe as well, things could end on a better note. And then there was Dom and the business …

Kate slipped the letter into her bag, whilst wishing her effort back in the attic to make Sye understand had been more fruitful. Next she searched for her driving licence, ready to complete the paperwork. As she opened up the wallet section of her purse, a folded piece of paper fell out. Kate had no recollection of how this had come into her possession. The last time the purse had been opened was the previous evening, to retrieve her credit card when settling up with Phil at the pub. The piece of paper hadn't been there then. The writing on it was strong and black, scribbled across the page. Kate read what looked like random sentences with words crossed out, others added – it was a work in progress.

Cautious, trembling fingers turned the sheet over, revealing a neater copy, initialled by the poet.

Timescape

A place to be.
Peace of mind, of soul,
to join together, forever
beyond ourselves.
A world of passion
to escape within ...
breaking
the chains of disenchantment,
the shackles of disappointment

A dream, that never ends with grief,
beyond this world ...
that flies and dances
for an eternity
with me, with you, with us

An ocean of pure existence distilled from
crashing waves ...
no more worries, cares or demands
of others,
just your needs ... *our* TIMESCAPE

Peace of mind, of soul,
to join together, forever
beyond ourselves
in the Timescape Sea.   S.H.

The incongruity of reading Sye's longed for commitment to her, there in the greasy waiting room, made Kate ache for their attic and the coast; its potency tugged at her, tempting abandonment of any inland pursuit.

And yet.

Part of her was soaring – this was what she had been listening for; Sye's declaration, winging his message to her in these few lines.

And yet.

Part of her began to realise how much his strength was growing, alongside her willingness to connect with him. The more she gave, the stronger he became with his manipulation of time and space; evidence of which was encapsulated in this one small piece of paper which proved it *had* been him there in the night causing her fitful sleep. But there was still confusion and contradiction – in the fact that those night emotions Sye had imposed on her were of fear and anger, *and yet* … this poem emitted self-assurance and peaceful confidence. It didn't add up, it was like one of those clever optical illusion pictures which could be seen as something different depending on the interpretation of your mind's eye. It was as if there were two Syes – one living in a volatile state and the other existing in placid contentment.

Waiting there for Terry, still holding the poem, Kate contemplated her options: cancelling the trip, ditching everyone and everything as Sye seemed to want – or going back to Warwick to face her responsibilities before joining him in their promised Timescape. Whichever she chose, Sye won in the end.

'Excuse me for saying but you look like your car just failed its MoT. Are you ok or are you recovering from a late night at the pub? I don't know how Phil does it, it's 9.30 in the morning and there he is with two beautiful women in tow.' Terry held out the pen and the paperwork ready for her to sign.

All Kate wanted was to get in the car. *What was this man rabbiting on about?*

'Who was that with him anyway?' He plainly wanted the full low-down on Grace.

Not needing this conversation in her present state, Kate cut it off quickly. 'I think Phil will tell you when he's good and ready,' she retorted, realising immediately that her words sounded sharper than she'd intended.

He stepped back. 'Sorry I asked.'

'I'm sorry too, I didn't mean to snap, my mind's elsewhere, got to get back to civilisation … pressure of work, you see.'

Aware that she had now committed two offences in the eyes of Terry Nettles, Kate's heart sank. She'd blown it. Delay was ensured by her unwillingness to chat freely about Phil and Grace, compounded by the capital offence of insulting the place he and his ancestors had probably lived in since the beginning of time as they helped weary travellers along their way. He moved around the vehicle in an unhurried fashion, painstakingly noting on a sheet every minor scratch, and one or two not so minor dents, before making her sit inside the car with him to record any minute scuffs or stains on the upholstery. The progress of doing all this was impeded further by his need to tell Kate every tedious story relating to each offending mark.

By the time the document was signed Kate's impatience was about to boil over, but she kept a pleasant smile fixed to her face knowing that if she said anything else which could be interpreted as a further slight, the process would slow down even more.

'I'm sorry I was short with you earlier,' she said when he deigned to pass over the keys. 'I'm just stressed out, sorry, I'll tell you all about Phil when I bring the car back.' A statement regretted as soon as spoken, but it cheered Terry up a little; he actually smiled as he clambered out of the car and tapped the roof to signal the beginning of her journey 'home'.

Once the signs for Kings Lynn had passed, Kate found she was almost too tired to contemplate what remained of her three hour journey to Warwick. To wake herself up she wound down the window and attempted to put on some music. She fumbled for the radio and pressed the on-button – the sound that came blaring from the speakers at its highest volume possible was the George Harrison track; the sitar not lilting and haunting this time but wailing and screeching at a high pitch. When the car in front slowed at a roundabout Kate managed to stop just in time, her shaking fingers trying in vain to find the volume control as the lyrics screamed out, assaulting her ears – the words no longer wistful, inviting her into Sye's Timescape, but venting a deranged, discordant rant.

Kate pulled in at the next layby and steadied her hands on the steering wheel, acutely aware of the intimidating anger somehow reaching out to her from Sye. His fury was indisputable. Confusion seized her – when she'd tried to explain why she had no choice but to go to Warwick, he'd chosen not to respond, so why now?

A good half hour went by before the exhausted driver of the world-weary hire car pulled out of the layby. Kate had sat there staring through the windscreen once more weighing up the rights and wrongs of what she was doing. To abandon everyone casually would be to follow in her parents' footsteps; she knew too well what it felt like to be discarded without any empathy whatsoever – there had to be a better way. In addition that now familiar small voice was trying in vain to be heard. An inner voice that wanted her to wake up and face the fact that it was undeniable that Sye presented two opposing personalities: one full of benevolent promises and the other whose actions incited fear.

23

HAUNTED

'Look at them all – Joe's not talking to Mark or Kate, and *she's* avoiding being alone with Mark – the only one everyone is speaking to is Sadie.' Batty leant closer to his wife, 'This is what it'll be like at my funeral, thank goodness I won't be around to go through it twice.'

'I knew she'd be the one.'

'Who do you mean? Sadie or Kate?'

'Kate, you know that's why I got her here.'

'Yes, yes I know all that, but what do you mean by *the one*?'

'The one to drag Joe's problems into the light.'

'Is that what this is about then, I thought it was to sort out Kate and Mark.'

'It *is* you old fool – everything comes back to Kate and Mark, I keep *telling* you.'

'It's time to put the chicken on the barbecue, where do you want me to wheel you to?'

'Somewhere I can watch what happens next,' said Angela, trying to place an optimistic note into her tone of voice.

* * *

Kate had started to slice an iceberg lettuce in the kitchen, pressing down on the back edge of the large knife with the palm of her hand whilst trying not to think of using the implement on Angela as it crunched through the leaves.

Mark appeared at her elbow. 'What's that lettuce ever done to you?'

Kate threw down the knife onto the chopping board. 'Just being here ...'

'What, the lettuce?'

'None of us should be here, not altogether anyway – I can't handle it. I wouldn't be surprised if they've invited Dom as well, but I expect you'd like that, wouldn't you!'

Mark blushed.

'That's Angela for you,' she said. 'Forcing us all into the same corner!'

'They haven't invited him, have they?'

'I wouldn't know,' she replied, 'I knew nothing of this until I let you in at the front door expecting it to be Joe.'

'But why such anger, surely that's for me ...'

'Look I know it was my idea for me to stay on in Norfolk, but I didn't expect to be so ... redundant that quickly.'

The thought of Mark and Dom together – *with neither of them needing her* – forced any anger to disintegrate into pieces and re-form as pure grief at the loss of them both. She picked up the knife and began to fanatically attack the iceberg again. No *Sgt. Pepper's Lonely Hearts Club Band* to tune into this time. No help from Sye to casually make sense of the rapidly changing emotions tumbling away inside her head, and certainly *no* conjured-up ethereal world where consequences didn't matter any more. It had been so easy in Norfolk, looking at this here-and-now life from a distance.

Mark held her wrists still, to stop the manic process of

annihilation. 'I don't get what you're talking about – I'm the superfluous one since you've got your lover in Norfolk!' He let go, stepped away and stared at her for what seemed like eternity.

He knows! Has Sye's reach come this far!

Kate started on a second lettuce; slicing it slowly and methodically, her eyes glued on the task to prevent him seeing the truth she was grappling with. Sye wasn't her lover yet, but she *had* been unfaithful, in a manner that could never be explained. Mark stood there waiting for a response with Kate cognisant of the fact that the longer she left it the more she admitted guilt.

Sadie raced in, a little out of breath. 'Can I take the salad out?'

The lettuce lay on the chopping board without any sense of purpose whatsoever.

'Do you want me to take over?' said Sadie. 'You both look a bit sick, shall I make the salad for you?'

Kate wasn't listening, her hand dropped by her side and the knife slipped out of her grasp onto the floor. Sadie picked it up, cleaned it efficiently under the tap and placed it back on the chopping board. Thrusting the bowl of tomatoes at Mark she said, 'Look, you chop the tomatoes, and I'll do the rest.'

Kate fled the kitchen. As she passed the open door to Angela's bedroom, she glimpsed the photographs arranged in a neat row on the dressing table and went to take a closer look. One displayed a youthful Mark with Fran on their wedding day. Next to that was Joe standing at the quayside on holiday, wellies on, holding up his bucket, which – from the shine in his eyes – must have been brimming with crabs. Then, close by, stood one of Mark and Kate on *their* wedding day. Joe's place in the photo parade struck a chord; sandwiched between two marriages – the boy out there in the garden today no longer recognisable as the same child in that centre-stage position. *Why does everything have to change? Or is it just me that's changed?*

'You alright?' said Sadie from behind.

'I'm fine, really, I'm fine.' Kate blinked back her tears.

As had happened on first meeting, she was startled by the girl's appearance, amazed how anyone as pretty as Sadie could in all seriousness look in the mirror before leaving home and think she had done well with the raw material. Her jet black hair was tied untidily up high on her head with random bright pink strands – some of which hung loose down the side of her face. A nose stud competed with several ear adornments for pride of place and Kate presumed there were other piercings lurking in hidden places. However, despite her initial misgivings she'd warmed to Sadie's easy, open, friendliness.

'Can I show you something?' said Sadie, as she fiddled with one of the pink strands. 'I got this yesterday.' Giving Kate no chance to decline the offer, she unzipped her trousers and displayed a small heart tattooed on her left hip. It was sore and puffy.

'That looks painful.Wherever did you get it done round here?'

'I went to Birmingham with a couple of girls from school, we all got one. Emmy's brother's friend has this place …'

'You should keep an eye on it Sadie, perhaps show your mum.'

'You gotta be joking me! I haven't even shown Joe yet,

'cos I don't want to put him off. I want him to get one too – got to choose the right moment to ask him.'

Despite her qualms about this piece of information, Kate smiled at the thought of one so young already schooled in the art of knowing the value of the "right moment".

'I can see he means a lot to you,' said Kate, acutely aware that any influence a member of the family could have on Joe's choices in life would probably be easily out-trumped by someone like Sadie.

'I know you'll think I'm stupid and it sounds like something out of a teen mag, but we're good together. I mean, I've had this thing for him for ages but it wasn't till the party that he needed me too. We're cool together now.'

'What party?'

'You know, when his dad came back and there was nearly a knifing. It was real bad, what with his so-called mates inviting Mic Spears and that lot – don't come much worse you know, he's a complete psycho. Well was, anyways. He don't come to school now, too ashamed I reckon – you know being put down by a teacher in front of everyone. They say that his mum found out and sent him to his dad's in London. What a hero Mr Haughton turned out to be. He's well cool.'

Kate looked shocked.

'Sorry,' said Sadie. 'I didn't realise you weren't in the know – you ought to be told – especially about all that other stuff with Joe.'

Seeing that Sadie was now in free flow sitting cross-legged on the floor, inspecting her black nail varnish as she talked, Kate felt obliged to join her there. The two of them leant up against the bed like two schoolgirls sharing confidences and Kate steeled herself for what was coming next.

'Will you promise me something?' said Sadie. 'If I tell you a secret, a big secret. You know, like you won't tell no one.'

Kate nodded.

'Cool. Anyways I think it's all ok now. It's stopped since the party. Since we've been together, there's no new scars. He covers his arms but sometimes he forgets when he's with me – I watch him see. I'm pretty sure it's stopped now.'

As this sank in, all Kate could say was, 'I'm ... I don't think I *can* promise this – I have to tell Mark.'

'Please don't, not now things are better – look I'll tell you if it gets bad again. Lots do it, for a while, but when things get better they get over it, honest.'

'You might not be able to tell me,' Kate said.

'Sorry?'

'I might not be around.'

'Oh shit, are you ill? What is it?'

'No, it's not that – it's, well – I'm here to finally end it with Mark before going back to Norfolk for good, but now with all this that you've told me, I don't know what to do. I don't want to damage Joe any more than I have already.'

Kate struggled to understand why she was pouring out all her problems to a teenager she hardly knew – whose mouth was now so wide open that a glinting tongue piercing announced supremacy of place amongst all the other body adornments.

Sadie continued, 'I think you should know ... it's not you that's caused this with Joe and it's not his dad, well it is sort of – look he just needs to *talk* to Joe. There's lots more stuff.'

'Not drugs, not that as well.'

'No way. I thought he might be, but now we're together I know he's not into that. You're going to think I'm real stupid but …'

'I won't, go on.'

'Don't laugh … I think he's … haunted.'

Kate didn't laugh.

'Not by an actual ghost, I'm not *that* stupid … it's like in his mind … it's his mum you see, sorry, his birth mum, not you … look I'm not saying this right.'

'You're doing fine.'

'I found this notebook. I shouldn't have. You see he was ill after the party, throwing up everywhere.' Sadie mimed the action with feeling before she went on. 'The notebook sat there next to his bed. I stayed the night. Stayed awake all night too. Mr Haughton knew, he ok'd it. I wanted to understand what was getting to Joe – I waited until he went to sleep and then sat on the bog and read it.'

'Charming – go on.'

'It was a list … sort of … well in the front was a sort of letter written by Joe, when he was little like – it looked like …' She jumped up, searched around for something to write on and found a pad Angela kept by the side of her bed. 'Look I'll show you.' Sadie wrote with great concentration as she formed the letters which mimicked a child's first handwriting.

Deer Mummy I can rit my leturs Joe xxxxx.

'And it went on like that. On each page his writing and spelling got better so he must have been getting older. All the things he could do like, you know like tying his shoe laces or riding his bike. He started to date it all too, every little … what do you call it … ?'

'Milestone?' offered Kate.

'Cool – that's it. There was a big gap when he started our

school. When he began again it became a list of problems, what with his dad working there and the bullies and that. And then writing the letters to his mum came back; *long* letters. He tells her everything.'

'In that case there must have been lots about me, the wicked step-mother,' said Kate.

'No not you, never you.'

There it was, thought Kate, confirmation of her own failure with Joe. 'He'd edited me out of his life then,' she said flatly.

'No … I think p'raps he thought his mum might be jealous.'

'Now *you're* starting to sound as if she's still around.'

'She is, to him.'

'Have you told Mark all this?'

'No way. I thought he wouldn't cope – that it'd be too upsetting, bring it all back like.'

'Joe's a lucky boy to have you, Sadie.'

'No it's me that's lucky – he's so … loving … it's like he needed someone to hug, desperate like.'

Kate was racked with guilt – *and I was never there for him, much too busy, much too … self-centred?*

'You were right not to say anything to Mark. Leave it with me. We have to help Joe as much as we can and you seem to be halfway to doing that by simply being around.'

Sadie responded to this with a smile which lit up the gloom that had descended.

'We'd better make a move,' said Kate, 'let's see what's going on at this god-forsaken gathering.'

'It's not that bad,' replied Sadie as they both got up from the floor. 'I'm glad you didn't think I was stupid like, saying

Joe was haunted.'

In order to avoid having to respond, Kate tore off the page on Angela's notepad and ripped it into small pieces. However, when she looked up, she saw Sadie was still wanting reassurance.

'No, you're not stupid,' said Kate. 'We all have ghosts from the past, waiting for us.'

'It'd be cool to meet one.'

Kate changed the subject: 'Where does Joe go after school? Does his notebook answer that?'

'That's the one thing he's never written down – I know about Angela's worries though, in fact it was me that told her about Joe. But I've found out something else that I can't tell her. I followed him – I bet you think I'm proper sad – but you see it's alright because Batty knows. It's him who often picks Joe up, round the corner from school. Angela's not in the know – but it's got to be alright if it's Batty, hasn't it?'

24

SEIZE THE DAY

Kate sat with Batty on the swing seat, wrapped together with a blanket around their knees, watching Sadie try to get Joe and Mark to kick a football around. With Sadie in the middle of the two of them she would pass the ball sent to her from one side of the great divide to the other, trying every so often to feign a miss which would bring about a successful direct transfer between father and son.

Kate elbowed Batty gently in the ribs. 'Time to come clean.'

'Don't know what you're talking about.'

'Where do you take Joe after school?'

'Who told you about that?'

'A little bird with piercings.'

'How does she know?'

'Training for MI5 I reckon – anyway, please put me out of my agony, what are you up to, it's not for some kind of therapy stuff is it … have you got him seeing someone?'

'You could say that.'

'Things are far worse than I expected then?'

'Singing.'

'Singing?'

'Proper singing lessons, I'm paying for them.'

'What on earth … oh Batty … why all the secrecy?'

'I'm surprised you have to ask. Look at my son, Kate, he's only ever really communicated with Joe through that football and that's not even happening now. Mark hasn't listened to a note of opera, or anything else I shouldn't wonder, since the day Fran died. Am I right?'

'True,' said Kate, rubbing her hands together to warm them. 'He's never allowed music to get close to him,' adding to herself – *not like Sye.*

Batty gave her his share of the blanket. 'You see Fran haunts them both because they've never let go, they both keep her locked inside – they need to let her free, but they need to do it together.'

Kate and Batty watched them kick the football from one to another; Sadie had done a good job and now could be seen sitting on the side-lines, shouting encouragement like a team manager at a training session.

'You ask me about the secrecy,' Batty continued. 'How could Joe tell Mark that all that indoctrination with the beautiful game, the team spirit, the macho male preserve has been a waste of time? How could he tell him that what he wants is to be an opera singer like his mum? And how could he let it be known to all those bullies at school? Joe was between the devil and the deep blue sea, so that's where I came in – it was hard work getting out of him what was wrong, but I got there. I promised not to say, mind you, not even to Angela, and that's been hard.'

The ball was kicked in their direction, Batty caught it, hesitated over who to throw it to and chose Mark. 'He's struggling to tell Mark that he doesn't want to go on to sixth form at school, he's found a two year music course at

Leamington College where he can specialise in singing. If he works hard and does well he can apparently take it on further, apply to some place in London, can't remember where. He's adamant he doesn't want to do sport at Loughborough, you know, where Mark went. The music teacher at school has been supportive, but that's another secret – Mark can't stand him. I'm going to have to be the one to tell Mark but I've got to get Joe to agree and choose the …'

'Right opportunity.'

'You took the words right out of my mouth.'

'How long has this been going on – why didn't Joe tell me?'

'I don't want to be unkind but you've hardly been around, too busy with your grand job, your hopes for a baby too – look I don't blame you for that – but not coming back, what's that all about?'

'Not now Batty,' she replied. 'Why didn't he tell Angela – she'd have been there for him, unlike me?'

'He's afraid she'd tell Mark – before he knew if he was good enough. His mother set a high bar you know.'

'And is he good enough?'

'Oh yes – his voice is superb – it's his real inheritance from his mother. That's where she is, there inside him, training his voice, pushing him on.'

'Yes, I think I'm beginning to understand that, but Fran needs to be exorcised, let out. Joe's got to do that or he'll never experience success in his own right.'

'I see what you mean, but how?'

The idea came to Kate instinctively. 'He needs to stand up and sing – in front of us all.'

'He'd never do it.'

'What better time than when we are all here together. Go and ask him Batty, you can persuade him, he'll do anything for you. Then it would be out in the open. Mark will be forced to see Joe as he really is *and* to listen to Fran being released from her hiding place – they'll all be free then.'

'I don't know.'

'Mark is more understanding than either of you gives him credit for, he just hides from the truth when he can't face it. Once he faces up to stuff he can be very strong.'

'Oh I know that, he is my son you know.'

'So give him the chance to see *his own son* clearly, for real – then, when we all know, Joe won't have to only share his secret with you and his mother any more.'

'I'll try.'

'Go and talk to him, *now* Batty. *Carpe diem!*'

And then Batty astonished her by standing tall in front of the whole gathering and reciting:

'There is a tide in the affairs of men,
When taken at the flood leads on to fortune,
Omitted, all the voyage of their life,
Is bound in shallows and in miseries.'

Everyone stopped whatever they were doing and stared.

'I don't know what you're all gawping at, I did a lot of acting in my time, at school. But I didn't have the courage to tell my father what I wanted to do with my life, so I followed in his footsteps as expected and, as you all know, worked in the shop … you did that in those days.'

Kate observed how Mark now reflected her own feeling of disconnection. While Sadie laughed and joked with Angela

– an incongruous pair, yet obviously at ease with each other – he listlessly tapped at the football with his foot; the earlier kick-about had ended abruptly when Batty had pulled Joe aside to engage in ernest conversation.

Moments later Batty spoke, getting everyone's attention with his stage presence for a second time that day. 'Angela thinks she has surprised you all today with this gathering, but that's not all.' He smiled and nodded encouragement to his grandson, 'Joe has something else up his sleeve.'

Joe looked down at his feet as if willing them to run from everything he feared.

Batty put his arm back around the boy's shoulder. 'You *can* do this.' He pushed Joe forward with an encouraging pat on the back.

No one spoke.

Kate crossed her fingers and hoped that Joe wouldn't cut and run. He avoided looking at his father and searched instead for Sadie; achieving that, his eyes fixed on her.

Batty stepped in again, 'It's from *Joseph*, isn't it?' He smiled at Joe, 'Your namesake.'

Joe pitched his voice uncertainly and sang the first line of *Close Every Door* and stopped. It was painful to see how much he was shaking and Kate wanted to rush over and hug him, to protect her stepson from the ridicule he feared. But she didn't, she waited and listened.

It was worth the wait. He mumbled an apology and started again. From tremulous beginnings, his voice gained confidence as he sang the words written to express the despondency of a young man failing to achieve his ambition. By the time he reached the climax of the song, the full power of his voice triumphed alongside the hope for the future conveyed in the lyrics. Both Joseph and Joe, as one.

And there on that cold, sunny, late October afternoon Kate knew that both she and Joe had to face their own ghosts in order to move on. Joe had taken his first step in exorcising his and as he'd brought the song to a close, his shy demeanour had been replaced by something new; the enormous pride of captivating his audience – a pride far greater than when that small boy had held a bucket full of captured crabs.

Kate glanced over at Angela who was giving Batty a *how have you kept this from me* glare. She hardly dared to look at Mark, but when she did, despite the fact that his eyes avoided hers, she was thankful to see his face reflected Joe's pride. He was the first to lead the applause, and as he did so tears began to course down his face. This time there was no attempt to hide or wipe away the true extent of his emotions which he wore like a badge of honour in front of his son.

25

DEPARTURES

As the applause died away, Mark spontaneously took hold of Joe and hugged him – a full-on, heartfelt embrace – resulting in a combined glow of pride which warmed everyone.

Angela tried to give Batty a good telling off for deceiving her, while at the same time looking pleased with the outcome. Once she'd finished admonishing him for the secrecy, a new tack was taken – gratitude that his visits "to the betting shop" hadn't been so frequent after all. She then turned all her attention to Joe.

Sadie waited, outside of the family circle, with a smile of relief on her face – which changed to unadulterated adoration as Joe broke away from his father to walk across and pull her into the group.

Kate stayed seated. Deliberately. There was a contradiction happening. She felt split in two; between the knowledge that very soon she would cease to be a part of this family and an overwhelming desire to take Mark and Joe in her arms and hold the three of them tightly together. She wondered if she'd been the only one to notice her husband's reaction during the recital. At the beginning, Mark had been clutching the football; halfway through, he'd let go and it had fallen to the ground soundlessly whereupon his foot had tapped it out of the way.

She congratulated Joe and left the family to discuss his future career, escaping with a feigned migraine.

Alone in her room she reached for Sye's poem which lay hidden under her pillow. His anger, if it had ever existed at all, seemed far away and forgotten as she read, over and over again, the words drawing her back in his direction. As her eyes fell heavy with sleep – the poem still in her hand – someone knocked on the door. It opened and Mark stepped into the room.

'Thought I'd see if you were ok.'

Kate screwed up the poem and aimed it at the waste bin. It fell on the floor. Mark walked over, picked it up and held it briefly before dropping it into the bin.

'What's that all about?' he asked.

'Nothing, a list of things I had to do before I left Norfolk, all sorted now.'

'Have you left? Have you come back for good?'

'Oh Mark … don't, I've such a headache, I can't …' Kate pulled the duvet over herself.

'I'm sorry,' he said, 'I know we have lots to talk about, loads of stuff to put right.'

'But not now. You need to go and celebrate Joe's wonderful talent. Everything else can wait.'

'I guess you're right.'

'I am,' said Kate, hoping he'd leave. But she couldn't resist adding, 'I've arranged to go to the office to see Dom tomorrow. He'll be pleased to hear about Joe – he's far more into music than football, isn't he?'

Mark coloured up. 'Probably,' he mumbled. 'I haven't

seen him recently.'

Kate was convinced he was lying; the honesty in his eyes which attracted her when they'd first met was missing.

Any further discussion was cut short by the appearance of Sadie, who had some uncanny ability which enabled her to pop up whenever Kate thought there was no escape from a confrontation with her husband. Mark looked less than pleased at the interruption.

'I wondered if Kate would like a glass of water?' Sadie asked.

'No, thank you, all I need is to get some sleep.'

'No problem. And ... Mr Haughton, Joe was looking for you,' said Sadie, holding the door open for him to join her.

Before Mark took the hint he reached out and touched Kate's hand but she pulled it away, tucking it under her cheek as she turned over with eyes closed. She was aware that he shut the curtains before returning to the celebrations, the noise of which reached a crescendo in appreciation of a champagne cork hitting the ceiling in the kitchen.

Kate got up and tip-toed over to the waste bin to retrieve Sye's poem. Opening it up, it looked like it had been written years ago with the creased paper beginning to tear in places. She ironed it out with her hands, re-folded it with care and put it back under her pillow. Kate had the feeling that she and Sadie had somehow swapped roles – the latter now being the responsible adult, and herself behaving more like a love-sick schoolgirl. Her head began to throb, a real pain, not pretence this time. Punishment, thought Kate, for inventing it; the dull relentless throbbing tortured her throughout the night, impeding sleep as she realised how even simple lies can come back to bite you.

* * *

Stirring the milk into her coffee, Angela took her time to spread the toast with butter and decide between marmalade or Marmite. She had encouraged Batty to make an early start on the allotment, taking advantage of another able-body around the house. Consequently, it had fallen on her guest to organise the breakfast tray and bring it to the sitting room. It pleased her to be alone with Kate, who sat on the sofa opposite, waiting to tidy away and trapped until the last crumb was eaten. It was time to unmask Kate's future plans and ensure that they wouldn't harm either Joe or Mark. Having been successful, both with getting Kate back *and* bringing about yesterday's gathering to provide the platform Joe needed, Angela was on a roll.

'I haven't thanked you properly for coming back,' she said. 'I thought my letter had got lost in the post.'

'Sorry, I didn't check the post-box, it's at the end of the drive, I'd been too busy to look.'

'Too busy?' asked Angela as she spread her favourite ginger marmalade on the four small triangles of toast she'd painstakingly cut.

Kate got up and began to tidy the room; she plumped up the sofa cushions and straightened the photographs. 'Oh, I've been doing this and that, visiting galleries …'

'And making new friends?' Angela prompted without looking up.

Kate's hesitation was a moment too long for Angela.

'Yes, sort of,' said Kate. 'Margret, my landlady, and Phil and … Grace of course.' She gave in, sat down again on the sofa and told all about Phil and Grace.

Recognising the intention to deflect the inevitable

question, Angela waited until the story was finished and then simply asked outright.

'So there's no one else then?'

Kate swallowed, smiled and flippantly said, 'I suppose you could count Terry Nettles, a throwback to the fifties – don't worry I can assure you he's not my type.' A phoney laugh and a theatrical grimace followed.

Angela pushed her plate away and looked past Kate to the unwanted football now sitting in the corner of the living room, aware that the ball she had aimed at her daughter-in-law had been kicked off the field.

'I'd best get off now,' Kate said, gathering up the tray. 'I'm going to the house while Mark's at work and I'm meeting Dom for lunch.'

'You'll be back for supper then?'

'I'll ring later.' She put the television on for Angela and bolted, shutting the sitting room door as she went.

Angela grabbed the remote and turned down the volume to hear clearing up noises in the kitchen followed by footsteps retreating to the guest bedroom. There was quiet for a while until the sound of movement in the kitchen could be heard again, briefly. The instant the front door shut, she reached for the walking frame and manoeuvred herself onto her feet.

The trek to the kitchen took much time and courage to do on her own. It was as she thought: there was a note addressed to *Angela & Batty* folded on the kitchen table, thanking them for their hospitality. It went on to explain that as Kate intended to concentrate on sorting the business and would be working all hours with Dom, a hotel would be better. There were some further comments regarding the success of the party and that she was sure Joe and Mark would get on better now they could be more open with each other. Kate said nothing further about herself.

There was the need to sit at the table for a while to recoup the energy required to get back to the comfort of the sitting room. The two dogs watched with doleful eyes, full of disappointment at the departure of their guest. By the time Angela had repeated her struggle back down the hall and was again ensconced in her chair, there had been ample opportunity to contemplate the fact that further intervention was required.

She picked up the phone and dialled Mark's mobile number.

* * *

Staring out of the kitchen window of what used to be her own home, Kate saw that the garden hadn't been touched since their holiday. All the debris of autumn was strewn on the lawn from the two Corkscrew Willow trees she had planted on the far boundary, the grass left unloved and uncut. In front of the trees was a wooden football goal which had once stood on well-scuffed soil, not the long grass of today.

No one was about – both Mark and Joe would be at school, so she could pack up some winter clothes and get out without any unnecessary complications before having lunch with Dom. She knew a face to face meeting with Mark had to happen but wanted to put off the inevitable a little longer. When everything was packed, Kate planned to send him a text to arrange to meet up that evening, hopefully on neutral ground – perhaps in the hotel bar. Before that though, there was Dom and business to see to, sorting practical and legal matters relating to the Agency. Hopefully, by tomorrow evening she'd be ready to leave.

A key turned in the front door. To Kate's dismay, it was Mark: the moment she'd been dreading had come too soon and there could be no running away. He wandered into the kitchen and picked up the post she'd laid out on the table as had been her routine when they'd lived together as husband and wife. Rewind, she thought, and it could have been that nothing was any different. But it wasn't normal for Mark to be home in the middle of the morning.

He looked up from the envelope he'd started to open. 'What's next then?'

Kate couldn't answer.

'Look if you've come back to sort things out – I've the rest of the morning, got a couple of frees, no one will notice.'

'That's not like you.'

'You're right, but I don't feel like me – I haven't since the end of the holiday – it's like this is all happening to someone else.'

Kate sat down at the table. 'I came back because there were things to resolve. One of them was to help sort Joe out. But I wasn't needed anyway. Angela and Batty had it all in hand as usual.'

Mark sat down opposite. '*Please* don't start that all again.'

'No I won't, but you have to realise just how undermined I used to feel, even Angela admits it now. In fact we have the beginnings of a whole new relationship … it's a shame it's too late.'

'Why?'

'Because …'

'I know, don't bother explaining … because in your head you're not here with me. There's someone else, back in

Norfolk, isn't there?'

Kate's intention was to deny his accusation, but her face betrayed her. 'You wouldn't understand ... it's not like ...'

'Don't say any more – I can't handle this – get your stuff and bugger off back in that rubbish car ... I would have expected Phil to sort his *girlfriend* out something classier than that thing!'

Mark stormed out into the neglected garden. Kate went to go after him but thought better of it. He'd jumped to the wrong conclusion but she was still guilty of the same crime. Instead she stood at the open back door and watched as he ran down to the end of the garden where he started pulling down the goal posts he'd once built while an excited eight year old had waited, hovering from foot to foot. Kate watched as Mark vented his anger on the wood, pushing on the posts with all his strength to dislodge them, first with his feet and then with his hands. Lost in the intensity of the moment, she almost leapt out of her skin when a hand touched her shoulder.

'Sye?' she said.

'What? Who? No it's me silly,' said Joe who had slipped into the kitchen to join her at the window. The stale smell of unwashed teenager wafted in Kate's direction and brought her back to reality.

'Why aren't you at school?'

'Didn't feel too good, think something I ate at the BBQ didn't do me any favours – threw up last night all over ...'

'Too much information Joe.'

'Anyway, what's up with Dad? I thought he was ok with me singing and not being his star footballer. He was cool with it last night.'

'I don't think any of what he's doing out there is to do with you Joe – your dad's trying to cope with a lot, because of me – none of that anger's directed at you.'

'So you're the target then?'

'Oh yes – and himself.'

She automatically brushed Joe's hair out of his eyes; he automatically recoiled.

'Sorry,' said Kate.

'You're forgiven,' he said.

'Your dad needs you now more than ever. I know he didn't always handle things the way you needed him to when your mother died, but he did what he thought was right at the time. Whatever is going wrong between the two of us shouldn't come between you and him, he has such good intentions … he's a good man, a wonderful father.'

Kate determined to stay dry-eyed; what she had to say to Joe was too important to be drowned in tears. 'You see, sometimes your dad can't locate the right words in his brain – help him Joe, you have to. When you sang yesterday you were a young man, not a stroppy adolescent – no, don't get cross. I can see where your anger came from now. I've also seen how you open up and talk to Sadie. Do that with your dad and he'll learn from you. We've all been shoving everything inside and I think it's you who holds the key. You can teach Mark to tell you how he feels – if you do it, he will too.'

Joe gave the appearance of taking it all in – growing up before her eyes.

'I thought I was expected to follow *his* lead, you know, in the past. When I found I didn't want to go in the direction he wanted, I didn't know how to tell him. So I stopped talking to him, it was like his fault and it made me angry with everyone.'

'You've told him now – and you did it in the most beautiful way possible – that was an awesome performance yesterday.'

Joe smiled. 'There's more where that came from.'

'What you need to do now is make sure you get the right training if you're serious about singing as a career – and stop smoking or you'll ruin that wonderful voice.'

'I've given up already, Sadie made me promise yesterday.'

'She's good at making people do that,' said Kate.

The back door opened. Mark glared at Joe. 'Study day? Again!'

Kate attempted to carry on her conversation with Joe regardless, unsure as to when there would be another opportunity to get across what she'd planned to offer.

'You may as well hear this too, Mark. Joe, if you go on to train as a singer, I want to help pay for it – with some of the money put by from my parents' house sale.'

'What's this, guilt money?' Mark interjected.

'What do you mean?' said Joe.

'Kate hasn't told you then, that she's running back to the arms of her new man.'

Instead of putting Mark straight on the subject of Phil, Kate couldn't resist retaliation. 'Thanks a lot Mark, are you going to also tell him that I'm not the only one seeking pastures new!'

Regretting her words, and realising that it wouldn't be wise to elaborate about Dom in front of Joe, she ran down the hall, out of the front door, got into the car and told herself to forget any idea of packing – it was definitely time to start again in every respect.

Mark chased after her as she reversed out of the drive onto the semi-circular road in front of the estate of houses. He sprinted across the lawned area, taking a short-cut to the far set of gateposts which had stood sentry to the main house long before its conversion, and planted himself in the centre of the road seconds before Kate reached the spot. It was impossible to drive past. Half expecting Mark to move, half preparing to stop, she noticed a figure step out from the trees bordering the lawn. Dressed as usual in his flared jeans but this time with an Afghan coat around his shoulders, it was unmistakably Sye who positioned himself next to Mark. His whole attitude expressed indifference as he stooped to light up a cigarette, using his coat to shield the flame.

Kate slammed her foot on the brake and prayed; to kill both men simultaneously would have been a dramatic judgement of culpability. To her great relief the car stopped inches short of doing so. She hardly dared to look up, in case she might see them both standing there together waiting for a response from her.

When she did lift her eyes it was to see Mark with his hands on the bonnet, his chest heaving. There was no sign of Sye. Kate sat at the wheel, needing to escape, yet also wanting to clamber out of the car and search for Sye amongst the trees. But she knew he'd gone and that he waited elsewhere. As she contemplated reversing and driving across the lawn to the other exit, Mark stood to the side and waved her past. Kate slowly pulled up next to him, wound down the window and spoke, trying to make her voice sound controlled.

'I'm sorry it's come to this, but you know it's not me alone, it's both of us, we lost our way – our path together. We both have new ones now.'

Mark looked down at her, full of confusion.

'Concentrate on Joe. He still needs lots of support. Ask Sadie about the notebook, but not when Joe's there,' she advised, thankful to have achieved what she'd planned with regard to her stepson. She'd done her best.

He stepped back as Kate slid the gear leaver into place and slipped out of her old life.

26

A TASTE OF FREEDOM

Dom sat with his feet up on Kate's desk in a scruffy pair of jeans and a faded T-shirt which had shrunk in the wash. Its logo supported his Uni football team from the days when he'd hoped to be more than just friends with the goalie. Watching those few matches was the closest he'd ever got to a football – before he witnessed the object of his desire hanging out with the captain of the rugby team. It had put him off all sporting types for good. Until Mark. Today's apparel represented a new freedom, or perhaps a return to the freedom of his youth; his working wardrobe full of smart suits had been declared redundant.

Whilst waiting for Kate, he re-read the email she'd sent the day before:

Hi Dom, you're right, it's time to call it a day with the Agency, let's meet for lunch and take it from there. I think we need to move fast and make this as painless as possible. It was never going to be for ever was it? See you tomorrow – 12 at the office? xx

Like a divorce, he thought, there would now follow the sharing out of everything: the office furniture, the memorabilia from their many past advertising campaigns and of course the money, if any profit remained once the business had been wound up and the tax man had stolen his chunk. It was imperative that they agreed on everything, any animosity after all this time would destroy him. But Dom was not depressed that morning. He was elated! It was a whole new experience, to have no plans for what would happen next or where life would take him. It had been more years than he could remember since he'd been on a high such as this without having taken or drunk anything to bring it on; a natural endorphin rush, brilliant!

* * *

At 12.45 Kate let herself into McKinley Nichols and called out, 'Dom are you there? Sorry I'm late.'

'In here, gorgeous,' came Dom's voice from the end of the corridor.

She walked through to her office, past the framed stills of trendy adverts positioned on the walls for all to see. Finding him at her desk, Kate couldn't resist saying: 'So who's been sitting in my chair then?' She pushed his feet off the desk. 'Wow, what's happened to you – I see you've become a football supporter now.'

'I can be anything I like, once I'm free of this place.'

'My email didn't come as a shock then?'

'No, a blessed release – it's been – bloody. I can't do all this without you and I've come to realise I have no useful creativity in my bones either, I just lived off yours – all that stuff you did sitting in this chair. I agree it's time to face myself and do something new.'

'What will that be?'

You see, I told you this part would be easy.

'No idea at all,' he said with a smile. 'But it feels good knowing I'm going to have some space in my life. Think I'll take a gap year – I feel it's owing to me.'

'It'll do you good to get away, where will you go?'

'Don't know, don't care. The thought of sitting on a plane with nothing to do, with no stress and no demands being made is enough right now. I'll think about the destination later.'

'You tempt me to join you. Sounds blissful.'

I don't mean it.

'I'm not going yet – I … I need to straighten out some personal loose ends before I go.'

'Need some help?'

It's alright, I won't let this hold me up.

'No thanks, I'll be ok,' he said.

Kate felt shut out – but then, if it involved Mark, she didn't really want to know.

Dom vacated her chair. 'Before we talk about the business, can I say something?' he said. 'Thanks for being so forgiving when I came to tell you about what happened with Mark. You were amazing. I want to say sorry again. I hope now you've had time to think about it, you don't feel I've let you down.'

'I didn't come here to go over all that for a second time,' replied Kate. 'We've all been at fault in our own ways but it's best not to pick at wounds. You and I have got such good memories from University, and from our past success with the Agency, let's keep those intact so we can summon them up when we're in need.' She sat down and began to look through the pile of paperwork which Dom had allowed to build up on her desk. 'Let's leave it and concentrate on winding things up without too much sentimentality. It's a business, not a marriage.'

So there's no need for jealousy, Sye.

Dom seemed relieved to change the subject and glanced at his watch. 'Let's have lunch and decide on the best course of action – with the business that is. This afternoon we can come back and get down to the finer details.'

By the end of the afternoon Kate was satisfied with the plans to close down McKinley Nichols. Everything had been negotiated without any disagreement and she was more than happy to let Dom handle the detail. It was the natural way to go – after all, it had always been his job to oversee the non-creative aspects of the business.

She booked into a small hotel near the railway station and, for the first time in a long while, had a surprisingly peaceful night's sleep – uninterrupted by fitful dreams. On waking she found the sun streaming in through the windows; her first thought was that perhaps it was a gift from Sye, he must know she was almost on her way.

Kate felt refreshed and full of optimism when she met up with Dom again. They both quietly got on with what they had to do and organised letters to their solicitor, bank and accountant giving Dom full authority to put things into action and act on Kate's behalf. She telephoned past clients who had to be informed, cleared her personal paraphernalia from her desk into a cardboard box and prepared to leave.

Dom came in and sat on the corner of her empty desk. 'What about all those pictures in the corridor, which do you want to keep?'

Nearly ready now.

'None, Dom, I'm done with it all, everything to do with my life here, I'm sorry if that hurts.'

I only need you now. I'll be leaving soon, don't worry.

'Don't take it personally Dom. It's me that's changed. I see life through different eyes these days, I can't explain. You'll appreciate what I mean, if you do what you say and travel. Life *should* keep changing. It's taken me a while to recognise that.'

'Yes, we were stagnating here. It's a good job we're doing this or we'd still be exactly where we are now when we draw our pensions and left wondering at the waste of it all.'

'Good, I'm glad we agree. Do what you like with the pictures.'

'I'll hold on to them for a while, in case you change your mind.'

'I won't.'

I promise.

'I still won't get rid of them yet, ok?'

'If that's what you want.'

'Where can I get hold of you if we need to discuss anything about the business, are you staying on here in Warwick?'

'No. I'll ring you sometime soon, but the point of those letters was to give you the power to wind things up without me.'

'I take that to mean you're going back to Norfolk and everything is over for good between you and Mark?'

Soon, Sye, soon.

'I think you know the answer to that. Let's not go there Dom. Some things are best unsaid.'

'Ok,' he replied. 'Perhaps one day you'll be able to talk to me about what's going on. If I go away, I'll keep in touch somehow … with you, and Mark if he's still wants my … friendship … as I said … *if* I decide to take off, and I'm not sure yet that I will … it depends on …'

Kate wasn't listening any more.

'Anyway, hold on a minute, don't move.' He rushed off down the corridor leaving Kate relieved that the conversation had terminated; it was going to lead them onto tricky ground and she wanted to avoid hearing anything about Dom and Mark's relationship at all costs. The more she thought about the two of them together the more everything in the past became a monumental mistake, a sham. Her earlier sanguinity was receding fast; the questions had returned and hung about on cobwebs in her mind, being spun again each time she tried to brush them aside. Had Dom loved Mark more than his friendship with her? And, had Mark been subconsciously aware of this? Was that why he'd turned to Dom so soon after their split? The unsaid question was far greater than simply – *who's been sitting in my chair?* Kate could see that she *had* been unfaithful to Mark, but she'd tried to be honest, to end one relationship before committing fully to another, and she'd also tried to put some of the wrongs right with Joe. But if Mark and Dom had been attracted to each other for years, no wonder her marriage had failed.

When I get back to you, I shall wipe them all from my mind. They will disperse into the breeze like the parachutes of a dandelion clock and it will be up to them to decide where they land – I've done my best here, there's no more I can give them.

Dom came back with two glasses which he placed in her hands. 'Let's open one last bottle of champagne and end this how it began – to celebrate our new beginnings – yours and mine! And ... well, I only hope that Mark will eventually see it that way too.'

This time she couldn't believe how brazenly he'd spoken and how much it hurt. There was that sound again; but this time the champagne cork exploded, outside and *inside* Kate's head. Somehow she managed to place the glasses on the table without throwing them at him.

'Save that for Mark,' she said.

Kate picked up her box overflowing with the past and left Dom holding the very full bottle to consume alone.

27

RETURN

There was one last phone call to make. Kate rang from the car before she started her journey.

'Angela?'

'Kate?'

'I'm so sorry I disappeared like that yesterday, to be honest with you it was sheer cowardice.'

'Thank you for admitting that. I know you don't want me to ask, but is there any hope for you and Mark?'

The question had been expected. 'It's gone beyond that.'

'He still loves you …'

'You may think he does, but things aren't as they seem – everything here has gone for me, I'm sorry Angela.' There was quiet down the other end of the line. 'Are you still there?'

Angela cleared her throat. 'So what are you going to do now?'

'I'm off to meet my fate in Norfolk.' Kate tried to sound flippant, but failed.

'You're not going to do anything stupid, are you?'

'I think my whole life until now may have been stupid, so what's new?'

'Kate … you don't sound like yourself, come over now, talk to us.'

'I think I've done all the talking I can. I'll be alright. Look after Joe and Mark for me.'

'I thought doing that was what *I'd* done wrong all these years, now *you're asking me to*?'

'Yes Angela, you see you and Batty do it rather well, much better than I ever could.'

'Don't be silly, don't go – stay a little bit longer.'

'I have to go now.'

'Look, talk to Batty, he'll want to help you.'

'No, I have to get the car back today. I *have* to go ... tell Batty thanks for everything, he's done a great job with Joe. Oh and tell him I want to support Joe financially when he starts his training. I'll sort something out with my accountant. I'll put the details in the post, Joe'll get a letter soon.'

'Kate ...'

'I'm going now, I wish Mark and I could have been like you and Batty ... what you have is so special ... but you know that. Bye.'

Unlike Dom, Kate didn't feel at all free as she started her journey back to Norfolk. For a reason she couldn't comprehend, her ability to converse with Sye had come to an abrupt halt.

What now filled the vacuum were thoughts of Mark. It felt like she was sliding from one side to the other on a see-saw. Yesterday, when she should have been concentrating on those around her, all that was in her mind was Sye as she'd slipped closer and closer to where he was urging her to jump off. Today, ironically, it was the opposite; following her conversation with Angela, the point of balance had tipped in Mark's direction, right when she'd planned to be free of landlocked Warwick.

Driving along the dual carriageway it was Mark's face that haunted her – his pride as he watched his son singing, his anger as he razed the goal posts to the ground, his courage as he stood in front of the approaching car, and his expression as he looked down at her, confused and disorientated by events. She knew that if there had been no Sye, Mark *should* have won her over: his actions, his physical presence and his warm response to Joe at the barbecue *should* have made her feel that there was also a chance to rebuild what had once been good in their marriage.

But anyway the luxury of choice had been erased; it was now Mark and Dom, she was convinced of that. The loss of both of them in one fell stroke crushed her. It became impossible to shut out the memories of the past they had shared. Memories such as the three of them lying on the grass together – those champagne picnics while Joe played – spoilt now by the thought that maybe, back then, Mark and Dom's feelings for each other had been growing under her nose.

Two and a half hours later Kate turned off the main road onto the country lanes and came across a signpost to Bircham Windmill. Despite still having a way to go before she reached the coast, she decided to take a break and see if their café was open. The last time she'd been there they'd all climbed right up to the sails, but this time Kate found it closed for the winter. She got out of the car and walked around the base of the windmill in the vain hope that someone might be about.

Questions grew in Kate's mind.

Why did it keep happening? This being shut out. As with Mark and Dom, in the present. And in the past? From

Joe. And even further back? From her parents. There was no one about to see Kate's tears; no one to witness the soundless scream which erupted from deep inside. It was an admission that there were no options left. Everything had gone in Warwick – collectively they'd all blown it. And there remained no choice as to where she was headed – Sye was pulling her closer by his silence now, forcing her to seek him out. Any strength of will she once had to fight him appeared to be gone.

Her thoughts were disturbed by the lone sound of a Canada goose vociferously honking encouragement at the front of a V formation flying overhead. Then the whole flock joined in, as they advanced with resolute purpose. Like those at the rear she knew she mustn't hold back – she *had* to follow Sye's lead or else she would falter and she was far too tired to fly alone.

Before getting back in the car, Kate rang Phil to give him an approximate time to collect her from Terry's garage as they'd previously arranged. Setting off towards Fakenham, she turned on the radio half expecting *that* song, hoping for some sign from Sye, but instead the radio refused to work at all – complete silence, whichever button she pressed. Damn it, Terry would expect to be paid for that – nothing had been wrong with the radio when she'd set off, but now it was all played out.

The Fakenham Teddy Boy kept Kate to her promise to give a full up-date on Phil's love life, so by the time the bill was finally settled with the loss of her deposit for the broken radio, Phil had arrived to collect her. Terry shook his hand with vigour, accompanied by a twinkle in his eye, but Phil came across as being very subdued – to the extent that Kate began to worry that the tale just told had found a different ending in her absence and that Grace now regretted her decision to come back to England.

'How's Grace?' she asked hesitantly, once they'd left Fakenham behind.

'Oh *she's* fine. I couldn't have coped without her.'

'Why?'

'It's Margret. She's not turned up for work – at all – can't understand it, she's never let me down before. I went to her place, and could have sworn her face looked out of the window, but she wouldn't answer.'

'You must have been mistaken, it all sounds a bit of a mystery. Is there a possibility that she's got a sick relative to attend to and rushed off to help? She hasn't a mobile – so perhaps that's why you haven't heard.'

'No, she would have left a note and she's never mentioned family – it's always puzzled me – no one has no one really, do they?'

Kate tried to lighten the mood, 'Maybe she has a secret life? A lover hidden out in the Fens? Or she's a spy. You know, one of those sleepers and they've contacted her for an important mission.'

'Be serious Kate, it's worrying. Her bike's thrown down outside the cottage, without a lock on it or anything.'

'How long has this been going on?'

'The whole time you've been away.'

There was silence between them as Kate contemplated the seriousness of what Phil had said and the mystery that was Margret.

'Come to think of it Phil, whenever we all talked, up in

your flat, she never told us anything about herself, but then again we never bothered to ask.'

'Perhaps we should have. Were we both too full of ourselves?'

'You're right, perhaps we're guilty of that … we should have,' said Kate.

When they arrived back Kate decided it would be best to stay at the pub for the night, as even though she'd still got the keys there'd be no heating on at her place and certainly no food to eat. Phil offered to take her suitcases upstairs while Kate walked straight down the road to Margret's cottage without even saying hello to Grace. It was as Phil described, with the bike thrown down – unloved. When she knocked on the door, she too was convinced someone looked out – then nothing more.

As she walked away from Margret's the sense of being watched remained and, as she approached The Old Pilot's House with dusk descending, that same impression emanated from the attic window. It was as if everyone was waiting for her return.

Part 2

"The flesh endures the storms of the present alone, the mind those of the past and future as well as the present …"

Epicurus

28

ACTS OF VANDALISM

Margret stood outside and listened. It was too quiet. No one could be seen through the kitchen window; what *was* on view gave her no choice. She found the door unlocked and opened it a little at a time, holding her torch ready to use as a weapon if necessary.

China and glass from the cupboards lay broken on the floor, chairs tipped over, the kitchen table upturned and the books from the stairs strewn everywhere. It couldn't have been Kate who had just arrived a few minutes ago and it was unlikely that some freak seismic vibration had taken place. It was obvious to Margret that this frenzied chaos had been caused by an intruder in a cataclysmic moment of rage.

The bedrooms displayed the same mayhem. Half expecting someone or something to jump out at her, Margret entered each room still holding the torch and praying she wouldn't have to use it. Discovering no one on the ground floor, she went up the first flight of stairs and stopped in front of the wardrobe which had been left at an angle across the small landing. It proffered an invitation to that place avoided for so long, at least until a few days ago. For the second time that week Margret climbed the stairs to the attic; placing her feet on this occasion with caution, to avoid the slightest creak.

On reaching the middle stair, Kate's voice sliced through the air – Margret listened, sat down on the step and tried not to move or make a sound.

* * *

'I can't believe you did that! What possessed you?' shouted Kate.

Sye's fury matched hers with a quieter, sinister, edge: '*You* wouldn't understand.'

As he spoke, he stared out of the window at the harbour now shrouded in a darkness only a place without street lights would know – in contrast with the attic where hundreds of small candles burnt around the edge of the four walls. The space they stood in had become a beacon, its light reaching out beyond, across the marshes and out to sea. His earlier words came back to Kate, *Don't come at night, or someone might see the torchlight.* So what was he doing advertising his presence? Nothing was making sense any more.

Kate attempted to calm her voice, to reach Sye, the poet, the artist … her future lover. 'I thought you were the one to help *me* see the way, now you're inviting anyone that's passing? I've followed your lead, I've done as you asked and listened.' She began to blow out some of the candles; the smell of molten wax filled the air. Sye turned to see what she was doing. The coldness in his eyes stopped her.

She tried once more to reach him: 'Even in Warwick I listened. I've kept my part of the bargain. I could tell that you were angry when I left here, confused by my actions, but while I was away, you spoke … to me … you were calmer, once you knew I was definitely coming back.'

'I knew nothing of the sort,' replied Sye, still steely-eyed, unmoved. 'And as for reading my feelings, pure imagination on your part. I've made no attempt to connect with you since you left me, none whatsoever.' He turned away again.

Sye's words were like a slap in the face, shocking Kate into the comprehension that an overactive imagination had been playing games with her mind. It was all too much to take in. She gripped hold of his arms and physically battled to make him face her. All she achieved was to see the emotionless look of disinterest in his eyes as he shoved her to the floor.

Despite the shock, she picked herself up and stood in front of him. 'If it's me you want to punish, why commit such pointless annihilation downstairs, those weren't just my possessions but Margret's as well. What has she ever done to you?' Sye actually laughed at this, inflaming Kate further. 'Is it that you want to destroy everything that isn't here in this precious room of yours? Anything out of tune with your sixties' utopia … everything that isn't *you*!'

This time Sye made no response whatsoever. Defeat rang loud; all hope lost. She had woken like Sleeping Beauty to utter confusion rather than to her rescuing prince.

Kate's voice gave away her desolation. '*I kept my promise … I came back as you wanted … I listened … but now all I need are my eyes to see what you are for real … a destroyer. Please Sye,*' she pleaded. 'Tell me what's going on … what have I done to deserve all this?' She was aware that her elbow was sore from breaking the earlier fall and held her arm close to her chest for comfort, attempting to rub away the pain.

Sye began to move from one window to another as if the gloom outside would reveal something he was waiting for. 'I said you wouldn't understand, you don't need to – your understanding doesn't matter any more.'

'How can you say that? What's happened to our needing to be equal in our desire for each other? You said each existence would complement the other. Where's all that gone now?'

'So many questions … it's gone where everything goes in the end,' he said.

'Oh stop being so enigmatic,' interrupted Kate.

'Into the ether that's where … along with Lennon and Kennedy, *everything and everyone* except me!'

'And why should you be different! Perhaps everything and everyone out there is seeking a connection too and your experience is … ordinary, normal, nothing exceptional!'

'Great – a whole universe of lost souls – that's something to look forward to.'

'But you found yours, you've found *me*!' Kate reached out with both hands to Sye to hold on to a once perfect dream; hands which slowly dropped to her sides in the full realisation of what she had been seeking … a flawless reality which could never exist.

'It's not you, it never was you!' Sye pushed past, ignoring the space she stood in, to look again out of what had been their Timescape window.

'What do you mean?' asked Kate incredulously.

'It's *her*. I told you, you're not listenng, you were irrelevant.'

'I don't understand.' Uncontrollable tears were burning her face. She felt like a child who'd been told that all the adult fictitious stories formulated to bring about well-being, joy and excitement had been blown apart all in one go; this time Father Christmas and the Tooth Fairy had been detonated in the same blast.

A voice came from the direction of the stairwell. '*I understand.*'

Kate peered through her tears to see Margret standing motionless at the top of the stairs. Her eyes were locked on Sye; they were not angry eyes but full of something else … sadness, tinged with pity … and then … *longing.* Margret's hair was loose and wild, and around her neck was what looked like a shoelace strung with several rings.

'At least you kept one promise.' Margret spoke with great control, never taking those eyes off Sye.

'Yes … I suppose I did,' he said.

In the split second Margret had appeared at the top of the stairs, Kate could see that Sye had become weakened by the effort of sustaining his 'existence' in the same place in time with both women. He took several faltering steps to reach the wall next to the stored paintings and slumped down to crouch there with both hands pulling his head tight into his body. The three were imprisoned, transfixed in what had become an eternal triangle locked into the silence of the room. The candles formed long shadows joined by the beam of Margret's torch which firstly illuminated Sye and then flickered onto the three canvases next to him. Kate watched the beam draw Margret to the paintings and heard a cry of anguish.

'What have you done to the paintings … oh what have you done? No, not these!' Within what had become a small unsteady pool of light, Margret turned them one at a time, as Kate had done before, the torch painfully revealing that each canvas had been badly damaged. With them all facing the room Margret stepped back … the pool of light grew, the extent of the vandalism fully unveiled. Each had been slashed, sliced through without pity. Moreover, it seemed as though that destructive act hadn't satisfied the perpetrator; the paintings were also defaced with gold paint splashed across their surfaces. The brush had been an instrument of anger, wielded recklessly, but with great passion.

Margret shone the torchlight onto Sye. 'If there was any thought in my mind that you really had returned to make things good between us, I couldn't have been more wrong, could I? You mean to destroy everything again!'

'I remember, you said I was a selfish bastard back then.' He spoke without emotion.

'Yes I did,' replied Margret. 'And it looks like nothing has changed, so much for hoping.'

He shielded his eyes from the torch and spoke to Kate. '*She's* changed. So much … I recognised her, that day on the embankment. It was the way she kept heading towards the house and then stopped to look back out to the sea. She used to do that every time we returned from the beach – drawn back to the dunes in case she missed something.'

He looked at Margret. 'You never could turn your back on the sea for long.'

'Of course I've changed … partly the normal aging process which you wouldn't know about – but part deliberate too.'

'Deliberate?' said Sye with disbelief.

Margret switched off the torch and sat, just a little away from him, with all anger worn out of her. The candlelight took over, softening the atmosphere.

Kate stood there, surplus to requirements: taken over by a sense of fading away, of becoming progressively distant from events taking place.

'After your …' Margret's fingers reached for the rings

hung around her neck, '… after your suicide … I left. Feeling was bad in the village about your influence on Will, and guilt consumed me. I went to Italy: made a living sketching portraits in the streets and ended up doing the same in the homes of wealthy Italians, a sort of guest attraction at their dinner parties.'

'Some leap – made it with your own name this time?' Sye interjected with a sarcastic note in his voice.

Margret ignored him. 'I stayed away a good ten years but in the end I had to come back.'

Kate couldn't cope with being left with what felt like invisibility – perhaps this was how Margret had suffered when she and Phil had been full of their own stories. There was a need to move closer to Margret, in an attempt to form some sort of solidarity with desperateness, which, for reasons she couldn't fathom, they both seemed to share.

'No one really remembered me,' Margret continued. 'I'd changed out of all recognition. My mourning you … us … and all that was wrong with us, led to this weight gain. Some people drink, some turn to drugs … or both, as you well know. Some give up eating, anorexic they call it now, but I went the opposite way,' she said ruefully. 'So it was no wonder no one could see the girl I'd been when I'd lived here before – I'd also grown my cropped hair long again so that *all* that other me had gone … I got the reputation as the local hippie. I liked that.' Margret smiled at the recollection. 'It's easy to be someone else – I'd had practice before and even grew to believe in it myself.' She paused, absorbed in memories.

Nothing stirred inside the triangle.

'It got easier and easier as most people I'd known back

then either died or moved elsewhere and so many places became holiday homes. I kept away from the pub initially, avoiding it much as I did when you were alive.'

'So you got back into painting your landscapes then … when you returned …' Sye mumbled. 'But there's only the three here … not much to show for so many years.' He covered his head with his hands again as if attempting to figure all this information out and somehow hold together his waning energy.

'It took a good while before I could face painting anything at all. These three aren't recent. I began them that final morning before the storm came, while you were still fast asleep in the dinghy – both you and nature gathering energy to wipe out everything. Painting that first picture prepared me for what I somehow knew was to come. The second painting was hardly my work at all – I became the conduit – the storm took over, it controlled your destiny, the view from the window and the paint on my brush. Finally, calm was restored and I painted the last one, the reality of what was left behind. As soon as those pictures were finished they were too painful to look at so I turned each one to the wall and stopped painting, as I said, for a very long while … every time I tried to consider a new landscape all that was in my head was this view.'

Sye continued to cradle his head into his chest, his long fingers laced together to form a protective barrier. Not daring to address her own despair, Kate could only listen to Margret.

'I couldn't bear anything that reminded me of you. Your promise to return possessed me. I tried to fight it in Italy, ignore any need to come back, but in the end I had to. I tried living here in this house, had this attic blocked with the wardrobe, but I still couldn't stand looking at the view … not for a long time anyway … it was too distressing. So I sold most of my earlier paintings, managed to scrape together a small deposit and bought one of the fishermen's cottages. Even there I covered the window which looked over the staithe. I had to earn a living somehow … so I rented this out to holidaymakers and did seasonal work at the caravan site, and eventually at Phil's of course.'

'Phil's? He's still around?' asked Sye, looking up, showing his bewilderment.

'No, Young Phil is the son of the one you loved to provoke each night at the pub … although I did work for Old Phil for a couple of years before he retired. He was the one person who, I suspected, had a pretty good idea of my connection to you, but we never spoke of it – not a word, not even about Will.' A long look passed between the two that Kate couldn't gauge; a shared memory not spoken.

Sye broke the silence, 'I'm sorry about your paintings.' The light in the attic was too dim for Kate see if there was any true honesty in his eyes; she mistrusted every movement, every word he spoke now.

'Sorry! Hardly!' Margret shouted. 'You were never sorry then, so why now! My paintings have always served your purpose! You've never been sorry about anything in your life – or your death so it seems – you manipulated and contorted everything!'

'It started out for your own benefit, you know it did.'

'But it soon became for *your* own good, didn't it? You were the perfect con-man but it bankrupted you in the end!'

Kate could be quiet no longer, 'Look you two, you're

losing me …'

Sye glared at her. 'Shut up Kate, this doesn't concern you.'

She opened her mouth to speak again but decided better of it as Margret dragged one of the wrecked canvases to Sye and held it close to his face.

'You destroyed everything that night, pretending to play the hero in the storm. But even then I knew it was your choice – you never intended to live – you committed suicide and you know it!'

'I set you free,' he said weakly.

Margret let the painting drop to the floor. 'Oh you are *so* wrong there … you left me tied to you for ever. Waiting.'

'Well I've paid the price for that, haven't I? Stuck in this hell-hole tunnel of time hoping that Kate would help release me.'

'And what price would *she* have had to pay?'

Sye didn't speak. Kate wasn't sure she wanted to know.

'I know too well what you wanted from Kate,' continued Margret, not waiting for Sye to come up with an answer. 'But it would have consumed her – or left her with no future existence worth living, just as you did with me. Those words you left me with were … so cruel.'

'What words?' asked Kate.

Tears were streaming down Margret's face. 'The promise he made … that he would come back for me no matter what – to be with me without the shackles of our history, our deceits. To rekindle our *Magical Mystery Tour* in a perfect world … and I was fool enough to believe him.' Margret turned back to Sye, speaking with more control now. 'I kept the poem you know; all that time in Italy. But when I came back I threw it on the floor up here and that same day had the wardrobe put in place.'

'That's where I found it,' said Sye, showing signs of real difficulty to collect his thoughts and speak fluently. 'The first time I felt present in this room ... I was hardly here ... and then one day ... I found I could pick up the poem and read it again ... it seemed to bring me back further into whatever this world is ...'

Both women waited for him to gather the strength he needed to continue.

'... but you never came ... I was looking for the girl I left behind ... I gave up for a long time ... until Kate ... look I can't go on, not with you both seeing me, turn away ... *please.*'

Not for his benefit, but to spare Margret, Kate took her by the hand and led her over to the window. Observing her friend's reluctance to look out she whispered, 'It's alright, there's no storm.'

'But I came here so often,' said Margret. 'Preparing the holiday lets. Why didn't he *see* it was me?'

'Yes why didn't you pick up on her thoughts as you did with me?' asked Kate, resisting the temptation to turn around.

Sye replied with slightly more power in his voice. 'I didn't even try to see beyond the woman she'd become and there'd be the radio, always on, so loud, so many voices, drowning out and blocking everything. I was weak, confused by the sounds and ... afraid. The people below changed all the time, it scared me.'

'So why *me*?'

'You and your family were quiet, your thoughts *found me.* I'm sorry.'

Kate deliberately turned to face him. 'I don't believe that, how can I?' The reference to her family brought her back to the present. 'What happens now, I've burnt all my bridges to be with you? Help me Margret, what can I do?' Kate's head was spinning with a full sense of the warped reality she had accepted from Sye.

'I don't know,' said Margret continuing to stare into the darkness outside. 'I've been lost in my own tunnel for over forty years – yours is just beginning – there must be some light somewhere.'

'*Margret,*' said Sye with a note of disparagement, 'I think you mean *Mae.*'

'Mae – you changed your name too?' asked Kate.

'Oh … one more little deceit. When I came back from Italy, I heard that song *Maggie May* on the radio … you know … well *you* wouldn't Sye … Rod Stewart?'

Sye looked blank. Margret ignored him and directed her explanation to Kate. 'It made me think about an old fishermen's song the children used to sing at the school, but different spelling – Maggie M-A-E – like me … so I made connections – from Mae to Maggie to Margret. Don't you see? It was another reason no one remembered me. Until Sye recognised me from the window just before you left for Warwick.'

'So his anger then wasn't because I had left, it was for himself, for failing to *see* you before.'

Margret made no response; she picked up the canvas and replaced it between the other two. She flicked the torch back on and became immersed with inspecting the damage.

Sye slowly got up and moved as far away as possible, to the smallest window, looking inland. He leant his forehead on the windowpane as Kate had seen him do before, staring out. Then, seemingly having gained nothing from the view, he placed his cheek against the glass – closed his eyes. For the first time Kate actually saw him fade away and fully understood the enormity of it all; that in order to be part of his world, she too would have had to take on this precarious existence and end her own life as Sye had apparently done.

29

MAE

Kate gasped.

Margret looked up from the paintings and scanned the attic for Sye – corner to corner, window to window – in vain. She ran to the door leading to the external steps and checked if it was still locked. It remained padlocked from the outside. Her chest heaved with loss and confusion and then, as if recalling an appointment to be somewhere else, she made to go below giving Kate little time to recover from the scene just witnessed.

Concern for Margret's sanity and well-being overrode Kate's own anguish as she followed quickly down the stairs and out of the house. Where the hell was Margret going? And what would she do when she got there? The older woman led the way, paying no heed at being followed – down the lane and along the footpath which led to the staithe as well as to her own back gate. Kate was fearful of what might happen next: was Margret's destination the security of home or the waters of high tide? She tried to keep up and follow the flicker of Margret's torch. Suddenly even that had gone and Kate was forced to feel her way along the brick wall at the back of Fisherman's Cottage to find the gate left carelessly ajar. It was too dark to take in the details of the small yard but she could just about make out that the back door had also been left open. She hesitated on the threshold; it was almost as gloomy inside but a light from upstairs lit the stairwell a little. She heard Margret walk across the floor of the room above – then everything went very quiet. Worried by this abrupt lack of activity, Kate rushed up the stairs.

On entering the upstairs living space which spread across the whole width and length of the cottage, Kate was immediately aware of the similarity with Sye's attic: the bare floorboards, the mattress lying on the floor in the centre covered in a faded patchwork quilt along with cushions of all shapes, sizes and patterns. But there the similarity ended as the rest of the room was a well-used artist's studio with many canvases leaning against the walls, sometimes three or four deep. An easel stood near the inland window. Another window, which ought to have looked out onto the staithe, was boarded over and used as a place to pin sketches and photographs of landscapes. Margret was kneeling on the mattress with the same large art book she'd found on Kate's stairs open in front of her; she was picking at the edges of something stuck to the inside cover.

There was no acknowledgement of Kate's presence. 'Is it ok ... me being here?' she asked quietly.

Margret paused for a moment, before she returned to her task, nails frenetically tearing at what looked like a black and white photo. Taking silence to mean assent, Kate warily edged across to look at the pictures fixed to the window boarding: all were of inland views, never the sea.

'Can I?' Kate pointed towards the canvases leaning against the wall – Margret looked up and nodded.

Kate began to examine Margret's work and found more

proof of Sye's deceit. The paintings were all similar in style to those in Sye's attic but in each corner were the letters M A E. The brushwork was unmistakable, but less anguished; the landscape and the artist at one rather than at odds with one another.

Still prepared to be rebuffed, she knelt down next to Margret who had succeeded in peeling the photograph off the book. Kate carefully took hold of it by one edge in order to see more clearly a young, happy couple standing in the foreground with a windmill behind. There were others posing with them, long-haired, flared-jeaned teenagers all as laid back and carefree as the young man in the centre. A young man who was undoubtedly Sye. The girl had Margret's smile, dark hair to her waist, wearing a bikini top and flared jeans painted with flowers. Around her neck hung a garland of buttercups. Margret tolerated Kate's perusal of the photograph for only a second before snatching it away to hold it tight to her chest.

Taking the hint, Kate chose to be practical and recalled that her mother's answer to all disasters had been a good cup of tea – or a strong gin. She left Margret enfolded in her memories and went downstairs to explore the kitchen which was basic in the extreme, with little in it to comfort on a normal day let alone on a day you'd come face to face with a ghost. Kate could find no alcohol at all so she made a strong cup of tea.

On her return upstairs, she found Margret curled up fast asleep, still clutching the photograph. Suddenly aware of her own exhaustion, Kate sat on the floor and nursed the warm cup while she allowed herself to face her own feelings. Was it really still the same day she'd left Warwick? The day on which she had irrevocably chosen to not only chase her dream but to reach out with both hands and live it. Her fool's dream.

And instead? The depths fallen into had been far worse than could be imagined. Kate lay down and covered them both with the quilt, hoping that if Margret woke, she too would be disturbed.

There was no question of going back to Phil's as promised, leaving Margret alone. With no knowledge of what the next day would bring, Kate fell asleep, her last thought to worry that Phil would now be even more concerned … but there was nothing she could do about that …

Kate's sleep was that of a body physically and emotionally drained, so much so that she failed to be stirred by Margret's movements. When she eventually woke, next to her on the floor was a fresh cup of coffee in a blue chipped mug with Mae written on it in cream letters. She heard the inland window being opened; the cool morning air reached in.

'Good, awake at last,' said Margret, 'I thought your coffee would get cold.'

Kate sat up and could immediately see there was something about Margret that was different. Traces of Mae? It was about the eyes somehow.

Margret stood at her easel and started to paint. 'It's only fair that I tell you it all now – I'm sorry I didn't last night, I wasn't ready – it's been such a long time. So often I've wanted to tell you and Phil more about myself, but couldn't. I'd become this person I'd invented and deep down there was some kind of loyalty to that girl I used to be. I don't understand what stopped me telling you, my parents are either long gone or have lost the will to find me.'

'Your parents?'

'The funny thing is that now I can see they weren't so bad, but back then in the sixties I saw them as coming from another planet. Our generation believed we were unique – convinced in our minds that no one had ever been young before we came along. Now I realise all teenagers think that.'

'That I do understand. Joe …' began Kate.

'But these days it's so different – they've so much freedom now – we'd only just begun to be liberated by the pill. Such a small pill that changed everything, at last there was sex without fear of pregnancy and boy did we celebrate!'

'How did you meet Sye?'

'I was seventeen, on a geography field trip to the windmill down the road – a whole group of us escaping from our all girls school in Leicester and ripe for our first experience of sex. Sye turned up with some friends and hung about. At that stage he thought he was either a great artist or a great poet – most days he failed to decide – but I was so impressed by him, and wanted to paint too. That's when we fell in love. He used bring me to the staithe, to sit with my legs dangling over the edge of the jetty, and I'd make sketches while he scribbled poetry. Once we stayed up all night to see if smuggler ghosts would silently steer their ships up to where we sat …'

Margret paused, reached for the necklace of rings and cradled them in her hand. 'My teachers didn't even notice I was missing that night – they didn't much care about what we were up to. Every day they left us all to our own devices most of the time and disappeared into the fields to smoke dope for hours on end and … well, you can imagine. Shall we say, I think they had just discovered the pill too … oh the headlines that would make today!'

'Did you stay then, in Norfolk with Sye?'

'No, not straight away – I went back for a month but my parents sensed I'd changed and pulled up the drawbridge. They refused to put me through art school and said I had to settle down and have a "respectable career" – none of this "arty-farty" life for *their* daughter. Yes, those were the actual words my father used. It got worse and worse, they wanted to put me in a box, their box, and stick a label on me.'

'So you came back.'

'Yes … I packed a bag and hitchhiked.'

'You must have been deranged. You could have been attacked, raped, murdered even.'

'We didn't think twice about travelling about like that then, everyone did it, we all thought that free love equalled a happy, safe world. I didn't have any problems anyway – I struck lucky, some middle-aged chap with his secretary I reckon, the way they talked, on their way to what people used to call a dirty weekend in Hunstanton. You see everyone was at it.' Margret grinned.

'What do you mean, struck lucky?'

'Because they never came forward when I went missing. Sye would bring in the newspapers and there was never a word. It seems my teachers didn't say anything about Sye either – they must have had a guilty conscience too.'

'Most probably fear – even in those days surely they would have been jailed for the drugs and the like if anything came out.'

'They must have kept quiet because the papers didn't report that the police had any interest in looking in this part of the world. I'd left a note saying I was going to London to study art so that must have kept everyone busy, searching there. I lay low for a long time, cut off all my hair, stayed in the attic, made love and painted.'

'But didn't anyone recognise you from the papers?'

'No. I only made the nationals for about a week, nobody here took any interest. Six months later I spoke to the village Mr Plod, looked him straight in the eyes and there wasn't a flicker of recognition. I became so confident that I even ended up helping out at the local school, until it closed.'

'When was that?'

'Around 1967 I think. I remember because that's when everything turned sour.'

Lost in thought, Margret needed a prompt to continue.

'Tell me about your painting.'

'I'd become a very successful painter, quite well known actually,' she said in a matter of fact way, showing little pride.

'How did you do that without your parents finding you, I presume they didn't?'

'Sye became the artist.' Margret picked up Kate's now empty mug, paused and ran her finger across the letters of the word Mae. 'We sold my pictures in his name. In reality he was the poet, his painting was pretty bad, and I was the artist. Unfortunately the poetry wasn't terribly good either.'

Margret began to clean her brush in the old plastic washing-up bowl sitting on a trestle table set up along one wall of the room. She chose another brush and returned to her easel; the shade required was carefully mixed and tested before she settled into being totally engrossed in the work. Kate began to think that perhaps this was all the information which was going to be on offer that day.

A while later Margret spoke again. 'He wrote his poetry

with little success so he took on *my* success. It seemed such a good deal to begin with. He used to take my paintings down to the street markets in London. Then I got one accepted for the Royal Academy Summer Exhibition and was picked up by a gallery nearby. So then it was the real thing – an exhibition, big do, champagne. Sye loved it, taking all the glory and he knew my paintings so well that he got away with it. I was simply glad to be free to paint and leave all that to him.'

'What went wrong?'

'He got jealous.'

'Sye – I would have thought you …'

'No, Sye was jealous of my talent, of all the praise that came my way, indirectly through him. It made him feel worthless. His poetry got rejected time after time while I became more and more successful. That poem we talked about yesterday was his last.'

'You must have been paying for everything too – from the paintings, from your job at the school?'

'Well he rented the house from his last remaining relative – his very wealthy aunt. She came to visit once. I found out then that he only paid her a pittance, despite the fact that he was always boasting that the reason I had a roof over my head was purely because of him. But I paid for everything else while he became increasingly resentful that all the money coming in was from me.'

'So if she owned the place, how come it's yours now?'

'He'd started leaving me alone, spending every evening at the pub. In the daytime he'd vanish to the beach and smoke pot. During the last few months he was generally high on something and wasn't really in a fit state to go to London. It was in the middle of one of these binges, his aunt turned up – she wasn't impressed.'

'I'm surprised she didn't throw him out.'

'I persuaded her I could cope with him. We hit it off actually – which didn't go down well with Sye, not at all. I think she wanted to absolve herself of what had basically become a non-existant family bond. She agreed we could stay on there, on condition that I took on the responsibility for looking after the place, as he was – in her words – "a total waste of space". So, you see, things were seriously unravelling long before the storm came, even she wanted no more to do with him. It's a good job he never knew that she changed her will too and left the place to me.'

With stiff joints, due to her cramped night's sleep on the mattress, Kate got up, stretched her limbs and went over to look at the painting Margret was working on. Mae, the artist, was functioning on two levels: she was absorbed in making her brushstrokes in the present, whilst reliving the past in words.

'After the storm, after he'd … gone, I wrote to her, told her what had happened and slipped in a cheque for the rent which was due. The cheque was sent back with a note – *Keep it, the house I mean, you've earned it*. I didn't believe it. And then I left anyway and went to Italy. When I came back the place was in a terrible state – damp saturated the bedroom walls, and plant life covered the windows downstairs – but the attic was dry, my paintings survived. There was an official looking letter on the doormat: she'd died six months before I returned.'

'At least you had somewhere to live,' said Kate as she watched the last gentle touches of paint bring life to a sky above a landscape which included the same windmill as the one in the photograph found yesterday; but this canvas showed no people standing at the foot of the building, merely an empty path leading to the front door.

'But not somewhere I could bear to be … I had spent so much time alone there, days and nights of wanting Sye to come home while at the same time fearing the sound of his key in the door.'

Any previous image of Sye which had been presented to Kate had shattered, supplanted by the real version: a being who had once used a vulnerable young woman for his own ends and now years later had reached across time to use the same skills of manipulation, in the same place but with a different victim.

Margret broke across her thoughts, 'When I saw the state the house was in I was tempted to give in, go back to my roots – but there was too much guilt to deal with, on both sides, and I couldn't cope with it, not with everything else. I did go back to Leicester once – stood across the road from my parents' house and watched a young family arrive home from school. It was winter, snowing, and they were laughing and throwing snowballs at each other, oblivious to the fact that such sadness must have belonged to the house they lived in. I tried to trace my parents then but no one knew where they'd gone. Perhaps it was deliberate, to leave no forwarding address, to punish me if I came looking.' The paintbrushes were cleaned again and laid to rest.

Kate was aware that so far they had only reached the end of the first act and waited with apprehension for what the next might bring.

Margret put her coat on. 'I'm ready for that walk along

the bank now – but not to the beach, not yet.'

They started out, with Kate pulling around herself an old donkey-brown duffle-coat of Margret's that was several sizes too big but successful in keeping out the cold. As their silhouettes progressed along the embankment, Margret set the pace and they walked without speaking until they reached the bench on the first turn in the path.

'This will do,' said Margret.

'For what?'

'You'll want to know how Sye died.'

Kate was staring out towards Scolt Head. She looked back inland, taking in the world that Sye and Mae had lived in together – very little had altered since then. To her left was the Boathouse and the village, with the creek winding its way, past where they were sitting, out to the sea waiting beyond the dunes and the unsullied virgin sands. It was a place that had rejected and turned its back on the modern world, one which had defied change for far more years than those existing between 1968 and now; those lost decades for Sye were a blink in its timeline.

'The night before the storm we had our worst row ever. He'd taken to drinking with a local lad, Will, who helped out at the shop and sometimes down at the Boathouse. Will was impressed by Sye, and what he represented, and Sye would often boast to him of his trips to London. I suspected that he was also introducing Will to the drugs he'd pick up on his visits to the city.

'I went to the pub at closing time, I'm not sure which of them I was more worried about. Sye had just come back from London; he dumped his bag, wouldn't speak to me and went out. I was anxious about what he might get Will to mix with his alcohol. When I got there the pub was already closed. I found them weaving down the middle of the road arm in arm.'

30

JULY 1968

Sye put up his hand to play-act whispering into Will's ear, 'Watch out, we're being followed.'

He glared at Mae, '*Ill met by moonlight proud Titania!*'

Will looked blank. The two of them giggled as they tripped over their feet: Batman and Robin on a bad day. Mae put herself between them and took hold of Sye's arm. Without physical support Will toppled and fell onto the road.

'Get off. Look, you've damaged him now!' Sye pushed Mae away and attempted to give his hand to pull Will up. It took several tries before they managed to make a good grip and a lot of effort before they reached some form of equilibrium, standing upright on their feet, with arms around each other again, laughing.

'Sye, please come home – we need to talk.'

'To talk? You must be joking, use your eyes, I can hardly walk.'

'You need to eat something, soak up all that alcohol – and the rest.'

'Why do I want to talk to you? I've got Will here, we do friendly talk, don't we Will? Not arguing talk like you do.' He poked his finger into Mae's shoulder.

She stood her ground. 'It's you that's full of bullshit – if

Will was sober, he'd see through you.'

'That's right, well done Mae.' Sye sat Will down on a bench, swung his arms to left and right with a flourish and bowed to her. 'I am the King of Bullshit – that's right, King of Bullshit, Lord of … Nothing. You … are the shining star, the one who has everything. You should hear them praise you, I mean me, I mean you … you know what I mean.'

'Come back and talk to me Sye. We can change things, travel abroad – you've always said anything is possible. We can be free …'

He shouted right into her face. 'It's you that holds me back, you stupid cow!'

Mae stood there, motionless.

He moved in, closer still. She smelt the heat of beer and whisky on his breath and turned her head to avoid the spit as he bellowed, 'Did you hear what I said, you are the one who imprisons me, ties me up … in a world of lies, and you … you are always … QUEEN OF THE WORLD!'

Sye took Mae by the arm this time and marched down the road. 'Make way for the King and Queen of Bullshit.' He marched them back to where Will was sitting. 'William, stand up, bow down before the Queen.' Will attempted to stand but couldn't quite co-ordinate his limbs properly. He sat back down on the bench and waved at Mae instead.

She didn't see it coming – Sye's fist as it smashed across her face.

It was Will who reached out to break her fall but even so she found herself staring at Sye's boots wondering where the next blow would come from. She felt Will's comforting arm cradle her.

'LEAVE HER! She asked for it!'

Will obeyed instantly and withdrew to the far end of the bench, his eyes averted from the scene. Sye grasped Mae's wrist, pulling her up from the gravel which had bitten into her hands, and thrust her away from him. 'Go and paint, turn all that straw into gold up in your ivory tower – I shall stay with my true companion tonight.' He bowed towards Will this time. 'Come with me young man, we shall sleep well tonight.'

They stumbled off together onto the small beach while Mae, still in a state of shock, stood alone on the top bank and followed their progress. Aided by the moonlit sky, she looked down on them and wondered whether Sye would have forgotten much of what he'd done when he sobered up the next day. In every breath she took there was the question – which was worse, the daily emotional distress he handed out or the physical attack just endured? Her hand rubbed her bruised cheek as she asked herself what she had done to deserve such pain. Perhaps it was her punishment for choosing Sye above her family, perhaps it was all her fault, perhaps she *had* asked for it.

Trying to get their attention, she shouted as loudly as possible, 'There might be a storm tonight, I can feel it in the air!'

There came no response to her plea as Sye led the way to their two dinghies which lay beached on mud only recently left by the ebbing tide. They lurched past Sye's dinghy, feet slipping and sliding, and almost fell over the rope which secured it to a makeshift buoy. Finally, after much banter and deliberation, they flopped down and leant against Will's smaller boat which was attached carelessly to the stern of Sye's.

Mae remained up on the bank, aware that the beach might well be flooded by high tide the next morning and prayed that if a storm came, it would not be too wild and the swell not so drastic as to cause much destruction in the creek full of boats. She walked up and down, sat on the grass, stood up again and watched and waited for about an hour. The two men below her sat talking, having climbed into Sye's boat where they proceeded to light up and pass a joint from one to the other. Sye ignored her, Will occasionally waved.

For what must have been a further hour, Mae tried her utmost to interpret their mumblings which were randomly interspersed with bouts of laughter before Sye stripped off and ran down to the water's edge. Will threw off his clothes and followed – they ran in and out of the water like two children, as carefree as she and Sye had once set out to be. It wasn't long before Sye began to tire of the game and returned to the boats. Mae continued her vigil as Will attempted to pull Sye back towards the water – the two raising their fists in mock anger at each other, then seeming to come to some agreement whereby they began to search around for their cast-off clothes. When they eventually collected together a random bundle they tried in vain to put on each other's trousers, this time behaving like old men, bent and cowed. Somehow Sye and Will managed to dress and tumble into their respective dinghies where they pulled the tarpaulins over themselves, emerging almost comically to say the last word – one, then the other – until they both must have passed out.

Mae weighed up what to do. Well aware that it was now well past midnight a sense of impending doom forced her into action; she took the steps down to the boats and pulled back Sye's tarpaulin to try and wake him. It was futile, he was out cold. She found the same in Will's boat. There was no way to rouse them. The air was clammy, oppressive; the heat of the summer's day lingering on into the night – exasperated with itself for still being there. If indeed a summer storm broke, it would be sure to disturb them. The best Mae could hope for was that it would have passed before high tide later in the morning. It was only a few hours until dawn and by then, she decided, it would be possible to try and wake them again – failing that, she might be able to get help from the local fishermen who should also be up and about with their boats.

Mae decided to return to The Old Pilot's House; she could still watch from there. Tired and dishevelled, she struggled to avoid getting ensnared in the undergrowth growing either side of the sloping track which linked the embankment and the narrow back lane leading to the house. On reaching home she went straight up to the attic and leant out of the open window keen to hear any sound of Sye and Will waking or, better still, coming up the lane.

When the dawn arrived, a little before five o'clock, the swell was only just stirring, indiscernible to anyone not versed in the ways of the sea. The sky looked as if the whole world had caught fire; the red clouds illuminating the marshes and reflecting a pale pink onto the whitewashed Boathouse above its black flood line. It couldn't be resisted. Even though she was exhausted and the tide was rising, Mae began to paint the sunrise, soothed by its beauty, her youthful naivety believing that a morning such as this would be incapable of allowing nature to turn on itself in the shape of the storm she feared. Each mark she made helped her block out the pain caused by Sye when he had humiliated her in front of Will. She painted methodically to begin with, and then more feverishly – racing time – in case the crimson sky faded away to lesser hues.

Once satisfied with her progress, she again leant as far out of the window as possible. She could just see the stern of Will's dinghy still beached a good distance from the water's edge, so there was plenty of time for them to wake before high tide. The air seemed less threatening than it had been in the night. Comforted by this, she settled down on the cushions in the centre of the room, often used as a bed when she was exhausted from painting. Her arm and neck ached from the intensity of her work and her cheekbone still throbbed from Sye's attack. Finally, Mae slept.

The rain pelted down onto the roof and woke her; where the look-out window had been left wide open the floorboards were soaked beneath. Mae battled with the wind to close it. All that beauty had deserted the sky and the anger of the gods was spewing out; the sea had taken control, smashing everything in its wake. The tide was in full flood. The embankment had no visible height; water was surging dangerously close to the top and there was no sight of any of the groynes. Many of the boats and dinghies were waterlogged or capsized or, worse, ripped to pieces.

The wind forced Mae's slight body to take the path it chose on her behalf. She made it down the lane, expecting to climb up onto the embankment to get a good view of where Sye's and Will's boats should be. When she reached it, it was clear there was no beach left at all. The tide, not due to be full until ten that morning, was higher than she had ever seen before with waves even snapping at the sailing boats parked up well away from the beach, on the other side of the road. Some primordial beast had been let loose from the depths of the sea and finding no sustenance there was turning to the land instead. Boats of all shapes and sizes tied to moorings were being wrenched away, only to find extinction.

Will's boat had gone.

She could see Sye; he was holding back the tarpaulin he had slept under as he stared out to sea. They both realised the other dinghy was missing at the same time. Mae searched frantically for sight of the lost boat, and realised that like the night when they'd challenged the smuggler ghosts to appear, no vessel could be seen successfully negotiating the heaving waters. What once had been a narrow creek between marshland and shore had now become one furious swollen sea and still it was not high tide. The upsurge was incessantly conquering more land, taking its prize.

Mae yelled at Sye, 'I'll get a rope from the Boathouse, they must be awake over there, I'll pull you in.' She couldn't tell if he heard but saw him mouth some kind of reply, point out to sea and deliberately release the dinghy from the buoy; in a flash it was clear what he was doing.

'Sye don't do this … it's suicide … you can't save Will, it's too late!'

As he fought to take control with the oars, the dinghy was being dragged towards what was left of the embankment coming close to where Mae stood. She stayed as long as she dared, reaching out in a hopeless attempt to somehow grab hold of the prow, but the ground ahead of her was fast disappearing beneath the relentless tide. All of a sudden the wind dropped and she could hear what he was shouting.

'I have to find Will.'

'You can't, save yourself, I'll get help.'

'I'll come back, I promise.' Everything stilled around him, the storm taking stock before attacking again. 'Keep looking out for me, *keep listening* … I promise. *Promise me* you'll be here when I come back. We'll have it all then, I'll make it good for us.'

'Sye – you – can't – save – him!'

'PROMISE ME!'

The storm drove him back into the centre of what used to be the channel. Mae shouted after him, 'I promise … I …' Her voice gave up, its purpose consumed as the storm renewed its offensive and showed no pity.

31

LOST

Sitting on the bench with Kate, Margret untied the lace of her necklace and laid it on her lap; she pulled off the rings systematically and slipped each one up and down her fingers in turn until a fit was achieved. Kate could see that every single ring matched those that she had seen on Sye's fingers.

'Was there a local lifeboat ... was the coastguard called?' asked Kate.

'The nearest would have been ... probably, at Wells, further down the coast ... I think that's where ...' Margret didn't seem to want to carry on.

'*You think*?'

'I ... I was soaked through to the skin ... I ran to the Boathouse, keeping my eyes on the small speck Sye and his dinghy had become. I only turned away for a minute to bang my fists on the door, shouting for help; but there was no response. When I looked again the speck had vanished. I hurried back to the embankment – all I could see was debris being tossed around amongst the few fishing boats and dinghies which had managed to stay in one piece.'

'But was there a search?'

'When I got to the phone box, the line was down ... so ... I went up the main road, knocking on random doors, still shouting – trying to raise the alarm. The whole village seemed to be hunkered down, waiting until the storm had passed. I tried the pub but Phil's father didn't answer. It wasn't surprising. He always used to tell everyone how, if he couldn't get to sleep at night after clearing up the pub, he'd end up dead to the world in the morning – often even failing to open at lunchtime ...'

'So what did you do?'

Margret paused, 'What could anyone have done anyway?' A look of pure anguish crossed her face.

An illogical thought occurred to Kate. *Was this Margret or Mae asking the question?*

It certainly appeared to be Mae who answered, justifying events: 'It wouldn't have been right to risk another man's life out at sea in a vain attempt to find Sye, not when he'd made his own decision between life and death. He hadn't set out to save Will, he was no hero. We both knew there was no hope – Will's dinghy was barely seaworthy, he was always planning to work on it, but never did.'

'Margret, what – did – you – *do*?'

'He made a conscious decision to take his own life and to do it as selfishly as possible, forcing my promise, tying me to him.'

Margret contemplated her rings, slipping them around and around on her fingers, one by one. '*Mae* did the only thing she knew how ...'

Several passers-by: chatter, a child's scream of delight upon being lifted high up on to broad shoulders, laughter tailing away.

Kate waited.

Margret began again, slowly dredging up the past: 'Back

in the attic … there *had* to be another painting. The storm. While it thrashed at the window, one hand held the brush and the other the palette, but each brushstroke reaffirmed those words … *I promise …*

'When the storm died down later, much later, it was safe to open the window. The stillness in the air brought with it that kind of small relief which comes when pain has subsided a little … a new canvas was placed on the easel … a track carefully picked out on the record … the sound turned up to fill the room.'

Margret moved her hands slowly in a circular motion on her thighs. 'Mae closed her eyes and ran the palms of both hands over the blank canvas in slow, ever increasing circles, feeling its tautness until her fingertips reached the edges …'

Her hands stopped moving; she sat rigid, remembering.

'The sound of the sitar was mesmerising. The words prompted – look within and beyond yourself … there was a need to paint that stillness in the air and that breath of hope. But it was … a struggle, no, a *battle* is a better description. The destruction left behind still wanted to dominate … I can't explain, look at the painting, the third one, you'll see …'

'I've seen it, I know what you mean.'

'It took until dawn the next morning to finish.'

A moment of peace touched both Kate and Margret as they sat next to each other on the bench staring at the meandering pathways etched onto the mudflats by the receding tide.

The silence was broken: '*Please stop! Please stop!*' Margret shouted. 'Stop that noise, it's happening again!'

She held out trembling hands; her eyes fixed on the rings. Kate spoke gently. 'It's ok. *Margret*, you're with me.

There's no noise, nothing can harm you out here.'

Margret placed one hand on top of the other, interlocked her fingers for a moment and then began to rip off the rings, stuffing them into her pocket.

When all the rings were stowed away, Kate asked, 'That noise, was it from the past, in the attic ... was it Sye?'

'It wasn't him,' replied Margret. 'It came from downstairs, the door knocker. It was Phil's father looking for Will. Mae lied ...'

Kate looked at Margret straight in the eye; could see the panic welling up, about to flow over. 'It's ok Margret,' she repeated, 'take a breath, we're here in the present, take your time ... that's if you want to carry on, we could go back ...'

'No! It was me. I lied! I was too ashamed to tell the truth ... I'd ... slept while Will drowned ... and ...'

'Breathe,' said Kate.

Margret began to calm herself; breathing slowly and deliberately. 'I lied by omission; admitted the row but told him I'd left them sitting on the bench and that I had presumed Sye was nursing a hangover at Will's place ...

'When the coastguard was finally called – it was far, far too late. I waited for the knock on the door that would tell me that Sye's body had been found. It never came. Will's was discovered three days later, casually thrown up onto a beach by lesser waves than those which had taken him. It was Phil's father who walked down from the pub to tell me the news.'

'Didn't anyone say they'd heard you trying to raise the alarm during the storm?'

Margret looked back towards the village; Kate could only just hear the reply. 'No one said anything, no one said anything at all.'

32

DRAWN BACK

A passing dog-walker hesitated as if to join the two women on the bench. Her spaniel sniffed around wanting attention.

'Perfect spot isn't it? My favourite,' she said.

Kate agreed, fussed the dog – briefly. She pulled her coat further around herself to keep out the chill. Margret stuck her hands in her pockets and looked at the ground. The hint was taken, the dog bounded off.

'Looks like we're not stopping then,' said its owner with a disappointed smile.

'So now you know everything, almost.'

'Almost?' asked Kate.

'Yesterday wasn't the first time I'd seen Sye.'

'What? When did you …?'

'After you left, I spent the next day deciding whether or not to go up to the attic. I knew something odd was happening and the photographs had confirmed my suspicions. In the end I had no option but to try and put my mind at rest. When I finally entered that room the paintings were as I'd left them, not like they are now, but still intact. I looked out across the salt marshes and there it was, the word Timescape written in the dust on the glass.'

'I made that up.'

'No you didn't. I wrote it several decades ago – it was my word.'

'No, you're wrong – it came into my head one day when I was …'

'You *still* don't see! He put it there, in your mind, he was playing the same record and you were dancing to its tune.'

'I'm not sure I want to hear any more.'

'Yes you do, you need to hear it all, *you* need to be able to move on.'

'So do you!' Kate stood up from the bench to emphasise her point, but Margret grabbed at her arm and pulled her back down.

'You can, I can't,' said Margret. 'Listen, let me finish. When I was looking at the word on the window, I heard the music, the sitar reaching out to me across all those years. We were obsessed by the Beatles. They were our soundtrack – part of the air we breathed. It was that same George Harrison song I'd played the night of the storm; his words were our words.'

Kate put her hands over her ears; everything in the attic had been a lie – every experience, every promise – she'd been an understudy, second-best all along. Sye had never cared about her … he'd simply used her for his own gain.

'You *must* listen.' Margret pulled away Kate's hands and held them. 'I turned around and there was Sye sitting in the middle of the room on the cushions, smiling that carefree smile of his like he'd never been away and what's more, I was back in the time when everything was good for us.'

Margret clutched at her grey hair with both hands and shook it hard. 'Suddenly I wasn't like this any more, I was that girl from the photo. It was weird, but wonderful. My life without him slipped out of my head as easily as slipping those rings off my necklace. With this body gone I was young again – we danced, made love, he read his poetry while I painted – I was immersed in our world, as if the years between then and now had never existed.'

She looked at Kate, with the glowing eyes of a young girl ready to embark on adulthood, desiring everything she hoped life could offer. '*I was Mae.*' Her eyes clouded over. 'Until …'

'Until?'

'Until, lying there side by side, exhausted and ready for sleep, he told me what he wanted.'

'Which was?'

'My suicide. Two suicides – his and mine – to make one whole being. It was his act of suicide which left him half in and half out of human existence. If he takes me with him, he can move on and together we can be united, forever as one.'

Every particle of air remained motionless; there was not a single bird call or even the ever present low rumble from the distant sea. Kate then knew with absolute surety that this role had also been planned for her; Sye had schooled her to be a replacement for Mae, whom he'd considered lost. This time she got up from the bench and stepped away, needing to make a space between herself and Margret, to break the link between them that Sye had attempted to make with his manipulations.

'And what was your answer?' Kate lifted her face to the sky and inhaled the sea air to make sure that all her senses hadn't been stolen when she had been listening to his seduction.

'My answer? Anger was my answer. I saw right through

what he had done: promising the return of who I once was. I remembered the reality and walked away.'

'*That's* why he destroyed everything.'

'Yes.'

'So we can be free of him.' Slowly Kate formed the sentence, 'if – if we do the same, and somehow destroy that room in *his* time …' She gained strength from the thought; he'd demonstrated vulnerability in that flash of destruction and in doing so had provided the answer. Destruction was the key, but turned on him. Hope began to grow.

A cold blast of November air hit Kate's face. That hope was not reflected in her friend's words.

'You can be free of him Kate, but I never will. I've waited too long and I've a promise to keep.'

'But you said …'

'My gut reaction came first. I left him and walked right out to the sea. Along this embankment, past all those bends in the path where you think you've reached your destination, before turning the last corner and seeing the truth – that there's still a long way to go. I made it in the end and sat in the dunes for hours, looking down on the vast stretch of sand I had avoided for years – remembering all the pain and it seemed right for him to have suffered too.'

'So we can keep walking away from him, we can be strong together.'

'But it all changed last night, when he vanished like that, I remembered *everything*. Despite how wrong it was between us in the past, despite the jealousy and the cruelty which was growing inside him, part of me still feels that I should have worked harder at turning it all around. *My art caused his death*. At the time the guilt was unbearable – I almost committed suicide myself soon after, but the girl who was strong enough to run away from home was strong enough to get away again. When I eventually changed my name it was to free myself of Mae and all those memories. A sort of suicide you could say. But you can never *just* walk away Kate.

'I tried to shut out the past for ten years in Italy, but it felt like painting over a used canvas with the colours bleeding through – and that's when I found my limit. I was held on a thread and eventually came to the extremity of its reach; so I came back – I always end up coming back.'

Out of her pocket Margret produced the photograph of her and Sye standing by the windmill, and this time freely handed it to Kate. 'When I got home last night and picked up that art book he gave to me as a present when I left my parents – I opened it up and there, staring at me, was this photo. That's when I remembered all the good things. He saved me you see, rescued me from a world I hated … *it was so wonderful when we were first together*. When everything went wrong it really was all my fault. My talent ruined him, it earned the money for the drink and the drugs … and the boat. And what did I do? I slept while Will drowned, and I was responsible in so many ways for Sye's suicide – it all happened because of me. I decided last night, while you slept, that I owe it to him, it's my turn to save him, to undo it all.'

'Oh Margret.'

'You mean Mae.'

'No, I mean Margret, that's who you are *now*.' Kate snatched the photograph and ripped it in two; to her surprise, there was only a passive reaction to this damaging act.

Margret dragged herself up from the bench to start back and murmured, 'I've got so tired of waiting.'

Kate looped her arm through Margret's as she tried to think of ways to turn this all around. Margret had rescued her by pulling back the curtain of delusion that Sye had so carefully drawn across her own grip on reality. Light was flooding in, diffusing the personal darkness Kate had almost walked into. The pure relief of being free of it all took over and made her even more determined that Margret should have that feeling too – to be reprieved, protected from Sye. Kate understood now that she had a massive debt to pay Margret; it was up to her to somehow deny Sye the satisfaction of sharing his appalling fate with another living being.

'So he doesn't know that you've changed your mind?' Kate asked.

'No, that's why he went berserk ... attacked the pictures. He still thinks I don't intend to keep my promise. I have to go and tell him. In 1968 I promised to wait. He's right, it's time to be together – in a happy, peaceful existence.'

Any good feelings regarding her own deliverance vanished as Kate saw she was powerless to stop Sye's psychological games, his hold over Margret was too strong. 'Make *me* a promise,' she said. 'Get some sleep, some proper sleep, before you return to the attic.'

The two women walked back along the bank. The breeze had picked up and Margret's progress was hampered by her hair which whipped around and blinded her at times. On these occasions she would turn to let the wind free her face, stop and stare out towards the sea while Kate paused too and waited. They passed more everyday walkers, living ordinary lives, some with dogs, some with rucksacks and walking sticks, others with young children wrapped up against the cold and already complaining about the length of the walk. Each person smiled, nodded or said 'Good Morning', to which Kate numbly replied, in the hope that normal contact might ground them both in some sort of reality. When they reached the end of the bank, Kate guided Margret away from the lane to The Old Pilot's House and along the footpath in the direction of the Boathouse, turning up the short road to the pub.

Margret pulled away. 'No, I can't face Phil, don't tell him what I've told you, *ever*.'

'I won't, but we need to let him know you're ok. Leave it to me, you can sleep in the B&B, you need sleep before you do anything else, you promised me.'

'No, I didn't.'

'You need some energy for whatever lies ahead.' Kate looked at Margret and smoothed back all the unruly grey hair which – now no longer assaulted by the wind – covered her face like a veil. A wan smile spread across Margret's face.

Grace was setting the tables for lunch; Phil stopped polishing the glass he was holding and glared. 'Thanks for letting me know you are both still with us. Grace, look what the wind's blown in at last.' He noticed Margret's appearance, Kate's concern. 'Are you alright? You both look like you've seen a ghost.'

Kate steered Margret towards the bar. 'We were up on the embankment and she came over a bit faint … she's a little,' – Kate mouthed the word very quietly behind Margret's back – '*confused* … I don't want to leave her alone till she's feeling better. Can I take her upstairs to rest?'

'Sure, help yourselves, we're so pleased you're both ok,' said Grace.

Margret allowed herself to be led through to the stairs.

'Hang on there, we've got something we need to tell you,' began Phil.

Grace glared at him – 'Not now, Phil, it can wait.'

Kate helped Margret into bed and settled her down to sleep without any resistance. Thankful to have some time to think, she sat in the chair and went over Margret's story, but came to a brick wall when she considered how to prevent the horrific self-destruction that was about to take place. Her initial euphoria at the thought of destroying Sye had left as soon as she'd tried to come up with a feasible plan. What hope was there against the power he had mustered to draw her so close to the same abyss Margret faced? Defeat seemed inherent in all the options. Kate had no weaponry in this war for Margret's life, whereas *he'd* been able to summon up all those good memories from the past. How had he done that, what had he done to the mind of the one he'd treated so cruelly? It was not beyond Kate to imagine. In truth, Margret had been preparing for this for over forty years. Sye had seen to that.

Having failed to come up with any answers, Kate went downstairs to the bar, in need of company. Should she tell Phil and Grace? Grace had lived for some time in a country steeped in deities living in the hearts of those who believed in spirits; perhaps she would understand. But Margret had been so insistant about not telling Phil.

As she walked down the stairs she glanced at some of the photographs lined up on the wall. Starting with sepia prints of the quayside in front of the Boathouse, they traced a family history, becoming more modern with colour photographs by the time she reached the bottom of the stairs. Most featured people, boats and often a trusty dog. Of them all, one image held her – a young man up to his knees in water, standing next to an old dinghy. Underneath, handwritten, was – *WILLIAM 1948-1968.*

Kate became aware that Phil was watching her. 'Is she ok?' he asked.

'To be honest, I'm not sure. Who's this?'

'That's my Uncle William. I never met him. Dad's younger brother – died in the 1968 storm I think – it had a big effect on Dad, he never really talked about it or recovered from losing him.'

Another life stolen by Sye, thought Kate.

They walked into the bar together. Phil switched moods. He was bursting with something important to say: 'As I was saying before you disappeared upstairs, I've got some news for you – we're getting married!'

Grace was smiling over in the alcove, holding a tray full of dirty plates recently cleared.

Kate burst into tears. Phil flung his arms around her.

'Tears of joy, I hope,' he said.

The bar door opened and slammed shut.

'Get your bloody hands off my wife!'

Grace put the tray down and calmly walked over to Mark to introduce herself.

33

FACING FACTS

Mark kept apologising. He couldn't believe his own stupidity once the misunderstanding had been cleared up. Phil and Grace tried to lighten things by attempting to bring out the funny side and offered drinks all round, but this added to Mark's embarrassment. If he'd had a wish to be granted there and then it would have been for human beings to have a rewind button, or an erase mechanism to give him means to escape the discomfort consuming him. He grabbed a pint and fled to sit outside the back of the pub at one of the deserted picnic tables.

* * *

'I'll give him some time to take it all in and go out in a minute. I'm sorry he stole your moment, it's great news about you getting married.' It was Kate's turn to feel embarrassed, if Mark could jump to conclusions, so could Grace. 'Grace you have nothing to worry about, with me. Phil's a great friend, and that's it, nothing else, trust me.'

'Don't worry, Kate, the thought never crossed my mind, we'll celebrate properly another time.'

Phil held open the bar door. 'Go on, sort him out, he's suffering.'

'Keep an eye on Margret, give me a shout if you hear any movement up there,' said Kate.

'I will,' he replied. 'I don't know, that room's becoming a sanctuary rather than a B&B, first your mate Dom and now Margret.'

A cold realisation hit Kate: Mark hadn't been the only one who'd made wrong assumptions. The mere mention of Dom made her see that her husband's reaction earlier had revealed how wrong she'd been. *Relief* – and shame at the words she'd spoken to both Mark and Dom with such little proof.

'Are you ok?' said Phil, putting his hand on her shoulder.

'Mark's not been the only one jumping to conclusions.'

'What do you mean?'

'Sorry Phil, that's for another time, if ever. Nothing personal, but it involves someone else's life story.' She smiled at Phil and Grace who both looked confused at the drama that was playing out under their roof. And it was meant to be *their* day, thought Kate.

When she saw Mark sitting alone outside the pub, Kate stood and looked at the man who was the complete antithesis of what Sye had turned out to be. She sat down next to him; his tired eyes bored into the brick wall of the shed opposite.

'There's no autocue on that wall you know,' said Kate.

He put his head in his hands. 'If there had been a chance, a small chance for us … I've messed it up haven't I?'

'Not you. I'm the one who's messed up,' she said.

'You had a point, about Joe, Mum, the way I let things …'

'Not now, Mark.'

'Why?'

Kate took a deep breath, 'I've two things to ask you:

one is, that after I explain what has been going on here you believe me, and the other is that you help me – however you end up feeling. Or rather, *you help Margret*.'

'Margret? What's she got to do with …?'

'Everything. She saved me but I can't save her, not on my own.'

'I think you need to explain.'

'I'm trying to Mark, it's not easy.'

He turned to listen, straddled the seat of the bench and waited.

Kate gathered her thoughts and then continued, 'You need to stay with me on this, even if at the end of my telling you this story you question my sanity … but it's not a story, remember that. Accept what I say as true, it happened, *it's real*. I am, for the record, quite sane; I'm not sure how I've remained so, but I am now.'

'You're not making a lot of sense.'

'Whatever you think of me when you've heard everything, you have to put those feelings aside because the next thing we have to do is to help Margret. Don't even try to analyse our relationship, or rant at me or get into speaking the truth about myself that I already know. I'll give you ample opportunity later, I owe you that. But right now there isn't time. Margret could wake at any minute.'

'Ok, I get it, Margret first. If it helps make up for wrongly accusing you of being unfaithful.'

Kate blushed. 'You're not going to like what's coming, let alone understand it.' She searched for the right words. Where to begin? Would he even believe her?

'You've started now,' he said, 'you have to …'

'I *have* been unfaithful, not in body but in my head, in my mind. I wanted something I thought you couldn't give me and that was the moment Sye was watching and waiting for.'

'Sye?' It was the first and last time Mark ever said his name.

As Kate spoke, it was her turn to stare at the wall, her eyes taking in the shape of the red bricks, the pathways the cement had been forced to travel along, the nooks and crannies of age. Kate looked at anything except Mark.

Mark said nothing when she'd finished. Kate left him no chance; she started to shake uncontrollably and couldn't stop. Her own body seemed angrier with her than the recipient of such an extraordinary account of events. Perhaps he simply didn't believe her; in the cold light of day, sitting outside the pub in a world of normality, Kate hardly believed herself.

He took off his coat and put it around her shoulders. It was a gesture that seemed to take for ever; life in slow motion. 'Let's see if they've lit the fire in there yet,' he eventually said.

'Don't tell them.'

'But Phil needs to know what happened to his relative – that young man – Will.'

'Not yet. I wasn't there. It's for Margret to tell him, and hopefully one day she'll be able to.'

'You're right.'

'About time I was right about something, isn't it?'

'Remember what you said, I'm not getting into that now – Margret first, us later.'

Kate touched his hands, they were so cold. 'Thanks Mark.'

'Let's go. Shouldn't we check on Margret? We can make a game plan while she sleeps and then you'll be there when she wakes.'

'This isn't a game, far from it. I only wish it was.'

They walked back into the pub together. Mark looked sheepishly at Phil and thanked him for the beer as Kate showed him the way through the bar to the stairs.

Finding Margret still sound asleep, Kate sat herself at the small desk in front of the window and pulled out the crumpled poem from her pocket.

'What's that?' asked Mark.

'Their poem.' She looked up at him, 'I thought it was … I was wrong … I'm so sorry.'

Mark put his finger on her lips and then took it away. 'Read it again with new eyes, read it for clues and see if there's anything there that can break his hold on Margret.'

Kate re-read the poem and was mortified by her own previous pleasure in sentiments which now shouted their inherent selfishness: *no more worries, cares or demands of others, just your needs … our Timescape.* Those words accused her. She admitted her guilt and acknowledged a new world in which she was no longer the centre. Instead she knew that what was needed of her from now on, was to think about how she could affect those other than herself – to interact as part of the whole. She celebrated this missing part of herself slotting into place, the part that had never been nurtured or allowed to grow. It felt different and it felt good; she owed Margret.

Margret stirred a little in her sleep. Panic immobilised Kate's introspection. 'What can we do, how can we stop her? We need to protect her.'

'You *can* stop her,' said Mark quietly. 'Give her some self-worth, here in the present. She's got to see that Mae has long gone, left behind on that night in 1968 as surely as that man left behind true human existence. Make her understand that Mae is just an echo inside the woman she's become.'

Kate couldn't hide her surprise, 'How come you're so good at this, all of a sudden?'

'I've had a lot of practice sorting out the angst of others.'

'Since when?'

'At work, all those kids, all those teenagers with their problems. Half my job's turned into dealing with their welfare in that place.'

'So why couldn't you talk to me, or Joe?'

'Probably all talked out by the end of the day. And family's different. I'd have had to deal with my own feelings then. Other people's feelings are far easier to handle.'

He nodded in the direction of Margret, 'I don't think she should wake up and find me here. I'll be downstairs. You can do this, you know you can.'

When he left the room, Kate's panic returned; it was as if she was sitting on the top of a high rise building trying to talk a suicidal person out of jumping. But then, standing by the bed looking down at Margret, she realised that although she was about to speak to the older woman, it was Mae, the young girl, she was preparing her words to reach. Everything was out of kilter. Kate took hold of Margret's hand and for a moment it was that of the child she'd never had, in crisis and in need of a mother's well-chosen words.

Slowly Margret woke and sat up in the bed. 'You won't change my mind you know.'

'Please let me try.'

'You can try but you know how strong Sye is. You were willing to do this for him not so long ago. My tie to him goes way back. It's always been with me – waiting.' Margret smiled at Kate. 'You're so kind to try. Particularly as I stepped between you and Sye back there in the attic. I saw what you felt for him and what he had done to you. I'm sorry.'

'Don't be, you saved me. I don't think it was him I loved. It was what he was pretending to offer. Contentment. Freedom? Hardly! I think there is only one person who can find that for me and that's myself. I have to reach out for it, not wait for it to land in my plate like some sort of hedonistic feast.'

'So you're trying to save me to make yourself feel good.'

'That's not true,' said Kate, 'but to be honest I'm no longer sure who I'm trying to save, Margret, Mae, me? Perhaps all of us. What I do know is that I care about you and so do the people downstairs – Phil, Grace and … Mark.'

'Mark's here?'

'Downstairs. He came back.'

'You all have someone then …'

'You're *not* alone,' said Kate urgently.

'Margret isn't, but Mae is.' With a look of total determination, Margret threw back the duvet and got out of bed. 'My mind's made up, I'm ready to take the risk of whatever Sye has to offer. I've been alone for too long.'

Any argument was wasted.

Margret continued, 'Go and build a new life with Mark. He's a good man. Open up with each other and deal with all that was stifling your relationship. Don't leave it Kate, look what that did to Sye and myself. *We* left things and it destroyed us. This is something I have to do to make up for the past.' Margret grabbed Kate's hands, 'What have I got to lose? I have a choice – a slow decline into old age or reliving my youth with Sye. I choose Sye.'

'But that's not what he's offering,' replied Kate. 'Look at his track record. Everything is about *him*. This connection with you is about *his* survival not yours. He's using you. Having broken you in 1968 he's trying to do it all over again.'

Margret let go of Kate's hands and looked away. Kate felt sure she was wavering.

'I'll help you make up for the past,' said Kate, 'help you now, in the present … *you can have a future.*'

'But … you can't do that, it was all lost when I let him pretend to be me with the paintings – I gave away my identity. There's no way Mae can ever find herself now and become the person she set out to be.'

'You *can* get her back; *Margret* has fostered all that early talent, and with help you can become Mae again if you want and let her find herself as a painter.'

Margret hesitated and then shook her head slowly, 'There are too many wasted years in between.'

'No! I've seen those new landscapes in your cottage. Cut yourself free of Sye and you can sell or exhibit those in your own right. I'll help you. I'm winding up the business with Dom. You have two houses, one could become a studio. You can paint and I can run part of it as a gallery, do the marketing. It's what I'm good at. I could stay out here with you.'

'And what about Mark?'

'Mark and I? I don't know. Whatever happens we can work around it. I don't know if there is a future for us but I do know he wants to help you too. It's what *you* do next that matters to us both right now.'

'It's no good, I've made my mind up. You've helped me. By making me say my decision out loud, it's made it real. Be happy for me.'

Margret walked over and hugged Kate who could not find it within herself to reciprocate, submerged as she was in a state of utter failure and fear. With nothing left to offer she watched as Margret picked up her coat, put it on and left the sanctuary of Phil's B&B.

34

BEYOND THE DUNES

Kate ran down the stairs to see the door of the pub closing behind Margret. As she reached Mark she knew failure was written all over her face; he didn't need to ask the question. She hurried him outside, pushing through a surprised group of out-of-season tourists.

Together, they sheltered from the bitter east coast wind in the flint-pebbled porch; Kate was shaking and had to concentrate hard to put a coherent sentence together. 'She's going to do it … I couldn't stop her,' she whispered as two locals arrived, nodding acquaintance as they made their way into the pub.

Mark pulled Kate through to the car park and spoke in a low voice. 'Did she say how – how she's going to … ?'

'You mean commit suicide. Let's be honest and say it out loud. No, I haven't got a clue as to what she's planning but I'm in no doubt that she's going to the attic – Sye is pulling her to him. Believe me, it's Sye who will determine what happens next.'

'We *have* to stop her,' said Mark. 'But I suspect your *ghost* won't let us do that. He seems more than capable when it comes to the art of mind control.' His eyes sought Kate's as she coloured with guilt. The thought of how, in almost every way, she had been unfaithful to Mark hovered over them like a bird of prey.

'Believe me, I've tried to pull her away from him. I did as you suggested, tried to persuade her to chose life, not Sye – to see what she could have ahead of her in the real world.'

'I hope *you* can see that too,' Mark replied.

They made their way towards Kate's via the quayside, to make sure that Margret hadn't gone back home first. Their knock on the door at Fisherman's Cottage was unanswered.

'He must have given you some clue, a message or idea as to what he expected of you – some indication during all that time you were with him. Was there nothing in that poem?'

Kate stopped in her tracks. From the back pocket of her jeans she pulled out the poem again, but it tore in two; trembling fingers finally managed to piece it together.

'The beach – it will happen at the beach – look.'

Written in Sye's scrawled writing were those words deliberately chosen, not for her, but – for Mae:

Peace of mind, of soul,
to join together, forever
beyond ourselves
in the Timescape Sea.

Mark read the words and responded immediately, 'Right, I'll cover the goal while you mark Margret.'

'And in English that means?'

'Sorry – what I mean is, that if I get out to the beach and you check if Margret's at your place, we'll cover both eventualities.'

'I can't go in, he'll know I'm there. Sye's so strong now, he can see into my mind.'

'You said the confrontation with you both weakened him.'

'Yes, that's why he faded, but he always comes back stronger and with the knowledge of Margret's determination to join him – when that realisation happens – I'm so frightened of what he'll be able to do.'

'You've got to keep trying Kate. Get her out of the house somehow. But I agree, don't go in.'

'I'll try, but how do we know we're right, about the poem, about the beach? Stay with me Mark.'

'I'm confident your instincts are right … he planted the seed of what he wanted in your mind with the poem … sometimes you have to follow your instincts.'

'That's not done me much good, so far.'

'We'll have to trust mine then,' he said, pulling her close; Kate didn't push him away. She felt safe for the first time since Sye had sent her adrift. Then, without another word, he began jogging towards the beach. Kate watched him go, bereft of his presence; she had never needed him so much.

Moments later, she tried to open the front door of The Old Pilot's House – it was bolted. She lifted the heavy, wrought-iron, door knocker and slammed it against the door repeatedly – taking out on it her frustration, knowing that Sye was going to get the better of them all. Just as Kate decided she would have to break the kitchen window with one of the large pebbles edging the gravel drive, the bolt shot back.

Margret appeared in the doorway, looking composed, but pale. Her words to Kate were firm, 'Please leave me to do what I need to do. Don't try and talk me out of this again.' She wrapped her coat around herself underscoring her intention to shut Kate out and marched off towards the coastal path Mark had recently followed.

'So where are you going? I thought he only existed inside that room,' Kate shouted after her.

Margret stopped, turned and spoke as one converted to a cause. 'When I stand there at the water's edge, when the tide is right, the cycle will be complete. He'll be there. *Our Timescape moment will happen Kate*, that's the only moment in which we can be as one. *Don't interfere.*'

'But why the beach?' said Kate, reaching Margret and moving in front of her to block the way, wildly playing for time, trying to think of a way to inspire a change of heart.

'Because the beach is where ... the storm led him that morning. I've kept my promise you see. I kept looking out for him and now I have *listened to Sye* ... telling me exactly what happened.'

'You've been up in the attic with Sye? Is he there now?'

'He was ... he told me how his boat smashed into another and that he was thrown against the groynes much further out along the embankment; he managed to cling on to one of the posts and pulled himself along from one section to another. Somehow he made it up to the top of the ridge – you see Sye watched me walk away. *As you are going to do with me.*'

Kate grasped Margret's arm.

Margret wrenched away Kate's hand and fixed her eyes on the route along the embankment out to the dunes. 'You need to understand. He sobered up with the shock of the storm, remembered the night before and couldn't face me – or rather he couldn't face himself – so he turned to the sea instead. He apparently waded along the top of the embankment, which stood just below the water level. When eventually it disappeared altogether, he was forced to swim. As soon as he was out of his depth, it happened: one minute the sea was cold and angry, the next the water was warm and calm; it buoyed him up and carried him to what was left of the dunes – he described it as dreamlike, otherworldly …'

'How could that happen? The sea was destroying everything else,' said Kate. 'Perhaps he was still stoned, hallucinating … but he should have stayed put, he might have been rescued.'

'He – had – made – his – decision! Weren't you listening when I told you before! *It was suicide,* not some comic book hero adventure to save Will. Sye looked to where the beach beyond the dunes should have been – our beach – and chose to keep going. *It was my fault.* He said I drove him to it … my talent, my paintings … he knew he could never match my success and would always be King of *Nothing.*'

'No it wasn't you – it was his *own* selfish weakness, you have to see that.'

'DON'T!' Margret's angry eyes were somehow manifesting as Sye's now, demanding Kate to move out of the way. She staggered back in shock, powerless to stop Margret from getting past.

As Kate started to follow, Margret stopped and shouted, 'DON'T TRY AND STOP ME! Sye's so strong now. You've seen what he did to the house. He's capable of so much more. DON'T COME NEAR ME!'

Margret began to steadily chant those familiar words usually accompanied by the sitar in Sye's attic, and set off again towards the ridge to begin her journey. With each step away from Kate, the chanting began to die on the biting wind buffeting the embankment. Kate watched and waited, convinced that this incantation was Margret's way of tuning into Sye to keep his message strong and clear – blocking any other persuasive voices which threatened to weaken her indoctrinated thoughts.

When Margret had become a small figure in the distance, Kate followed behind, along the raised coastal path, never more aware that its fortification was the only defence holding the sea back from all it desired to engulf. Keeping to what she judged as a safe distance she was surprised at the effort it took to match the pace Margret set up ahead. Instead of slowing down as the lengthy trek progressed, which would be the case for most women of her age and stature, Margret took up a faster pace, hurrying to meet her terrible destiny. It would be up to Mark now. Falling even further behind, sight of Margret was lost – until Kate anxiously turned the last corner to spot someone disappearing into the dunes.

Frustrated at being unable to get there more quickly, Kate increased her pace and slipped on the uneven path, turning her ankle. A forbidding thought forced itself upon her consciousness – *this is where it all began, with a sore ankle – and now it will be where it all ends for Margret.* For the second time that day there was no bird cry, no sound from the sea; even the wind had given up its fight. This, Kate knew, was Sye's last manipulative message – all his doing. Terrified by what she was about to witness, Kate ignored the pain; propelled forward by fears, not solely for Margret. Sye wouldn't be expecting Mark, but if Mark intervened what might Sye do?

Kate reached the man-made wooden path leading to the sand dunes and painfully negotiated up and over the first mound to slide down the dip in the dunes, the loose sand causing her feet to disappear from under her. Looking up, Kate could see she still had to conquer the next, much steeper, incline to reach the summit of the last dune which would hopefully give a clear view of the beach. It seemed insurmountable.

Suddenly Mark was there. He tried to help her up the slope, 'Where's Margret? What happened?' he asked.

Kate stopped and stared at him, 'What do you mean? She must have passed you, you *must* have seen her.'

'No, she's not been this way, just a young girl a few minutes ago.'

'What did she look like?' asked Kate not waiting for an answer but making one last push to the top of the dune.

'Cropped hair, thin, pale,' came Mark's voice from behind her. 'I thought she was a bit odd – singing to herself – in a world of her own I think.'

'No – in Sye's world,' said Kate, '– *look*!' Mae stood at the water's edge holding hands with Sye. 'I knew it – we're too late – there's Sye with her.'

'Where?'

'There, standing next to her, holding her hand, that's *him!*'

'She's alone Kate. The girl, not Margret.'

'What … *see*, he's there, he's leading her in, now!'

Kate was aware that Mark was staring at her as if he was beginning to really doubt her sanity; but the girl she called Mae *was* wading out into the water with Sye, up to her knees in the surf, her coat thrown down not that far from where the white breakers met the sand. Kate limped to the water's edge. The unrelenting tide reached much further up the beach than she'd seen before; coming ever closer to the dunes.

'Margret ... Mae!' Kate stripped off her coat, threw it on top of Margret's, dragged off her boots and socks and felt the pull of the sand forcing its will between her toes as the waves stole the ground underfoot. With the next wave, a warm surge encased her. The air was infused with a stifling heat, comparable to stepping off a plane in foreign climes. Next came the sweet smell of imminent rain heralding a breaking summer storm. An electrified sheet of lightning sliced through the threatening clouds into the turbulent waves and the world turned turquoise as the light caught the edges of the clouds, reflecting onto a sea which had slipped back in time to that freak July storm in 1968.

'Kate, stop, don't go in.' Mark's voice reached out, lost behind, as the ruptured sky gave way to torrential rain. Kate could see the rain had formed a wall between the time and space she inhabited and Mark on the other side, standing on dry sand, confused, beached and unable to act. She looked back into the storm at the same moment as Sye turned languidly to meet her gaze. He smiled, and let go of Margret's hand to punch his fist up to the sky – a small gesture but clear in its triumphant purpose. Despite the oppressive heat engulfing Kate, the blood in her veins chilled.

35

STRANDED

Kate knew she was beaten. It was over. Sye had won.

In desolation she went to turn towards Mark but her eye caught a small movement within the rising arc of the next wave. It was Mae turning too, appearing to step away from Sye. One step towards the shore. The huge wave which had begun its swell far out in the ocean, reached its zenith and plunged into foam strong enough to knock the slight young girl off balance. She disappeared below the surface. As Mae fought to regain her footing, Sye reached out and grabbed at her arm.

With surprise Kate perceived what was happening; Mae was not only struggling against the ebb and flow of the waves but also struggling *against* Sye! He was trying in vain to hold onto the life he wanted. Another strong wave came. Although it wasn't deep at that point, Mae was torn away from Sye and went under. He searched frantically, splashing the water all around in a blind panic that the sea would rob him of her suicide. Of course, thought Kate, for him Mae's death *must* be at her own hand; it had to be her choice – to give herself to the sea, not to be taken. And then, quite calmly, in contrast to Sye, *Margret* not Mae reappeared a couple of arm-lengths away from him. It was enough. She regained her balance and moved towards Kate, who likewise went to her – they met in the shallow breakers and held onto each other.

Both looked to where Sye was still standing, waist high in the sea, struggling to keep his balance every time a wave came. He stared back at them for what seemed like an eternity and as the strength of supporting one another empowered both women, they watched him get weaker and begin to fade. He then faced towards the seaward horizon, seeming to make a determined choice between the ocean and the land. It was a massive wave that took him under.

Watching, mesmerised, as wave after wave continued to wash over the spot where Sye had stood, the temperature dropped as Kate and Margret huddled together, frozen in the water and frozen in time.

Shuddering uncontrollably, Margret held Kate by the shoulders and looked at her squarely. 'I was never going with him, to be dragged back into the past ... your words, in the pub, saved me. *You offered me a future* – but I couldn't let him pick up that thought my mind ... I had to convince him I was totally his ... totally with him. By making *you* absolutely believe in my commitment to Sye, I convinced *him* ... that's why I sang every Beatles song I could remember all the way here.' She took a breath and gained more control, 'I had to keep my determination intact and block out what you'd said, to get him out here, away from the room – to fool him I almost fooled myself. I'm sorry I made it so hard for you.'

By the end of this speech Margret's skin was as grey as her hair, her lips blue. Kate somehow managed to drag them both towards the shore where they paused again to look back and stare in disbelief that Sye had truly gone, wary of him rematerialising at any moment to continue to haunt them both for ever.

Mark's voice broke the quiet that had replaced the deranged clamour of the storm, 'MY GOD, WHAT THE HELL …'

They turned to see his distraught face. He was surrounded in every direction by thousands and thousands of stranded starfish, washed up on the beach, victims of the sea along with Sye. The three of them were rooted to the spot staring from left to right to see how far the wash of orange and pink extended – stretching for as far as their eyes could see, glistening in what was now glorious sunlight. They had all been victims of time: the two witnesses to Sye's 'death', the confused onlooker and the myriads of inert creatures.

Margret was the first to move. Despite the cold and her soaking wet condition she ran amongst the starfish, picking up any that showed signs of life, shouting: 'Get them to the shallows … must get them to the shallows.'

Kate left Mark to gather up the coats and boots and approached Margret who was becoming increasingly hysterical in the struggle to return the starfish back to the sea. '*I must save them, I must save …*'

Margret sank down onto her knees exhausted, her trembling hands full of the lifeless creatures. When Mark arrived to offer the warmth of her coat, she looked at him showing no spark of recognition and dropped the starfish one at a time. They were all dead except for the last one left in her hand, it had lost a limb but it moved … there was still life.

The words Batty had spoken returned to Kate – *all the voyage of their life, is bound in shallows and in miseries.* And she understood the need to seize the moment in the same way as Margret herself had done when she'd let go of Sye's hand. Trying not to harm it further, Kate lifted the starfish from Margret's care. 'This one's mine to save I think,' she said, before wading back into the sea, up to her knees, to place the creature in its natural habitat. She hoped she'd given it a small chance of survival – to find its way to a world beyond the shallows out of sight of the death and destruction of its own kind.

On her return, she found Mark trying to rub the circulation back into Margret's hands. Kate took her in her arms again and once more they began to take benefit from the comfort of the other's embrace, whilst each wept silent tears.

Mark prised the two apart. 'Come on, make room for me, walking back will soon warm you. I can't honestly say I understand what I've witnessed, or … what I haven't witnessed. He was messing with my head as much as yours. But you're both still here in my reality. I presume you're real and he's no longer with us?'

'Oh yes,' said Margret. 'I'm sure he can't come back; he was so desperate … that moment was his Timescape window and I refused to open it.'

'I think the starfish suffered from his anger, his ending spawned this destruction,' said Kate, still unable to take her eyes off those who'd perished. Holding hands, whilst trying in vain not to tread disrespectfully on the dead, the three of them finally reached the other side of the barrier formed by those doomed creatures. They made their way up into the dunes from where they took one last look at nature's strandings littering the shoreline.

'Whatever caused them to be carried to the shore must have been a … freak of nature,' said Mark.

'Like Sye,' added Margret.

'I'm sure he's really gone,' said Kate. 'Can't you feel that the whole atmosphere has changed? The wind has dropped, the sea is calm now. We'll have an easier walk back than we had on the way here.' She grimaced as she sat down on the sand to put on her boots. 'How am I ever going to get back with this ankle!'

'Easy,' said Mark. 'Lean on me.'

Part 3

"The storm has passed:
I hear the birds rejoicing ..."

Translated from: La quiete dopo la tempesta
Giacomo Leopardi

36

THE GAP

Up on the highest point of the Boathouse roof: claws hold on tight, unblinking eyes look across the staithe to the sweeping bow of the horizon. A distressed landscape. All recognisable landmarks have morphed into something vaguely familiar … something from a previous incarnation? Tips of masts toss about, failing to offer a perch. The storm forces take off. She has no wings; expectation … to plummet.

*

Awake with a jolt, eyes wide open – the sensation of plummeting still with her; Mae closes her eyes in an attempt to return to the point of oblivion, but bad dreams always stop short.

*

Self-imposed wakefulness became a necessity – to avoid dreams which would, if given full rein, reach out to the past for material to work with. At night, deliberately conscious, despite the immense exhaustion Mae existed in during each day, she held her mind carefully in the gap between past and present. If she concentrated hard on nothingness, the gap would expand to become a safe place to be; and then sometimes she could allow herself to sleep. This effort involved blanking out every single past experience which had led, directly or indirectly, to anyone who had suffered at the whim of Sye. In this way her mind wiped out her previous existence; it was hard work, like preparing an old canvas to be repainted, sanding down the ridges to ensure none of the texture came through. Logic dictated to her fragile mind that by destroying the one persona, the 'other' she had become, could never exist either. That was the past and present dealt with.

But what of the future? So simple; without the recognition of 'self', there was no need for a future. And so the gap widened and engulfed her. 'Stay in the gap,' she said to herself. In that case she wouldn't need wings and as long as she didn't attempt to land anywhere – past, present or future – she would be safe. She would not plummet.

During the daytime she couldn't, wouldn't, speak. Why was everyone trying to pull her from the gap? They all seemed to think it their responsibility to wrench her away from the safe haven she had found, as if 'it' was the danger itself. They didn't grasp the concept as she did; they couldn't see what she knew was the right way to exist. All of them, Mark, Kate, Phil. Yesterday even Joe had asked her to go crabbing, to the staithe would you believe – the one place she knew was dangerous for her – did they think she could be forced from the gap? Too cruel. It made her tremble. 'Stay in the gap,' she said to herself.

But for Grace.

She set up her easel next to where Mae was working in the outbuilding Phil had cleared. It made a good studio, provided that the door was left open to let in the natural light. They worked wrapped up in layers of jumpers and coats, with fingerless gloves helping to keep their hands warm. Mae worked from her collection of inland photographs, painting clusters of buildings set in an empty Norfolk landscape drifting into the sky; buildings she'd never been in that belonged to other lives, other stories, not hers.

Grace had no expectation of two-way conversation. She simply explained to Mae that what she wanted to do was to use her own photographs from India to record on canvas the emotions she had experienced out there. She'd talked about how photographs helped retain the memories but that she wanted to somehow capture, in her own paintings, the sensory experience. Grace asked Mae to show her how to mix the right colours for the moods, the scents, the very taste of India.

Mae found that she was beginning to enjoy her attempts to share knowledge – still without talking – with purely a brush to express herself. In doing so, she began to rediscover her own ability to articulate emotion on canvas, by proxy when demonstrating at Grace's easel. It proved an impossible skill to teach – this innate ability; Grace would often grimace at her own efforts, but would always pick up her brush again and persevere, day in, day out. A new form of 'present' grew in their silence; working alongside each other, the gap within Mae's mind began to shrink.

It took weeks before Mae dared to freely express her emotions within her own paintings, but when she did, the formality of a photograph to trigger ideas became less necessary. As the year began to warm, coats and gloves were abandoned. New images of landscapes were created where the buildings became less important and nature ruled; depictions of stark cruel winters – with somewhere, almost secreted, an intimation of spring returning. Silently, she accepted that conflict and pain do create the artist.

When it felt safe enough, with several large canvases completed – proudly leaning against all the walls of the studio – Mae was ready. She had fashioned a stronghold around herself using her completed works, and from the positive energy formed within the physical space these paintings created, she began to face her memories – little by little. And little by little, Mae from the past grew closer to Margret in the present.

37

A CHANGE OF USE

Sadie stared out of the open window, right across the marshes to Scolt Head.

'These weekends are cool, I never knew anywhere could be so … massive,' she said.

Seeing her oblivious to everything other than the view, Joe rushed over to grab the whitewash brush she was holding – before it dripped on the newly polished floorboards. At last they'd finished their job of touching up the careless marks made by those who'd hung the pictures.

'Even so,' she continued, 'you can't quite make out the sea from here. You can hear it though, can't you? That rumble which I first thought was far off thunder, but now I know it's the waves breaking on the beach. You can smell it and you can sort of spot where the … you know … the rivery bit meets the sea, but then it tricks you – it vanishes over the horizon and behind the dunes. *Please* walk out there with me, why won't you?'

'It's too far,' said Joe, pulling a face. 'Kate and Dad were always trying to drag me out there when we were on holidays here. It's boring, walking all that way.'

'It wouldn't be boring with me.'

'Ask Kate, she'll go with you.'

'I asked her, she said she was busy. I asked your dad as well, but he didn't seem keen.'

Joe too easily remembered those past holidays when he would be forced to head out to the beach, and was surprised that neither his dad nor Kate had jumped at the chance to go with Sadie. Adults are so unpredictable, he thought. He looked around the attic which to him seemed much bigger than when they'd started, its four windows inviting the sunlight to illuminate the brushstrokes of each work of art displayed on the walls.

'I still can't get over being up here,' he said, keen to change the subject. 'Not after all those times when I used to lie in bed downstairs and imagine the attic as a black hole in space.' The contrast between his childhood imagination and present reality was as dazzling to him as the white space he stood in.

'Seems ok to me.'

'When we first came up, there was something creepy about this room.'

'What, that it was full of ghosts or something?' said Sadie. 'Think logically, with all this empty space, where could a ghost hide? I think somehow we'd notice one hanging about. Or perhaps it's holding on outside, by its fingertips, below the window-sill.' She leaned out to reach the catch and shut the window. 'That's that one sorted then,' she said as she high-fived Joe, her eyes laughing at him.

She continued to take in the view. 'If I were a ghost, I'd haunt the footpaths out there in the middle of the night and hope to gate-crash a zombie party! That would be real cool, better than being stuck in an attic waiting for someone to turn up one day.'

Joe stood behind her, put his arms around her waist and his chin on her shoulder. 'Your hair smells of paint,' he said.

'Thanks a lot, loser, *boyfriends* have to do better than that.'

'*Sor – ree,* but I like the smell of paint … it's felt good covering up these walls … it's like … we've painted out anyone who's lived here in the past.'

'That's fine then, we don't want anyone watching what we get up to, do we?' Sadie teased, before pulling up his T-shirt. 'Let's have another look.'

Her fingers traced around the tattoo on his shoulder which had their names clearly entwined. Joe seized Sadie's hand and spun her round to hold her again.

'Wish we had a mattress …' she said.

* * *

Lying on Mae's mattress in Fisherman's Cottage, Kate needed to rouse herself to get ready for the meal out in Burnham Market that evening. However, she was still mentally ticking off the extensive 'to do' list she'd started the day with. It had been exhausting, completing the final preparations for the Gallery opening. At last all the paintings had been hung and tomorrow Mae would see that almost everything was in place, as Kate had promised. It was annoying that the blinds hadn't arrived on time, however they'd be sorted out next week; being able to adjust the light in the room according to the time of day would mean that any damage to the artwork could be avoided, particularly when the sun streamed in through the large window. The notion of too much light had been quite a problem, but they'd been determined to overcome it.

To use the attic as the Gallery had been the right thing to do – they'd all agreed; to abandon the place would have given Sye the satisfaction of having won.

Over the first course Kate and Mark congratulated themselves on the successful completion of the work on The Old Pilot's House, now renamed The Pilot's Gallery.

'You've helped so much these last few weekends,' said Kate.

Mark poured the wine. 'It's been pretty good, considering.'

'Joe and Sadie have enjoyed it too.'

'And his birthday outing to the windmill.'

'Quite like old times,' she said.

'I can't believe he's sixteen now.'

Kate grimaced, 'Exams soon.'

'He'll be ok, he's been hard at it – and when they're done with, he can pack up the house while I work out my notice till the end of term.'

'That'll keep him busy, no doubt Sadie will help out too. She's better placed to keep an eye on him than we are, I wouldn't want to think of him falling back, getting depressed again. Are you sure all that's stopped?'

'He's good now he's looking forward to his future – much more than most of the kids at school. He's really single-minded about his singing.'

Much to Kate's discomfort, Mark began to praise her for pulling everything together with the Gallery. Alone together for the first time, she craved his chastisement … wanting to pay her penance.

She turned the focus back to Joe: 'I'm so pleased he's going to do the music course in Leamington.'

'Mum and Dad are excited about him staying with them in the week while he's at college,' said Mark. 'And of course Sadie's over the moon.'

'Those two have it all mapped out you know, if he ends up studying singing in London, as he hopes to, she's going to apply for the London School of Psychology – wants to do some type of counselling eventually – she told me today.'

'Now why doesn't that surprise me?' said Mark.

'Well she's had lots of opportunity for work experience …'

Mark shifted in his seat. 'I'd forgotten how sure you are at that age that life will fit the plans you make.'

The conversation came to a halt.

Kate delved around inside her head for a way to lighten the atmosphere but decided that whatever she said would probably sound glib. She smoothed out her napkin, folded it and waited.

Mark brushed his hand through his hair. 'I'm glad Batty's happy to drive all this way for the opening tomorrow. It'll make a good break for them with their stop-over in Cambridge tonight.'

'It's a shame we won't be able to get your mother upstairs to see Mae's work.'

'Don't worry, she's looking forward to orchestrating the refreshments from the kitchen, with her two waiting staff.'

'Lucky Joe and Sadie!'

When they'd finished their dessert, Mark pulled the conversation back to Kate. He held his glass up to her. 'It was a brilliant idea of yours to get Phil to sort out the outbuildings behind the pub for Mae's new studio.'

There he was again, trying to put her on a pedestal … 'It

wasn't my idea, it was Phil's – *and* to let her the B&B so she can go and paint at any time, day or night.' Kate emptied her glass. 'That day ... he could tell somehow we'd nearly lost her.'

Mark offered the last of the wine; she put her hand over the glass. 'No thanks,' she said. 'Grace has done a great job of befriending Mae and I saw Phil watching her paint the other day; if Grace isn't by her side, he slips in whenever he has the time.'

'Do you think he's worried that Mae might take off like she did before? How much does he know?'

'Not much – and it's really Mae who should do the telling, not me. We have to be thankful that at least the awful silence has gone and she's painting every day now. But I think she'll always be emotionally scarred in some way.'

'Mae's survival through all this – it's down to *you* Kate, all your efforts with the Gallery have been ...'

'No,' she replied, emphatically. 'You're wrong. It's down to *all* of us.'

It was midnight by the time they got back.

Kate offered Mark a cup of coffee before he had to return to the caravan in the pub car park which he rented out from Phil at the weekends.

'So how are you finding Fisherman's Cottage?' asked Mark.

'It's good, a bit basic but it seemed an obvious solution.'

'I thought you would have had enough of being alone in a building, perhaps I ...'

'Quite the opposite, I wasn't *ever* alone over there. At last I've got the space I need to sort myself out.' That's one thing that hasn't changed, thought Kate, I still have the knack of saying the wrong thing at the wrong time.

She tried to see if Mark looked as confused as she felt, but he studiously took two mugs down from the shelf and gave nothing away.

'You've told me about Joe and his plans, but how have you both been getting on together, back in Warwick?' Kate asked as she filled the kettle.

'It's fine. Thanks, as usual, to Sadie.'

'What do you mean?'

'Well it's like you said, work experience. If there are any issues she sits us down and makes us have a full debate ... she gets us going and then totters off on her high heels to push Angela around in that wheelchair. By the way there's a plan for a motorised scooter now.'

'Poor Batty! Can you imagine what it will be like for him with Angela terrorising the neighbourhood? He'll have to ride pillion so he can keep an eye on her. Rather him than me!'

'They've got even grander plans. Their house is full of glamorous cruise brochures.'

'Sounds like Batty has decided to *seize the day*.'

They took their mugs of coffee outside and walked through the back gate to stand looking beyond the staithe, up and out into the clear night sky.

'It's good that you and Joe have opened up to each other.'

'I'm not as hopeless as you think.'

'I don't think that.'

'I told you, I could always sort out other kids with *their* parents – just couldn't deal with all that stuff at home. I'd forgotten how. The day Joe sang at the party forced me.

It was the start. We're pretty much *well good* now – as he would say.' Mark smiled wryly.

'If you ever need to stay back in Warwick with him, over a weekend, or even go away together, I'm fine with it.'

Mark put his hand on Kate's arm. 'And us, what of us?'

At last spoken aloud: the question she'd been asking herself a lot lately. It wasn't as if she didn't know what she wanted any more. It was the fear of hurting him again that haunted her now. There was a need to be as sure as possible that all the threads that had led her to Sye had either been severed, or could be woven into a new pattern with Mark – along with the all the subtler shades they had each discovered since those first few notes Joe had sung so tentatively.

Tomorrow she would be closer to knowing; after the opening, when the punters had gone home. Then the bonfire she had planned for her friends and family to gather around that evening, would be lit. In terms of art it was to be the one 'site specific installation'– designed to enable each spectator to form their own interpretation and to hopefully take away a new view of the future.

'I'm so sorry I let you down.' Kate asked herself why the words seemed so feeble, so pathetically inadequate?

'You didn't.'

'I don't know if you realise exactly what was going on in my head that week in Warwick.'

'Shush … listen, let's leave it all there where it belongs – in the past. And so much may not even have really happened. Remember, on the beach … my experience wasn't your experience. I never saw him … he didn't exist in my reality.'

'But my thoughts were real, I made it easy for Sye.'

Mark shook his head, 'Let's not play the blame game,

sometimes both sides make mistakes. We both got it wrong. I should go now, it's late, we've all got a big day tomorrow.'

To her frustration, Kate was awake far earlier than intended; it was much too soon to put the "big day" into action. She put on some warm clothes, drank a glass of milk and locked the back door of the cottage as she left.

The light was beginning to break over the staithe, merging with the mist clinging to the salt marsh on the other side of the water. Kate took a few steps along the footpath towards the Boathouse before she paused, unsure whether to continue in that direction or set off in the other towards the embankment and out to sea. She thought back to when she had chosen the sea path on the day she'd sent Mark and Joe home at the end of their holiday. Today her indecision was brief, it was a route to be spurned and Kate wondered if ever she would feel able to stand on that far beach again.

To shake off any small part of her that had been tempted to return to that particular stretch of sand, she hurriedly made her way to the landing stage where its weather-beaten mooring posts loomed in front of her. Those sentinels of the land stood steadfast in their purpose at the edge of the jetty untouched by the many tragedies they'd witnessed in the past. They reminded her of the strength there was in surviving against all odds, and filled her with the knowledge that having withstood the ravages of a storm there was a good probability that others ahead could be unfalteringly faced. She stood with her toes over the edge and looked down between her feet to the water below. It was calm and content, reaching across the channel and all the way out to the seaward horizon; its stillness urged her to feel the same.

38

GHOSTS

The opening was a great success. To Kate's relief the art world which nestled within the North Norfolk landscape came out from its winter quarters to celebrate the spring and the wonderful new talent which had emerged within its midst. She shone with pride for Mae, who, despite her initial panic that morning, had visibly grown in confidence as the day progressed and the brilliance of her work was discussed by all. In fact, when they'd both been interviewed by the national paper journalist Kate had set up using her contacts, it'd been difficult to get a word in edgeways as Mae rose to the occasion and at long last presented her work using her own words.

While they'd cleared up after the event, Joe had serenaded them all and everyone joined in, caught-up in the moment, until Sadie dropped the champagne glasses. Kate remembered Dom on that last day in the office and the champagne they never drank together. Since the beginning of the year, he'd been 'doing' the capitals of Europe from which he sent a trail of emails in the form of a brief diary of his travels, littered with entertaining comments on all the new and interesting people he'd met. Amsterdam, Paris, Madrid, Rome – ending up in Nice where he'd looked up her parents and been persuaded to settle for a while. There'd been a postcard to wish them luck with the Gallery. He must have been worried it wouldn't arrive on time as yesterday she'd received another email with the same sentiments, but this time he'd finished with the question – has Mark forgiven me yet?

Tomorrow she would email him back to say it wasn't a matter of being 'forgiven'. She would tell him how they all had wounds to mend, caused not by Dom but by other events which had begun to spin out of control from different points in time, years ago.

When the last glass had been put away, Kate took Joe out into the garden. She needed help to move the three damaged paintings from where they had been left at the back of the building to the place where they were to be burned. When he'd asked her how they got into that state, she insisted on carrying them face down and changed the subject rapidly.

'Sadie did well today,' Kate said.

'Except for the glasses, she's not used to champagne and couldn't balance on those shoes any more. They're gross, I don't know why she has to wear them.'

'To reach up to your height I think!'

'She's awesome.'

'And she's here, in the present.'

'What do you mean?'

'We all need to live in the present and not allow the past haunt us.'

Joe said nothing; he stacked the three paintings ready to burn and added some unwanted building materials. He finally pushed in a collection of cuttings from the garden they'd previously gathered and stood back to admire his handiwork.

'You'll soon be ready for your new life,' said Kate. 'I know you'll get into University if you work hard at college.' She considered carefully what she said next. 'I'm glad you let your mum go free – at the barbecue – when you sang to us all.'

As he looked at her, she perceived that the old uncommunicative Joe was tempted to return.

'You don't have to say anything,' she said, smiling at him. 'But always remember you've so many people who believe in you – your grandparents, Sadie, Mark … and me.'

He returned her smile awkwardly. 'I thought I was really bad at first. You know, when I enjoyed all the attention at school, when I was five I mean. And when I didn't get it any more, I wrote her a letter, like she was real.'

Kate didn't respond for fear of saying the wrong thing and prayed that no one would interrupt them.

'*I made her real,*' he said, '*I believed she was listening.* I expect you think I was stupid.'

'No I don't, it was real to you. I know exactly what you mean.'

He started to cry and she held him like a child in her arms, despite his size.

Joe dried his eyes with his sleeve. 'Thanks,' he said. 'You and Dad, you're ok now, right? You're here for us?'

'I'll be here for you whenever you want,' Kate replied. 'You were wrong to feel guilt you know, it's the last thing she would have wanted.'

'That's what Dad said.'

'I think what she would have wanted more than anything is for you to sing. That's her gift to you.'

Sadie came out of the house wearing her shocking pink wellington boots and carrying a large yellow bucket. 'Look, the tide's on the turn, best time to go crabbing isn't it? You promised there would be time before we light the bonfire.'

Kate walked with them as far as the embankment and watched as they mooched off to the jetty together.

'Time for the present,' she murmured to herself.

* * *

Mae helped Batty take Angela over to the pub to get warmed up by the open fire. She added some extra logs and got the flames going with the aid of Batty and a constant flow of instructions from Angela. Having settled them into the two armchairs with a cup of tea, she left the pair to mull over the day and take a nap.

Sitting between Phil and Grace up in his room above the pub, Mae quietly told the same version of Will's death that she'd told his father after the storm.

'Dad's never spoken about him,' Phil said, when she'd finished.

Mae stood up to leave, but wished she'd said more. She struggled for the truth, to tell the whole story. Failed.

She tried again, 'Will was good to me that night. He didn't deserve …' She couldn't go on. Instead she said, 'Everyone thought your father to be so cheerless, for a publican that is, but those who knew about Will understood why.'

Phil turned to Grace, 'His worst moods come just before a storm. When he ran the pub, he'd lock the door and not open up until days later.'

Mae left them, went downstairs to the office and took

out her camera to look at the photographs of The Old Pilot's House: north, west, south, east … east … east. She chose one to print out before pressing delete on each of them, and marvelled at how simply they had been banished from her life.

No one noticed her slip the photograph behind the paintings on the bonfire. She didn't plan to be there while they burned; she'd be in her studio, painting.

* * *

Mark was the last to lock up and leave the attic. It had been his suggestion – to replace the wardrobe with a door to fill the space. Every weekend, he'd made it his business to be the one to open it in the morning and the last one to lock it in the evening. He always felt fine up there alone, whereas Kate wouldn't ever go up on her own. Just in case. Anyway, it had been impossible to be solitary anywhere in the building during the last few months as the place was either buzzing with workmen in the week or family at weekends.

He'd warmed to the idea of his new career: to help run the art workshops with visiting artists, make canvases, do general maintenance and be on hand to keep everyone safe. He'd also been thankful that Grace had agreed to help run the Gallery shop in the week – alongside Kate – until the end of the summer term when he would be free of his job back in Warwick.

He was about to turn off the lights when Mae called up from the bottom of the stairs, 'Mark, is that you?'

'Yes, it's me, come up and have one more look at what you've achieved, there was so much interest today.'

She joined him and gazed at all her work displayed around the four walls of the attic. 'I wanted to ask something,' she said. 'Why did you change around the two smaller pictures?'

Mark knew exactly which paintings she meant. One depicted a star-shaped body, faded coral pink, almost translucent in places, lying stranded on the beach and highlighted by a cold white light. The other, put up alongside, was a total contrast – exuding warmth from the sun-blistered orange and crimson arms of a starfish – giving off the impression that it was basking in silver shallow waters; certainly not dead at all. They were the two pictures he regularly found changed around. Whenever he returned them to their correct hanging, he would come another time to find the positioning had been altered again.

Somehow it reassured him that the 'being' which continued to lurk within these walls could do so very little. It was fruitless attention-seeking and no harm could come of it. Mark was confident that as long as those he loved and cared for all remained bound together, they would be strong enough to hold off any kind of interloper. It would be up to him to keep everyone's belief in their new found security intact. 'Sorry,' he said. 'I took them down to repaint a spot the kids had missed, and put them back all wrong.'

'That's alright then … otherwise everything was perfect … I can't begin to thank you and Kate …'

'This room, it's changed us all,' said Mark.

'Mark …' her voice faltered, alerted him.

'What is it?'

She looked him in the eye. 'I have to tell someone … it was all those people today, so many from the village. Here to support me. And then sitting with Phil and Grace, telling my story again … lying again.'

He took down and hooked the paintings back into their

correct places. Waited.

'The lie I told Kate – the village didn't turn their back on me in the storm, they didn't hunker down and ignore my cries for help. I never gave them the chance.'

'Why did you tell her that they did?'

'To hide my shame. I was so tired that night of the storm, so confused – first the humiliation and then ... he struck me. I felt helpless, so utterly useless. Yet I still kept watch. While I painted that first painting – the sunrise before the storm – I felt safe, soothed. When the storm came, chaos was everywhere, outside ... and inside my head again ... until the sea took him. And then? I was RELIEVED! Can you believe that? I hardly can. I ran straight back and retreated into painting the other two pictures. By the time they were finished, it was too late. So I've killed him twice, back then in 1968 *and* on the starfish day.'

'No you didn't – both times it was suicide.'

'But I should have tried to ...'

'Back then, no question about it, you'd been a victim of his drug and drinking habits and the emotional abuse which came with all of that. Then there was the physical attack and I suspect it wasn't the first, was it? No wonder you were confused. You were young, isolated, with no one to save you but yourself.'

'But what about Will, could I have saved him? I told Old Phil so little about what actually happened and here I am lying to his son now. I was so close to the truth today ... I wanted to tell Phil everything ... but couldn't. I'm still a coward.'

Mark weighed his words carefully. 'If you want to know what I think, it's that Will was tragically long gone and as much a victim as you were. He made his choices too and you weren't responsible for those. Nothing you could have said to Old Phil would have changed the fact that Will was lost, and there was nothing anyone could have done to save him by then. If you had told Old Phil the detail of that night, it wouldn't have changed the fact that Will was dead and it might even have made it all much harder to bear.' He paused before continuing, wanting desperately to give worth to his own experience by using it to ease her pain. 'Over time it's possible to blunt the knife-edge *imagination* creates as to your loved one's last moments. Facts stay sharp for ever. Of course, there's always what if … but Old Phil has had to suffer that, whatever account you gave him; you couldn't have spared him.'

'But should I tell Phil the truth now and Kate, what about Kate?'

'Look you've told me and what's it changed? You've probably told Phil enough to help him understand his father better and that can only be good. Leave it alone. Today marked your moving on at last. Not just for you but for all of us. That … *apparition* … wanted us all dragged back into the past and he failed. Don't let him succeed now. You've punished yourself for years and it's time to stop. Leave it back there and move on with us.'

Mae came over and placed a splayed hand over the image of the faded starfish positioned to the left of the other. 'I came to believe my own lies, but it feels good to have told myself the truth at last.'

'Facing yourself is the hardest, owning up to your inner demons,' said Mark.

'I'm working on it … and that's why I want you all to call

me Mae.'

'What? I presumed it was to do with all of this,' he said, looking around at the artwork. 'Because of being Mae "the artist",' – Mark indicated the quotation marks in the air – 'rather than Margret "the landlady".'

'No, it's more than that. It's for my parents: the least I can do … is to celebrate the name they chose.'

She moved her hand to the adjacent picture, to the starfish shimmering in the sunlight. 'Did you know, starfish have the ability to regenerate? They grow another arm when damaged. It takes time but they succeed.'

'Where did you pick that nugget of information up from?' asked Mark.

'Don't know, I must have read it somewhere.' She took her hand off the canvas, 'That's why I had to paint them, they are like me you see, before and after … that's why they *must* be hung that way.'

39

EMBERS

Grace, Joe and Sadie linked arms on the far side of the bonfire. Mark only needed one match to light it; the flame caught hold and leapt up into the night.

Kate fell out of the present, spellbound by the power of the blaze. She felt at one with all those through the ages who had reflected on their lives whilst staring at such primal flames. Transfixed, this one act of purification enabled her to see the truth clearly and without doubt. Whether or not Sye or any essence of him remained near this place no longer mattered. What did matter was the man who had struck the match to ignite the fire. The real, tangible, living man next to her who, from the moment she had asked, had supported her unconditionally; step by step towards this point – to share the warmth from the flames.

It was as if the paintings were relieved to get to the end of their existence; they settled into glowing embers more quickly than any of them had anticipated. It was a silent gathering. There had been an initial roar as the canvases accepted their fate, after which not even the far rumble of the sea breaking on the sands beyond the dunes dared to make itself heard. Kate brushed off the large flakes of ash which had come to rest on her clothes and turned away to leave the drifting smoke to the whim of the breeze.

Grace broke the quiet. 'In the Hindu tradition fire can be seen as both the sign of life or death. The creator and destroyer of life.'

Kate did not voice her thoughts: *And so we must each choose what we take from this.*

With arms still linked and Joe lighting the way with his torch, the three opposite set off towards the pub where Phil was preparing the evening meal and Mae had said she would join them all.

Mark held back, causing Kate to do the same.

'I need to tell you something,' he said as he kicked at a small block of wood which had fallen away from the fire and escaped the blaze. 'Mae said something today which made me think about how important it is to be honest with oneself.'

'Isn't that what we've both been trying to do?' she said.

'I need to say this out loud – I realise now how much I've always loved Dom.'

So much for moving beyond pain, thought Kate, a chasm opening in front of her. *Got it wrong again.*

Mark stared at the embers, not at her. 'It could never be the love he wanted from me though, because that was and *is* always yours.'

No. Got it right. She held his words close.

'When I read that postcard wishing us well, it hit me,' Mark continued. 'I love him as a friend and I miss him, don't you? And he loved us so much – never made a move or gave away his feelings before that night. What must that have cost him?'

'I know he's so sad, about the way things happened,' said

Kate.

'I admit I was out of my depth. You know what really shocked me about that kiss was the sudden loss of not being able to go back to what we had before, to that friendship.'

'Well, unlike Sye, none of us can leap about in time. The only option we have is moving forwards, thank goodness. All we can hope for is to invent a better future – I'm sure the two of us can find that with Dom again.'

'I hope so,' he said. 'Come on, let's go, we need to catch up.'

She set off, followed by Mark only a few steps behind. The sound of their feet crunching on the gravel driveway filled the silence the others had left, that is until she became aware that her husband had stopped. Kate turned to see that he had been unable to resist the desire to look back at the attic window.

Having paused, she waited and held out her hand for him to take.

ACKNOWLEDGEMENTS

I would like to express my thanks to Judith Allnatt for teaching me so much about the craft of writing and also to Victoria Bull who kept me going, chapter by chapter, with all her advice on plot, characterisation and editing.

To my friends – Jackie Cardwell, Sue Robinson, Patricia Coleman, Rosemary Bowett and Mary Pick – thank you for taking the time to read *Timescape* and for all your honest and valuable feedback. I would particularly like to thank Alison Symmers who took her interest and support one step further by introducing my novel to the reading group she attends. So another big thank you to my first unknown reviewers – your thoughts and comments made me feel brave enough to self-publish.

Thank you to my husband Bob for giving me the space to write and for your constant support and belief in everything I do.

Lastly, thank you Beryl and Peter for introducing me to the beauty of North Norfolk and to Bob, Kathryn and Ellie for making it such a special place in our lives.